VIVALDI'S LOST CONCERTO

Jennifer Mackenzie Dunbar

FIRST EDITION

ISBN 978-0-6485043-1-3

Shadows scattered across the room and thunder drowned out the mother's fading cries. A powerful tremor, born deep within the earth, shook the lagoon and its islands, as if God himself was impatient for this birthing to be finished. With a final desperate push, the child entered the world; his quivering body, frail but fighting, was veiled in a bloodied chestnut coat, like a runt fox cub. The mother fell into an exhausted sleep, grateful that this, her first child, had finally been ushered from her.

I cut the cord and sucked the mucous from his limp blue body, blowing into his flaring nostrils. He startled, as if surprised to be alive and his tiny chest rose and fell once, twice and then paused before fluttering again, struggling to claim his place among us.

I did not expect him to outlive the storm. Wrapping him tightly as another tremor shuddered through the room; I took the water, collected that morning from the font of San Giovanni and drew a watery cross on his crumpled forehead.

'Antonio Lucio Vivaldi, per picoli de morte, ti battezzandole nel nome del Padre e del Figlio e dello Spirito Santo.'

'Antonio Lucio Vivaldi, due to danger of death, I baptise you in the name of the father and of the son and of the Holy Spirit.'

A flash lit up the image of Saint Cecilia hanging above the bed, and in that moment, I understood that the heavenly hosts were indeed watching over us. I placed the panting baby onto his mother's swelling breast and prayed.

'Heavenly Father, if it is your will that this child survives, he will repay you a hundred-fold and dedicate his time here on earth to your glory, bringing to all mankind joy and inspiration beyond our earthly imagination.'

Extract from the diary of midwife Sister Margherita Veronese as told to her protector and scribe, the Abbess Minelli. Parish of St Giovanni, Bragora, Venice, March 4th, 1678.

CHAPTER 1

Scotland 2015

Fiona pulled the mirror's two side wings inward just as she'd done with her mother's battered dressing table as a child. There they were, the multiple reflections of the multiple Fionas. Straight ahead was today's Fiona, an adult at last. Anxious, as always, but thrilled too, to be finally back in Scotland the land of her birth. Aside her, the struggling student immersed in her books, safe at last in her one-room apartment. Further back the prisoner Fiona, frightened and angry. She pulled the mirror wings closer and the other Fionas emerged. A rebelling teenager full of rage, a school girl desperate for a mother's love. And there, far, far away, was a joyful Fiona, a small child listening to the sounds of her grandmother's flute. She heard it now as if it were being played right there in the room; the tune that had both haunted and enchanted her all her life; the tune whose mystery she'd come to the Scottish Highlands to solve.

Pushing the side mirrors back she looked straight ahead again. Fiona Morag Sinclair. Twenty-seven. A little damaged but a lot smarter. She pulled her hair from her face. The scars from the bashing that first night in prison were barely visible now. If she looked hard enough she could see the remnants of her many piercings, her only remaining adornment a small ring in her eyebrow. A salute to the past.

1

The memory of another long-ago reflection stole upon her. Of when she first woke in prison. Back then she'd only seen half a face reflected in metal toilet rim. Back then she'd been only half a person.

She investigated herself further, making sure that this person, this whole person staring back at her - calmer, smarter - was the real Fiona, not just another pretender who would run at the first sign of trouble. Run back into the oblivion of drugs.

She could hear Andy and Jean below, getting ready for bed. Their unrestrained welcome into their home had been more than she'd anticipated. The absence of the prying questions she'd expected, either through politeness or naivety, was a relief. They were happy just for her to be there, they said. Just sad that her Gran had not lived to see her again.

She turned away from the mirror and rallied her courage. Hadn't she overcome the shame of a prison sentence, enough even to finally finish her degree? Hadn't she proved she could walk away from those who would drag her down? Hadn't she formed friendships that would last a life-time? Facing up to family was her one last terrifying hurdle.

It was Aunt Jean's phone call, telling her of her Andy's illness that provided the motivation she could no longer ignore.

'He's not got long, lass, and he wants to see you before he goes. You can stay with us for as long as you like.'

Her tiny attic bedroom overlooked Oban harbour. She could see a ferry leaving for the islands: Mull or maybe the Hebrides. She'd once gone on a ferry with her grandmother to the island of Jura and seen the Corryvreckan in the distance. Her grandmother told her of the legend; that it had been created by a witch, a hag, to wreak revenge on evildoers. Fiona had clung to her grandmother, afraid of being swallowed by it.

'It only takes the evil ones, love. The good people, like us, it lets pass.' The story had stayed with Fiona. Was she good, or an evildoer? Or was she a victim of wrongdoing, like the old hag?

Watching the ferry's slow, determined progress as the daylight faded helped calm the whirlpool of fear inside her. "Anxiety" the prison psych had called it. Whatever its name, it had been with her ever since she could remember, threatening to pull her into its black bottomless vortex. Spinning her life into chaos like the dangerous, beguiling Corryvreckan whirlpool.

As the ferry disappeared and the sky turned a pale purple, the tune, her tune, began again. Its gentle sadness connected her worlds and she smiled. Scotland. Home at last.

'You'll do,' she said to herself, and once again the mysterious, haunting tune, the Vivaldi concerto, came to her and filled her with happiness. And with the happiness, a renewed curiosity about how she knew it, had always known it. Teresa, her violin teacher, had laughingly accused her of channelling Vivaldi when they first heard it together not long after it had been discovered. But she'd learned it from her grandmother. So how had she known it?

Fiona could almost feel her Gran as she sat back on the bed. She seemed to be at her side, pulling at her.

'Now is the time,' she heard her Gran whisper, 'and you are the one.' In the past she'd been alarmed by these contacts from her grandmother, she'd thought them a sign of madness, drug induced schizophrenia even. But she knew now they were just part of her healing. A relic, maybe of some Celtic gift. She only needed to accept it. Nothing else.

Jean knocked on the door. 'Do you have everything you need pet? We're off to bed.'

'Yes thanks. Jean, I really appreciate you putting me up before my residency starts. I can't thank you enough.'

'Och away with you. You're family. Of course we want you to stay.'

Jean was about to close the door when Fiona said 'Jean, you mentioned a suitcase from Gran?'

'Aye, I put it under your bed hen. She was so sure you'd be back one day that she made me promise to give it to you in person. Just an old recorder and some faded photos, I think. She said something about a great-grandmother and Culloden, of all things, too. It didn't make any sense to me or Andy. Guess it was the old age taking her.'

Fiona's heart leapt. She knew it would not be a recorder but Gran's flute.

Jean yawned. 'Goodnight, Fiona. Sleep in as much as you like. I've my volunteer job at the library tomorrow, but Andy'll be here.'

Fiona pulled the battered suitcase from under the bed. 'You've seen better days too,' she said. She remembered it from when Gran would come to stay with her and her Mum in Aberdeen. Back when days were endless and life full of promise.

Undoing its broken clasps, a musty waft of old heather caressed her, pulling a long-held sob from deep within. She thought she'd finished with the pain of missing her Gran, but the suitcase was full of old memories, too strong to push aside.

Piecing the wooden flute together she wondered how old it was. Hadn't they stopped making flutes from wood a hundred or so years ago? The damp had got to it and warped its once fine lines so that the joints barely fitted. But she played it anyway, drawing from it soft, sweet notes that brought her Gran to her side.

'Play our tune, Fiona,' she heard Gran whisper.

She played a bar or two and smiled. She'd taught herself how to play the tune soon after taking up flute lessons in prison. She'd been rusty at first, but it soon came back to her, how to get a note and hold it steady. Most of the Concerto was way beyond her ability. But the second movement with *her tune* she knew well.

Putting the flute aside she sorted through the photos. Most she'd taken and were of Gran and Mum, smiles wide but fixed. But Fiona could see behind the facade; she could see the war raging.

Her whirlpool began again and crept from her stomach to her chest. Faster and tighter as memories of those early years in Australia crowded in upon her. In the past there was many a time when all she'd wanted was the black nothingness it threatened. She would have rolled a joint to end the spinning. Spent days at a time unconnected, oblivious. Even now she sometimes longed for that soothing euphoric blanket. But those days were gone.

Shuffling the photos together, a piece of yellowed paper fell to the floor. Irregular in shape, as if it had been torn from a larger sheet, Fiona thought it was merely a wrapper for the flute. She was about to throw it away when she noticed some dim markings on it; on one side a hand-written treble-clef with some sketchy music notes and on the other, an inscription of some sort, barely visible. She could only decipher some of the letters. The first line looked like:

To El............... m sic a. . m.g.c..

The second line was a little clearer:

Comp...d by Ant.. ...aldi and tra..cri..d by ..ur f...nd ..ways, R.bb.e .er.

Turning back to the music Fiona propped the paper against her pillow, picked up the flute and began to play. The tune, her tune, Gran's tune, Vivaldi's lost concerto tune, filled the attic room with joy and many more questions.

CHAPTER 2

Australia 2010

Fiona pushed on her elbows, heaving herself up to sitting. The room spun, and a pain shot down her left side. She held onto her ribs as she eased her legs off the narrow prison bed, rested, and gathered her breath. Blood stained her thighs, the tear inside her throbbed. She barely made it to the toilet at the far side of the cell before the last of the acrid bile forced itself from her. The cistern's dull metal reflected her; half a face, one eye swollen shut, her eyebrow gashed and a cheekbone red before the bruising.

'Fiona Morag Sinclair,' she rasped. Half a face, half a person.

She fell back into the hardness of the bed, shamed and humiliated. Lying on its coldness, she felt every bone like a knife. She thought about Jake and the baby that never will be. She winced, remembering Jake's fury when she told him about the abortion.

Along the corridor she heard the sounds of the other women waking. Toilets flushed and water ran into steel sinks. The stench of morning pee and shit barely masked by the hard, carbolic smell of prison issue soap.

It was day one, for Fiona. A prison remand while she awaited her longer-term fate. Her hand went to her belly and its concave emptiness. It had been the right decision, motherhood was not part of her rehab plan. She refused to replicate Vonnie's role-modelling as a mother. She knew first hand what living with a parent's addiction meant for a child.

The week-long bender on ecstasy and anything else she could find had brought Fiona relief from the emptiness and anger that followed the procedure. In and out in a day. Baby gone. She'd been easily persuaded to break into the bottle shop. Off her face with drugs and grief. And angry, oh so angry at Jake's response.

But the syringe had not been her idea.

The hotel's CCTV camera had caught it all and it had only taken a day for the police to find her. She'd been full of promises when Jake collected her at the court house, bailed to appear the following week. But her promises were not enough. He left that afternoon taking all that was his, which was everything. Twelve months clean and the hope of a future destroyed in seven short days.

She ran some water into the sink and cleaned the blood from her legs. The guards had turned their backs when the other women, all lifers with nothing to lose, had taken her to one side. She'd been expecting it, both the official strip search, standing over the mirror, and the brutal follow-up by the women. Women desperate for some relief from the drudgery that was their life inside these walls. Relief from the knowledge that nobody cared any longer.

***

Their dealer had been waiting for her at the courthouse the day before. He'd shoved the small packet of crystals into her hand.

'Word is you're going inside, Sinclair. The girls are waiting for this. They need it now, you understand.'

But Fiona had flushed it down the courthouse toilet. One more bashing was worth it.

The social worker who'd written her bail report, Paul Kelty, had nodded to her as she walked to the dock. Fiona saw the fake smile masking the sadness in his eyes. That was not a good sign. The Magistrate read aloud the summary of Paul's report.

'Mr Kelty suggests you would benefit more from a period of supervised bail out in the community than from a prison term,' he mused, and for the briefest moment Fiona imagined herself walking out the front door instead of into the holding cell behind the courtroom. But his tone shifted as he looked at his watch.

'Ms Sinclair,' he said, raising his eyes above his glasses, 'you've pleaded guilty to Break and Enter with violence and five counts of Larceny. You have a lengthy record, although nothing for the last three years I see. You are now twenty-six years old, Miss Sinclair, and this offence is a much more serious offence than those of your past. You and one other broke into a bottle shop. Your accomplice was wielding a syringe. Your victims, the bottle shop owner and the young man who you threatened, were both traumatised by your actions. I have Victim Impact statements taken from them and one of them is here in court.'

Fiona looked to where he indicated. The young man, hair recently cut and wearing an ill-fitting suit, was seated at the rear of the courtroom. She had seen him arriving earlier. He'd stared at her, but she had no memory of him. There was a time when she would have tried to excuse her actions, pleaded that the syringe had not been her idea, but she knew now that it made no difference to him, this young man with a bright future ahead of him. When he met her gaze she felt shame, total shame. She knew nothing would erase what they had done to him.

The magistrate continued, speaking now to no-one in particular. 'I take into account Mr Kelty's background information about your disrupted childhood with an alcoholic mother. He says you had been drug-free for some time before this crime spree. But time is ticking, Miss Sinclair. You are, it would seem, at a crossroads in your life, where you can either choose a life behind bars or a life as a contributing member of our community.'

He paused and looked for a long time at Fiona before shaking his head. 'I agree with Mr Kelty that Bail in the community could be considered, Lord knows our prisons are full enough, but as the prosecutor has pointed out, your current circumstances give you no incentive to stay in South Australia and you are therefore a flight risk.'

It was in that moment that Fiona's hope disappeared.

'You will be remanded in custody awaiting the preparation of a Pre-Sentence report.'

The memory of that moment, when her world crashed and despair flooded in, brought on another retch. When the spasm finally stopped she wiped her mouth, padded between her legs with toilet paper and dressed in the prison allocated clothes. She'd ask to see the doctor if the bleeding didn't stop by afternoon. Her lies would not be new to him. He'd no doubt seen and heard it all before. For now, she just wanted to show her face at muster and get day one over with.

***

Two weeks in prison felt like two decades. Fiona startled awake to the menacing sound of keys, clattering like angered crows, as the guards worked their way along the cellblock. She'd quickly become accustomed to being woken in this way.

The lifers had left her alone since that first night. A few questions had been asked about her injuries by one or two of the newer guards, but no one was surprised when she insisted she'd fallen out of bed. Her bleeding had stopped that first day, although it still hurt to use a tampon. Her facial swelling subsided and she'd learned to sleep on her back to ease her broken rib. A prison nurse had put a suture in her eyebrow, warning her it would leave a scar. Fiona didn't care. Her biggest scars were on the inside.

Still half asleep, she could hear the guards gathering at the other side of the wall. Her eyes flew open as the memory of yesterday's events drove away all remnants of sleep. The feeling of despair that greeted her most days gave way now to something new. Not quite happiness but a vague, desperate hope.

And with hope the tune began in her head. A tune that had been with her for as long as she could remember; an elusive, melancholic melody that only came when the black thoughts disappeared. She sat up and there it was, on the grey metal cupboard; the flute. Her flute. Discoloured and dented, but hers, at least for now.

The screws had tried to take it away after yesterday's recreation period. 'It's a lethal weapon,' they'd said, smirking at each other. One of them had been around for years it seemed, the other looked as if he was just out of school. As they tried to take it from her, she'd hugged it to her body.

'I need to see the Manager then,' she'd said, breaking her vow to stay under their radar. Usually she would have given in or, if scared enough, screamed the place down. But a few years living straight had taught her how to use the system.

Seeing their hesitation, she continued. 'The Manager said she wants us to have a chance to learn music and Teres...' She faltered. Familiarity attracted suspicion. 'I was instructed by the music therapist to play every day.'

A small group of the women gathered to watch the action. Lis, the woman who'd overseen her bashing, was amongst them.

'Yeah, let's see what the Governor has to say about you trying to take it off her, Sir,' Lis said. Fiona scowled to hide her relief. Lis had sway at all levels.

The guards exchanged looks. She'd only been in for two weeks but Fiona knew they were not happy about the new manager. Probably because she was a woman and, for once, not an ex-screw. The older of them nodded. 'It stays in your cell then, Sinclair, and make sure it's in that box when you're going to your lesson.'

'Case,' Fiona corrected before she could stop herself.

The older officer stepped towards her. She could feel his breath on her face. 'What's that, Sinclair?'

'It's called a case, Sir,' Fiona replied, eyes down, just managing to disguise her disdain. Imbeciles, she thought. Wouldn't know a flute from a tuba.

She'd heard their contempt as they'd locked her in that night. 'Another bloody do-gooder social work idea. Since when did music and crims go together?'

Perhaps they're right, she'd thought last night as the cell door slammed and their footsteps disappeared. Perhaps I don't deserve it.

Now however, she was not going to give in to their contempt. She put the flute to her lips, just as she'd done as a child when playing with Gran's flute. Hers had been wooden and wobbly. Still, Fiona had loved its sweet sounds. She thought too of the tune, her tune, and realised, with a growing certainty, that it was probably one she'd heard her grandmother play.

The metal flute was easier to play but, at first, she only managed a wobbly squeak. She remembered what the music therapist, Teresa had said, 'Long and slow. Keep your lip steady.'

She tried again. A long single note filled the bare cell, penetrating deep into her memory, reverberating into the hollow blackness that lay, always, threatening, in her chest; her private dark whirlpool. As its echo died, she held the flute, arms outstretched as if making an offering. She felt its weight. The weight of history. The weight of hope.

Putting it back in its case she picked up the only other thing she valued in her cell – a battered photo of her with Vonnie and Gran. Her Uncle Andy had taken it the day Fiona and her mother left for Australia. It was the only one she'd agreed to be in and, somehow, she'd kept it through the years of couch surfing and the freezing nights spent in doorways during Adelaide's bitter winters and stifling summers. It had been with her in the crowded hostel rooms that smelt of the sadness of previous occupants. She'd even kept it in her pocket as a good luck charm when she shoplifted.

When she met Jake and set up home with him, she had it framed. But he smashed it during the row they had after he picked her up from the police station.

'You're no different from her you know,' he'd said, pointing to her mother, Vonnie. He knew it was the most hurtful thing he could say.

She stared now at the photo, trying to see more of what had been happening that day. Her mother was laughing, happy to be leaving Scotland behind. Gran was smiling too but Fiona could see her sadness. Fiona herself had simply stared. A teenager's angry stare. Once Stewart had been in the photo too, but her mother had cut him out. Stewart, Vonnies' great hope for a new life in a new world, gone as soon as her drinking became more of a burden to him than fun.

***

The morning siren wailed.

'Five minutes until muster,' the loudspeaker bellowed. Security flaps slapped, and keys clanged as the cell doors were flung open. Fiona pushed the flute case under her bed and pulled on her track pants, a singlet and t-shirt. The pants almost fell off her narrow frame. She'd never been anorexic but, for a time, eating had seemed surplus to requirements. When her whirlpool of anxiety was at its worst, food repulsed her. Even prison food, high in carbs, low in nutrition, had not added to her weight. The other women seemed to fatten their drug-depleted bodies when they were inside, but Fiona remained bony; her naturally androgynous body accentuated by the oversized clothes.

She could hear the sullen voices of the other women and smelt the guards, as they got closer. The smell of men. Tobacco, sweat and yesterday's aftershave. One or two women yelled out profanities as their names were called. Most just said, 'Present.'

Fiona suspected that the fear of yet another death lay behind both the apathy and bravado of the guards and prisoners alike. Just two days ago, one of the new girls had been found hanging. She'd been transferred from the juvenile system on her eighteenth birthday. The brutality of the adult prison had proved too great for her to bear. The image of her collapsed body, wrapped in canvas, still haunted them all.

'Sinclair.' They yelled through the flap at her. Fiona stood, waiting, her arms akimbo. The metal door banged open and her jaw stiffened.

'Present.' Scowling to mask her dread of another day, she stepped into the corridor, arms behind her head, legs apart.

No dead here, she wanted to say. Alive and unarmed. Just a flute and a history of pain.

***

Fiona had been the first to arrive at the recreation room when the music therapy session was announced over the loud speaker. Two young Aboriginal girls wandered in after her. She knew they must be at least eighteen to be incarcerated in the women's prison, but, to Fiona, they looked like children. They spoke to each other in whispers and Fiona guessed they were from the lands. Pitjantjatjara maybe. Desert people. She'd heard they stabbed an elder. She could see the pain in their faces, the emptiness behind their eyes. A female elder she'd once met at a shelter had once told her how their ancient culture and values had been almost destroyed. The law that kept people safe, she said, had been lost. Fiona looked at the girls' fragile bodies and wondered what horrors they knew.

Three wasn't much of a group but the teacher, Teresa Kelty - Paul's wife, Fiona had been told - didn't seem to care. 'More time for me to spend with you three,' she said.

The young girls were too shy to play at first. 'We're just here to get out of laundry duty Miss,' one of them said. 'No offence.'

'None taken,' Teresa laughed. 'As good a reason as any. While you're here you might as well have a shot at playing something. And what about you Fiona? Why are you here?' she asked.

Fiona hesitated. Complying with the prison system, especially rehabilitation programs, was seen by the older women as betrayal. The "them
and us" culture was strong inside. She was about to agree with the
laundry excuse when something about Teresa stopped her. Some years
older than Fiona, she wore her greying hair pulled in a loose knot, her
freckled skin unadorned by makeup. Yet Fiona felt an affinity to her
that she couldn't explain. It may have been the way she held her gaze,
with neither judgement nor pious benevolence. Just a steady woman to
woman curiosity. Fiona decided to be honest.

'I used to play when I was a child. And I would watch my grandmother,' she added. She could have said a whole lot more. About how
music made her feel, how it reminded her of Scotland, her first home,
but she pulled back. That's enough, she thought.

They played a few simple tunes, Fiona on the flute and the others on
recorders. Fiona thought she sounded awful, but Teresa seemed genuine
when she praised her.

'You've got a good ear, Fiona.'

Praise was not something Fiona knew how to handle. 'For a thieving
crim you mean?' She responded, her protective scowl in place. Teresa
ignored the taunt.

'You seem to really feel the music. It's as if you go somewhere else in
your head when you're playing.'

Fiona looked up. Teresa seemed to be reading her thoughts. Plenty
of social workers had tried that before and Fiona had learned how to
fight them off by simply shutting down or, if she was in a temper, telling
them where to go. She'd found that worked. They were easily frightened.
But Teresa was different, genuinely interested. She wasn't pretending to
know everything about her. And she didn't. None of them did.

'If you can come each week and practice in between lessons, I think
you'll learn quickly. How long are you…'

Teresa stopped and bit her lip. Fiona could tell she knew she'd broken
a rule. Never ask how long. The answer was always too painful. Fiona

shivered, remembering her duty lawyer telling her she might get three years. 'It's the minimum for armed robbery.'

'But I wasn't armed,' Fiona had argued. 'Someone else had the syringe.'

'Yes, your co-offender. The prosecution will argue that you colluded with him just by being there. They will try to charge you with being armed as well.'

Three years. The words drummed inside her head. The room around her disappeared and she felt like she was watching herself from above as the whole court day played out before her again. The handcuffs digging like talons, the pain as she banged her head climbing into the back of the security van, the smell of bleach and the stench of urine and vomit. She'd tried to back out, but she was pushed in.

The whirlpool enveloped her again. The whirring tightness that started in her stomach and spun ever faster and wider. It stole her breath and scattered her mind. The memory of the Corryvreckan story overtook her like a warning. She wondered if she would get past it. Was she good or evil?

The flute clattered onto the cement floor. Fiona startled, realising she was still in the recreation room.

'She does that,' one of the Aboriginal girls whispered. 'It's like the kurdaitcha man is talkin' to her.'

Fiona shivered, trying to shake off the memories.

'Welcome back to planet Earth,' Teresa smiled, her concern evident. 'Why don't you play again Fiona?' she suggested. 'Music can help. It makes you focus on the here and now. It might give you some relief.'

She played the same tune again. Teresa was right, it helped. It was as if the prison walls disappeared, the whirlpool inside her became a calm flat sea once more.

'Do you know any traditional folk songs?' Teresa asked. 'That's the music I play the most.' Fiona shrugged, not sure if the music she knew from Scotland could be called that.

'I know *The Dark Isle*,' she muttered. 'But I don't suppose you'd have that.'

'I think I have as a matter of fact,' Teresa said, diving into her bag. 'Did your grandmother teach you that?'

'Yes. And my mother used to sing it, before...' Fiona left the rest unsaid.

'Are all your family musical?' Teresa asked, shuffling through her music sheets. Fiona felt a rare flush of pride, as if she were reconnecting with some long-lost part of herself. She'd had plenty of social work reports written about her over the years, but nobody had ever asked her this.

'I guess they are, or were. Both my grandmother and mother are dead, and I don't see anyone else anymore.' The words tumbled out of her. Words she rarely said to anyone, let alone a stranger. She scowled to hide her embarrassment.

'Oh, I'm sorry for your loss,' Teresa said, as if genuinely concerned, ignoring Fiona's feigned hostility. Teresa played *The Dark Isle* through twice and asked Fiona to join in. The tune, simple and uplifting, filled the small room. Fiona saw the image of Gran smiling. You won't disappear, Fiona, she thought she heard her Gran say. *You're not evil.*

When they finished the song and the last lingering note disappeared, no one moved. They all knew something special had just happened. Fiona's were not the only tears.

The explosive sound of the metal door hitting the wall ended the spell. A guard strode in, his arms crossed over his bulging stomach. He pushed himself between Fiona and Teresa, facing Fiona. Four women, led by Lis, came in behind the guard, laughing at some private joke. Fiona remembered that the drug diversion session was being held in the room next. She was surprised to see Lis there. She wasn't a user. Not any more. She must have some other reason for being there.

Fiona turned away from the guard and put her flute in its case, wiping away her tears. Teresa moved too and stood beside her with her back to the women. 'That was beautiful,' she said, quietly. 'You should keep up lessons when you get out.'

It had only been a whisper, but the other women fell silent, as still as hunters. The words "get out" fell into the silence like a wounded animal. Developing the ability to hear even the quietest of conversations was a matter of survival in here. Everyone knew Fiona had another court hearing coming up. If she were getting out, she could be pressured into scoring for them, sending it in with their visitors. Even though she'd told no one they probably knew too that Paul - Saint Paul as they called him - had interviewed her for her sentencing report. Fiona could almost see the plotting on their faces. They assumed Teresa knew if he'd recommended Fiona be released.

The women gathered around Fiona and Teresa. The whirring in Fiona's stomach was almost overwhelming. But she knew what she had to do. She thrust the flute at Teresa, a cynical sneer on her face.

'S'pose you'll want your scabby whistle back then if I might be getting out. Wouldn't want to leave it with a scum thief like me!'

To her relief the other women laughed and joined in. 'No way, not with Thieving Fi. Not if you ever want to see it again.'

Fiona's heart raced. She badly wanted to hug the flute to her chest, but the stakes were high. She joined with the women and turned to face Teresa. *Us and them.*

The guard stepped away, pretending not to notice. Lis and another woman stood, hands on hips, arms muscular. Another two smaller, perfumed and decorated with rose tattoos, lingered alongside. Lis draped an arm around Fiona's shoulders, her fingers resting on her nipple. Fiona fought back the urge to grab her wrist and push her hand away. Play this one very carefully, she told herself.

'You'd better watch her with your old man too, Mrs Kelty,' Lis said to Teresa. 'She was giving him the look last week. Thought she was going to flash her tiny tits at him.' She twisted Fiona's nipple.

The other women laughed. 'Yeah, she'll be thieving him from you too if you don't watch her,' they chorused. Fiona drew closer to Lis and watched for Teresa's reaction. She desperately wanted to keep the flute, but a slip now would cost her dearly.

To Fiona's relief, Teresa seemed to know the game too. Turning sharply to Fiona she said, 'Keep it for now Sinclair, but I'll need it back if and *when* you leave.'

***

One week out from court Fiona's case was deferred for another month due to some mistake at Corrections. They'd lost her report when some clerk or another had resigned. Paul Kelty phoned to tell her. His sheepish apology did not help to soften the blow.

'Have you any fucking idea what slackness on your end means for me in here?' Fiona yelled. He apologised again and said he would phone her the following day, once she'd had time to process the news.

The guards noticed her anger and she was moved into a shared cell. Bad news often ended lives in here. Her cell mate, Lanie, was about her own age. She'd recently gone down for murdering her ex; the father of her child. Fiona had known Lanie for years, from the many hostels they'd stayed in. They used to look out for each other, literally.

They'd pick out a shop with clothes hanging at the front. Fiona could put on the small talk when she needed to, and when she took out her piercings she looked pretty normal, unlike Lanie who had a tattoo of a snake on her neck and shaved her head. They'd arrive at the shop at the same time, but separately. Fiona would go inside to the racks at the back and engage the shop assistant in some banal small talk. If there were two assistants, she'd usually manage to attract the other one's attention too, making a comment about what she was wearing or some such drivel. Lanie would be taking things off the racks at the front of the shop, as if she were going to try them on. When she heard Fiona say 'Oh, that looks fantastic' to the assistant, Lanie would take off, shoving the clothes into a bag. They knew where all the CCTV cameras were and all the laneways leading out of the mall.

They'd never get much for the clothes. Just enough to get stoned or high for another day. Pharmacies were trickier but more lucrative because they could sell the goods at near retail price. Hair salons were fair game too.

Once they'd been at a drug treatment group session and Lanie approached the hairdresser's shop next door, pretending she was making an appointment. She noticed one of the staff going out the back to get supplies. The following week during a break in their session, they went outside to have a smoke. Lanie looked over the fence on the pretence she'd seen a cat.

'Idiots don't lock the back door into their store room. It's full of hair products!' she whispered to Fiona. When the social worker went inside ahead of them, Lanie was quick to seize the chance.

'Give me a leg up Fi. There's an old crate of some sort on their side. I can fill up my bag, throw it over to you and be back before the stupid bitch gets back. If I'm missed, say I'm in the loo.' One of the other girls, blonde hair, blue eyes, butter-wouldn't-melt type agreed to waylay the social worker if she needed to.

They did this for three weeks before the hairdressers started missing stuff and alerted the Social Worker. The group session breaks were supervised after that, but Lanie and Fiona had made enough to keep their habits going for another week or two.

They worked like this for a couple of years, until Lanie moved in with her man when she got pregnant. Fiona knew he was bad news and kept her distance. It wasn't just the bikie gang he was in that scared her, there was a coldness about him that Lanie didn't seem to see.

The creep had tried it on with Fiona at about the time Lanie found out she was pregnant. She decided not to tell Lanie. She seemed so smitten and so vulnerable. Now she wished she had. Lanie's story might have turned out different. He'd beaten her regularly, even as her belly swelled. Fiona should have guessed when Lanie disappeared from their usual haunts. She bumped into her one day coming out of the Emergency Department of the hospital. Fiona was there getting another prescription for barbiturates. She still wasn't registered on any suspect list so all she needed to do was go to some random GP and say she was having panic attacks and they'd write it up.

Lanie was about six months pregnant at the time. There was no hiding the bruises, but it was the dead look in her eyes that frightened Fiona the most.

'Just leave him,' Fiona had said. 'Come back to the shelter with me. We can tell the police.'

Lanie shook her head. 'He'll find me no matter where I go. It'd be even worse. Don't worry Fi, he's got his coming.'

A week later Lanie evened the score, permanently.

As the cell door was locked on their first night as cell mates, Lanie filled her in on what had happened since they last saw each other.

'It was when he kicked me in the stomach that I knew I had to end it. I waited until he was out of it. I used his knife, the one he'd threatened me with so many times. I knew enough to go for his artery. The blood spurt hit the ceiling, Fi.' Lanie looked at Fiona as if searching for something. Praise? Judgement? Fiona did neither.

'And your baby?' She asked. She'd always wondered about it but finding out would have meant contacting people she'd been trying to avoid.

'I had a little boy. He was tiny. Born premature. You know Fi, they kept me cuffed even in the hospital, right up until his head was showing and then they only took them off because I needed to lean forward. Bastards. They said it was to stop me escaping. As if. I couldn't stand, let alone run. The midwife was crying the whole way through and pleading with them to take them off, but she just made it worse. They get off on seeing us women cry.'

'So where is he now?'

'The welfare workers were waiting outside the labour room. I was only allowed to hold him for a couple of hours before they took him away. They wouldn't even let me feed him, Fi. They assumed I was still using. Dumb fucks. Even I know none of the shit gets into breast milk.'

Fiona wasn't so sure but now was not the time for a biology lesson. Then Lanie began to whisper something. Fiona leaned closer.

'They said he was born addicted, Fi.' Her fragile face held all the guilt of the world. 'They gave him to my Mum. She's got him until he's eighteen. She called him Buddy after some singer she liked when she was our age.'

Fiona had no idea what to say. The horror of Lanie's world crowded upon her. She hugged her and wondered about the baby. Would he ever know his mother's story? She thought of her own pregnancy and the abortion. She thought of Vonnie too. She'd always hated her for not getting off the booze and being the mother she needed. But right now, it was Lanie she felt sorry for.

Lanie pulled away and wiped her eyes. 'What about you Fi. I thought you'd got clean?'

'I did. When I saw how he was beating up on you and heard what you did.' She looked at Lanie, wishing she could take the words back. 'What you had to do to get out of the relationship… Well I really began to see how stupid it all was. Then I met Jake at a party and he said he'd help me get clean. He's Joe's cousin.'

'Joe the dealer?'

'Yep. They're like chalk and cheese. Jake's the odd one out in the family, the rest are all doing drugs of some kind, mostly steroids. Anyway, we had the hots for each other straight away, but he made it really clear he had no time for women on drugs. I went into detox that week and a month later I moved in with him.'

'Just like that? Straight?'

Fiona nodded. 'Don't get me wrong. It was tough, but not as hard as I thought. I went on methadone for a while. Even went to TAFE and did some training in hospitality, picked up a job at a Mexican take away.'

'So what went wrong?'

Fiona had not told anyone other than Jake about the pregnancy and she suspected Lanie wouldn't be totally understanding of the abortion.

'Life,' she said. 'Life happened.' They hugged again, two silly girls who had become broken women.

***

Sharing a cell with Lanie meant that Fiona couldn't play the flute as often as she wanted. Lanie slept a lot, not always from natural causes. The lessons continued to be the highlight of Fiona's week. Teresa brought new tunes for her and she got better at reading music. The tune, her tune, came and went. The whirlpool came and went.

The rest of her days settled too. Seeing how good Fiona was for Lanie helped keep her in Lis's good books. Lanie had always been a favourite of Lis's. She'd tried to pass on some pills to Fiona a couple of times but Lis soon realised that she was not risking it. Anyway, Fiona knew that Lis thought she would be more use to her on the outside.

She enrolled in the drug treatment program, too. She knew she wouldn't hear anything new, but it passed the time and it would look good next time she went to court. The group leader was a social worker she'd met before and Fiona knew that at least she wouldn't lecture her.

'Part of stopping using is working out why you use,' the woman said. 'Talking it through can help but sometimes it's hard to work out what to say. They say pictures are worth a thousand words, so I've brought these.'

She pulled out a box of pictures cut out from magazines and spread them out in front of the group, asking each of the women to pick a picture that told a story about their lives.

Fiona picked an image of a doll inside a box. Its tiny body seemed to be wedged in and it was pushing against the sides. Fiona could feel the constriction, a sense that there was no escape. With its blank face and staring eyes it might as well be dead she thought. Someone needs to take it out and love it. She realised it wasn't just the doll she was thinking about.

She volunteered to speak first.

'Sometimes I feel like I've been put into a box that is too small for me. It stops me from doing things even thoughI know I can get out of it, if I want, but I don't, because it's safer in the box. It's what I know.'

She thought she was making it up, to get it over and done with, but as the words came out she realised it was true. She did think her life - the life she'd found herself living - was too small for her. She knew she could be much more than she was. As the realisation washed over her an image of her grandmother came to her. She remembered her saying as they'd hugged goodbye, 'Don't let anyone or anything stop you from being you, Fi.'

She looked up and the social worker nodded, as if letting Fiona know she understood. The next woman to speak was new to the prison and thinner than anyone Fiona had ever seen. Thinner even than Vonnie, just before she died. The young woman's skin was chalk white. She held up a picture of an overweight woman.

'I think she looks like me,' she said. The group stayed silent. They'd all seen anorexia before.

The next woman was a friend of Lis's. She chose an open can of spaghetti. 'That's my brain,' she said laughing. The other women laughed too. 'It's full of tangled thoughts that slide against each other,' she continued. 'One big ugly mush. So, I keep the lid on.'

The social worker asked, 'If you could pull one of the threads out that helped all the rest to untangle, what would it be about?' The group expected her to make another funny comment, but she paused, thinking about it. 'The baby.' She said. 'If I could get rid of that memory, every-thing would be all right.'

Even her friends in the group looked puzzled. She'd never talked about a baby before. 'It looked like him,' she said, looking up, knowing all eyes would be on her. She'd made a decision. 'He looked like his father. My father.'

A ripple of shock rang around the group. They'd all experienced some pretty horrible things but even the tougher women were close to tears. Fiona gulped back her own reaction. No wonder these women are fucked up, she thought to herself.

The social worker was barely holding it together. 'That must be hard to talk about. Do you want to say more?'

'No,' said the woman. 'It's my shit. My can of spaghetti in my head,' she laughed. 'I just don't open it.'

A sober mood fell over them all and the women kept their stories light-hearted as they continued around the group until the break.

Lanie came up to Fiona and almost nuzzled into her. Physical con-tact was one of the few forms of release they had. 'My story seems like nothing now,' Fiona said. 'I just need to decide to get out of an open box,' she joked. Neither of them laughed.

CHAPTER 3

Australia 2010

Fiona packed her few belongings in a bag marked "Property for Collection prisoner 18052010." It was standard procedure on court day, even if a person's chances of release were minimal. She didn't have much, just the clothes she'd worn when she came in and a few things she'd managed to buy from the store: toiletries, underwear and a pair of cheap runners. She'd given the flute back to Teresa the day before. Since the incident in the Rehab block they'd never discussed what would happen if she got out. The less said the better. But now was crunch time.

'I'll keep it for you, whatever happens,' Teresa promised. Fiona wanted to believe her, but she knew things changed quickly on the outside.

An Offender Aid worker had brought in a pair of black jeans and a cotton shirt for the hearing.

'You look like a bloke,' Lanie teased. 'You should pretty yourself up. Magistrates don't like dykes.' Fiona looked in the mirror. She knew she looked more like her father than her mother and she'd often been presumed to be gay. She'd even been to bed with a few women. When Jake had asked her about her past she was honest about that. He didn't seem to care. Their sex had been full on and probably what kept them together.

She put on some lipstick but wiped it off. 'Better to look like a bloke than a tranny,' she said to Lanie.

'Here put this on,' Lanie said, handing her the pale pink shirt she'd worn to court and managed to keep with her. It was silky and felt strange against her skin after the industrially laundered prison uniform. 'Hope it does you more good than it did me. I wore the top three buttons undone, but the Judge was a woman and I got life anyway.'

Fiona put the shirt on and buttoned it right up. An officer came to collect her bag. 'If you're released before four phone the office and we'll get it up from Property for you to collect,' he growled.

Yeah, like I've got a phone and a car or money for a taxi, thought Fiona. They have no friggin idea!

Thoughts of getting out were almost too much for her. She'd hardly slept. The whirlpool churned all night as she tried to imagine herself on the outside. She'd only been inside for eight weeks but already she found it hard to think about all the things she'd have to make decisions about if she was released. Even the small stuff seemed too hard. Without the Property bag she'd have no shampoo, no deodorant, no tampons. Nothing. And it would be a week before her first dole payment would come in and that would go on rent. In the past, when she'd felt like this, she'd have a joint or pills to calm down, but she knew she'd be urine tested in the first week or two. She'd have to cope without it. The thought terrified her.

The day before, Lis and four others cornered her in the exercise yard. 'Get as much as you can from Joe. He still hangs out in the Mall.'

The thought of meeting up with Joe terrified Fiona, not that she had any intention of scoring. But she couldn't say that to them.

'I won't have any money.'

'Don't worry about that. He's expecting you,' Lis said. 'He owes me big time for not shopping him.'

'Yeah tell him I'll give it to him how he likes it when I get out,' one of the others said. 'Unless you want to give it to him for me. He likes the skinny ones.' The group laughed. Fiona joined them. Even now, she had to protect herself from them.

'What? The Virgin Queen? No, she's saving herself for Saint Paul,' one of the others sneered.

The nickname had started when she'd turned down a few advances. She would have had an easier time inside if she'd "buddied up" as the screws called it. She could understand why it happened – straight women together. Lanie had crawled into her bed a few times but Fiona had made a decision to stay single. Just like relationships on the outside, the worst fights inside were between lovers.

As for the reference to Saint Paul, they goaded her about him since he came in to do her court report. Their radar was not too far from the truth. He was good looking in a dopey Hugh Grant sort of way and his gentle voice had coaxed her into telling him more than she'd told anyone else about her past. Normally she hated divulging anything about herself, but she was street-smart enough to know it was her history, mixed with a glimmer of hope, that would get her released. So she'd told him about her mother's years of drinking, and the homelessness as she tried to get away from her. He took notes and seemed unsurprised by anything she said.

'And education?' he asked.

Like most people, he was startled to hear that, despite everything, she'd passed Year 12.

Paul took his time writing the details of her past and she knew it would look good in the report. As they walked together from the interview room to the common room, she felt a strong surge of attraction. But Teresa was his wife and she was strangely attracted to her too. Not sexually, more an adoration. She'd never told anyone her feelings, but the other women seemed to know.

'Going to Wesley are we Fi?' one of them asked. 'Plan to see lots of Saint Paul and his cutesy wife? Nice threesome you would make.'

Fiona laughed as genuinely as she could. 'Not my type, either of them.'

'Just make sure you don't get too cosy with them. They'll shop you if they get the chance. We're relying on you, Sinclair.'

Lanie had pleaded with her too. 'Take some gear to the Southgate Tavern where the old girl hangs out. You'll easily find her, she's there at the pokies every pension day. Tell her to put it in Buddy's nappy when she comes to visit. They hardly ever check the babies. Best thing they ever did for me, taking the little screamer away from me. He makes a great carrier.'

Fiona knew it was easier for Lanie to pretend she didn't care about Buddy. She nodded and Lanie smiled. But they both knew she was lying. Fiona had no idea how she was going to stay clean herself, but she sure as hell wasn't going to come back in just for keeping someone else supplied, even if it was Lanie.

As she climbed into the prison van she wondered where she would sleep that night. Back in her cell or the Wesley House hostel? She prayed that it would be Wesley because if she was back in her cell, it would be for years.

It was Paul who suggested Wesley House, 'It's like a hostel but it's only for women getting out of prison. You can stay for a couple of months; until you get on your feet.' She said no at first but as the day got closer and nothing else was arranged, she gave in. She hated the thought of living with others; especially other crims, but at least she'd have her own room with her own key.

'Guess it's better than taking my chances on the streets,' she said to him. 'I haven't got anywhere else to go. I moved around a lot with my mother. It had all been public housing. When she died I thought I could stay on in her house, but the Housing said I couldn't 'cos it wasn't in my name.'

Paul shook his head. 'Yeah, that's the policy now. Reduced stock. Only for high risk. If you had children, then maybe...' He looked at Fiona and shrugged. They'd both heard it all before.

'What about before you were arrested? Where were you living?'

'Private rental but in my boyfriend's - ex-boyfriend's - name.'

'And your belongings? Can I arrange for them to be taken to Wesley if you get out?' Paul offered.

Fiona laughed despite her despair. 'I don't have belongings. My mother pawned most of what we had and apart from clothes, everything at the flat belonged to Jake.'

'There were some personal things at my mother's place but as soon as Housing realised she'd died, they sent me a letter via Welfare. They were going to let it and if I didn't come and get our stuff, it'd be ditched. What the fuck did they think I was going to do with it on the streets?'

'And how long ago was that?'

'Two years yesterday,' she answered, her voice cracking.

As Paul wrote his notes, she remembered the pitiful sight of Vonnie in her last weeks. *Liver Cancer* they'd written on the death certificate. But Fiona knew she died from broken dreams.

Paul passed her the tissues. 'I'm sorry Fiona. Sorry for your loss.' He knew better than to say more.

***

In the back of the locked van on the way to court, Lanie's silk shirt felt even more out of place. The whirlpool almost consumed her. She tried to think of her flute, to calm it down. She remembered what Teresa had said as she'd handed back the flute. 'If you get out Fiona you can have it again, at least while you're at Wesley House. And if you don't-'

'If I don't get out, I'm fucked,' she snapped. As always, Teresa ignored her anger.

'Paul said he was recommending that you be released on Bond. You'll just have to report in to Corrections once a week to a Probation Officer, stay clean and try to get work or enrol to study.'

'Back to TAFE you mean?'

'TAFE or Uni. You got good year 12 results. Why not? You could get a student allowance. I know it's going to be hard, Fiona, but whatever happens you've got support to call on. You don't have to do this alone you know.'

As she climbed out of the van, cuffed and flanked by two guards, Fiona wanted to believe Teresa. In her head, an old voice came in strong and certain. *Trust no one.*

Her case was billed for the end of the day. The courtroom was almost empty by the time she got called. Only her legal aid lawyer, Paul and the court sheriff were in the room. She'd been in the cramped holding cell for four hours, her back ached, and her legs felt like jelly.

The magistrate was the one she'd seen before, the one who put her inside. He didn't look up when she was brought in. A greasy strand of hair fell over his eyes and his cloak was crumpled. Fiona could smell the polish on the wooden bench. Despite the air conditioning, the room was stuffy and too warm, hanging on to the odours of previous occupants. The magistrate finally looked up from his files.

'Ms. Sinclair, I note that you are represented here today by a legal aid lawyer and that you have been given the benefit of a Pre-sentence report written by Mr. Kelty. Is the author in the court?' he asked, looking up over his glasses.

Paul stood. 'Yes, Your Honour.'

'Thank you for attending Mr. Kelty. Please be seated. I see that you have taken great pains to retrieve information of the offender's past, both here and in Scotland. I understand that due to her mother's young age at the time of Ms. Sinclair's birth and her lack of adjustment to parenthood, the offender spent much of her early childhood with her grandmother, where she received good care. You also explain that following the death of Ms. Sinclair's father in an industrial accident her mother became depressed and began drinking heavily. It was soon after this that Ms. Sinclair came to Australia with her mother and her new partner, an Australian, leaving behind all that had been stable in Ms. Sinclair's life.'

As the story - *her story* - flowed out into the courtroom Fiona's head spun and her legs folded beneath her. She felt again as though she'd drifted into another world and was watching herself from above. As she swayed forward, the court officer caught her shoulder.

The magistrate sighed. 'If the prisoner is unwell, we can adjourn to a later date. Although I-'

'No,' Fiona managed to say. 'No, I'm OK, Sir.'

'Very well Ms. Sinclair. We will continue.'

Turning to the lawyer, he said 'Will you advise your client to address me as Your Honour in future.' He sighed again, ran his hand through his thinning hair, and flicked to the end of the report.

'Mr. Kelty, you have assessed the offender as only medium risk of re-offending due to her having had a substantial period off drugs in the past. She has undertaken drug treatment and music education programs in prison. You note that she has a reasonable work history, having worked for two years in hospitality after doing some training. You also draw my attention to her possibility of continuing her education, having achieved, against the odds I must say, a good Year 12 pass.'

He looked up as he read this and stared at Fiona as if seeing her for the first time. Fiona knew that how she looked right at this moment could make all the difference. Did he see the woman or the crim? She pulled herself to her full height and accepted his stare. The silk shirt fell softly against her skin and she knew she looked better than she had at her last appearance. She made herself think about the Fiona she wanted to be. A woman who could study. A woman who could play the flute. A woman who was reliable and trustworthy.

Paul caught her eye. He nodded to her and whispered to the lawyer who stood up.

'Your Honour, Mr. Kelty the Community Corrections Officer has asked that you take into consideration that since writing the report Ms.

Sinclair has found accommodation at a supported shelter, should she be released.'

The Magistrate turned back to Paul. 'Yes, yes, I see Mr. Kelty that you have indicated that she was exploring the opportunity to take up accommodation at Wesley House. Not the most salubrious, nor, I am told, crime free of places, but better than the streets I suppose.'

Looking at his watch he continued in a bored voice reading from the report.

'You have informed me that, should I decide on a non-custodial sentence, she would benefit from the restrictions imposed by a supervised order where she could receive support and guidance from a Community Corrections Officer.'

The room fell silent as they awaited his decision.

'Ms. Sinclair, despite a period of two years crime free, your offending - namely the theft of property from a range of retail stores - has been increasing in frequency over the last twelve months and culminated in you breaking into a local bottle shop. Your co-offender was armed with a syringe, but I have noted that you claim to have been unaware of this until the break-in. Since the death of your mother, you have no doubt battled with grief, but frankly, Ms. Sinclair, if we all went about stealing every time we lost a loved one the world would be a sorry place indeed.'

He closed the file. 'I am sentencing you to three years in custody.'

Fiona gasped and began to topple.

'However,' he went on ' I am suspending the sentence and, giving due heed to the recommendations of Mr. Kelty, you will be placed on a community-based order, to be of good behaviour, to abstain from use of illicit drugs and to report weekly to a Community Correctional Centre where you will be subjected to random urinalysis.'

Relief swept over her.

'If, Ms. Sinclair, I, or any of my colleagues, see you before this court again in that time you will be given no such leniency and you will serve out the remainder of your sentence in custody. Do I make myself clear?'

'Yes, Si- Your Honour.'

'All rise,' the sheriff called.

***

Fiona got off the bus at the stop recommended by a court volunteer. Two young girls brushed past her, laughing. They headed for a nearby café precinct. Although it had only been a couple of months since Fiona had caught a bus or been amongst "straights", the speed of the traffic as it went past and the sound of the girls' laughter unnerved her.

She clutched the small bag a Salvos worker at the court had given her.

'Just a few things to get you started,' she said. Fiona had almost cried. A toothbrush and paste, a box of tampons, deodorant and two pairs of knickers. *Thank God for the Salvo's.*

Crossing the road to avoid the cafe crowd Fiona soon stood in front of Wesley House. Unlike all of the other hostels she'd stayed at over the years, this one was in a leafy suburb amongst what appeared to be expensive homes. The trees lining the street were laden with purple flowers. Jacarandas. Fiona remembered Vonnie telling her the name when they'd first arrived in Adelaide and how they'd gathered hands full of the fallen flowers and taken them home. That had been one of the good days.

The Salvo's worker had said something about Wesley House being Federation style. It meant nothing to Fiona but she could see now its distinctive old Adelaide look. A look her and Vonnie could never have afforded.

'It was donated to the Salvation Army by an elderly spinster,' the worker explained. 'She specified it always be used to provide shelter for homeless women, especially those leaving prison. It'll be a good base until you find your feet.'

She'd looked hard at Fiona as if trying to figure something out. 'It's usually the older girls, about your age, who can make a go of it there.

The young ones can't hack all the rules.' Fiona flinched at being called old, but she knew what the volunteer had meant. Most female druggies were either dead or reformed by thirty. The men seemed to last longer.

So, she thought, taking in the twisted wire fencing and the neatly manicured lawn, *this is it, Wesley House*. My home. Sighing, Fiona pushed the gate. The large veranda that ran across the front and down one side was covered with rusting corrugated iron and the painted cement was cracking. Two battered cane chairs with large overflowing ashtrays beside them were the only adornments. The windows had been modernised and secured with iron railings. The house faced the road and looked much like all the other houses along the street, although it was flanked each side by a six-foot hedge shielding it from inquisitive neighbours. Fiona wondered if they knew who was housed next door to them. She guessed that most would have a good idea. The occupants would not fit in with the usual Eastern suburbs' populace.

She knocked at the double-locked front door. An older woman let her in. Fiona knew her from other shelters she'd used but the woman showed no signs of recognising her. In fact, she barely looked at her. The door opened into a long corridor that fed six bedrooms, three either side. Three of the rooms were doubles and three singles. Fiona had scored a single room.

'You have the only key to the room, other than management,' the woman told her. 'We change the locks for each new resident. Yours has also got a chain lock put on by the last girl.'

'Woman,' Fiona said. The worker nodded. 'Yes, women who act more like juveniles.' Fiona steeled herself for a lecture. She wondered why the woman worked here if she disliked them all so much. She soon found out.

'I should know,' she continued. 'One of them was my daughter. She overdosed a week after her release. Her tolerance was down, you know.'

Fiona flushed with shame. 'Sorry,' she mumbled. The woman shrugged and Fiona could see the pain behind her anger.

'It's a shared kitchen and dining area,' the woman continued, ushering Fiona to the rooms at the end of the corridor. 'We clean it once a week and throw out anything that's in the fridge out of date or unlabelled. The girls, or women as you would say, don't use it much. Lord knows what they live on!'

Behind the kitchen was a lean-to with two bathrooms and a laundry area. 'The rule is use the bathroom on your side of the house.'

Fiona peered past the bathroom into the garden. Obviously a once well-kept lawn, it was now just mown weeds.

'You're welcome to do any gardening you like. No illicit plants, of course.

'Right, I'll leave you to settle in. There's a volunteer here every day but nobody overnight. No visitors after six. Stay straight and you'll have no problems with management. Muck up and you'll be out on your ear.'

Fiona's room was at the front of the house and was three times the size of her cell. She pulled the blind up and shuddered at the grill. At least I can open the window, she thought. As she hoisted the frame up a sweet waft of jasmine creeping from next door greeted her. *Beats the ever-present ammonia of prison,* she decided.

Unpacking took two minutes. She placed the crumpled photo of Vonnie and Gran on the bedside table. Now what? she wondered. She had lots she needed to do but no money to do it with. Hearing voices at the front door, she peeked out of the window, staying far enough back to not be seen. She recognised one of the voices as Angie's, a friend of Lis. She'd been one of the lookouts the night of Fiona's assault in prison. She'd been released the week earlier. Fiona heard she was at Wesley. She'd have to face her soon, for now she just wanted to stay in her room.

Her room. She hadn't been able to say that for years.

Putting the key into her jeans pocket, Fiona made a mental note to get a chain for it the next day so she could wear it around her neck. That way it would always be with her. She would never take it off.

The voices disappeared into one of the rooms and with the quiet came a craving. But not the usual craving, to be out of it, removed from reality. It was for her flute. Fiona imagined its weight in her hands but then steeled herself, readying to be let down. Teresa's promise had seemed genuine but Fiona feared that, like most of the promises made to her, Teresa's wouldn't stand the test of time. Her heart sank at the thought of the flute being given to some new person. Again, the cravings surged. She fought them off. Even these dark thoughts could not destroy the elation she felt at being free and safe. She had a room and the only key. She began to softly hum her tune.

The voices had fallen silent, so she made her way to the bathroom. Two women of about fifty were sitting outside, smoking and talking about their grandchildren. Fiona wondered what it would feel like to be homeless as a grandmother. She waved but they barely acknowledged her as she walked into the bathroom. She guessed they'd seen quite a few women come and go.

When she came out Angie was in the kitchen. Memories of her first night in prison swept over her and the whirlpool began spinning and she fought off the urge to get away. She'd had plenty of contact with Angie since the night of the beating but seeing her on the outside was different. The rules had changed but she didn't know what they were.

'So you made it out, Sinclair. Need any supplies?' Fiona knew she didn't mean food. She shook her head.

'I got some dope on the way here,' Fiona lied. 'I'm sticking to weed for now.' She knew well the politics of the using culture. Totally clean was bad, threatening. Us and Them. In or out. Using only marijuana was seen as tame, but allowable.

Angie stared at her before turning away. 'Suit yourself. Just don't come over all goody two shoes. You need to decide which side you're on Sinclair.'

There it was again. Us and them.

Truth was, Fiona had always felt on the outer, even when she was at her worst. Except for Lanie, there was something about her that the others, the ones who were in it for good, found threatening. She suspected it was her refusal to be totally potty-mouthed. She couldn't help using the language - the words - she'd been raised with. Fiona didn't think of it as posh but that's what she'd been accused of often enough. And she couldn't unknow the year 12 level knowledge she had, nor did she want to. But she knew it set her up for distrust. She went back to her room. Being free wasn't going to be easy. Being at Wesley might prove even harder than she'd imagined.

CHAPTER 4

Australia 2010

The communal phone rang just as Fiona arrived home from the prison. She'd caught two buses each way to collect her property only to be told it had been returned to storage and she needed to phone two days in advance. Fed up and tired, she reported into her Probation Officer on the way home. That at least had been straight forward. He'd kept it short and made a comment about how frustrating the prison system could be. He even offered to take her the following week when he was going there himself, but she declined. It would mean waiting for him for half an hour in the admin area and that wasn't an option.

One of the older women eventually answered the phone. She stopped Fiona as she passed. 'Are you Fiona?' she asked, passing her the handset. 'It's a Mrs. Kelty for you.' Fiona glanced around, relieved that Angie wasn't anywhere to be seen.

Teresa suggested they meet the next day at the nearby café precinct. 'No, not near here,' Fiona said. 'Too many people watching. Can we meet near where you live? There won't be any crims there.'

'You might be surprised,' Teresa said, but agreed to the arrangement. Fiona was taken aback at how elated she felt at hearing Teresa's voice. She tried to fight off the happiness, convincing herself she didn't want anyone else in her life. Other people brought pain. But with Teresa came the hope of getting the flute. It was a risk, Fiona realised, she wanted to take.

Teresa lived on the other side of the city, towards the sea. She caught a bus there, through the city stopping outside the central market. As the shoppers, mostly Chinese and Vietnamese, boarded laden with bags brimming with fresh herbs and smelling of spices, Fiona could see into the busy market. It had been one of her favourite places when she was younger. She remembered meeting a school friend there once and flirting with boys from the local private school. Life had been full of promise back then.

Leaving the city, the bus headed west along Henley Beach Road. She noticed the many café's and African restaurants. Vonnie had been friends with an African man once. He didn't drink so it hadn't lasted long. Fiona remembered his velvety skin and soft deep voice. He'd given her a drum but Vonnie had pawned that as soon as he left her.

She was the only person left on the bus by the time it got to her beachside stop. The sea was a myriad of blues and greens and drew a sigh from her she didn't know she was holding back. How could she have forgotten how beautiful it was?

Scanning for anyone she knew she made her way to the agreed café. She'd already planned that if she was spotted she would say she was scamming; getting ready for a bag snatch. She couldn't see Teresa and her whirlpool of anxiety rose. Looking at all the well-dressed couples and their tidy children reminded Fiona how much she didn't belong. She wished she hadn't agreed to the meeting. She was about to leave when she spotted her. The whirlpool slowed enough for her to remind herself that if she wanted to do things differently, she had to take chances. She waved.

'Hi. Good to see you. How are you?' Teresa greeted her.

'Can we go inside?' Fiona asked abruptly. She led the way to the back of the crowded room. It was full of thirty-somethings reading *The Australian,* as their children drank baby chinos. Fiona wondered how long it had taken them to coordinate their designer clothes. She noticed several handbags lying on the floor, half-open and unattended. Idiots, she thought.

She led the way to a table near the rear exit and sat with her back to the wall. It was a good place to detect anyone she didn't want to see. Good too for making a quick exit if needed. They sat under a speaker playing classical music.

'Oh, that's nice,' Teresa said. 'Vivaldi. My favourite classical composer. Not that I know much about classical music. Paul's the one for that in our household. Give me traditional folk music any day.' She listened a little longer. 'I think it's the Four Seasons.'

Fiona tried to listen but the whirlpool was spinning and her head was full of troubled thoughts. *You don't belong here. They're all looking at you. Get out.* She must have been frowning because Teresa looked a little taken aback. 'God. Sorry. This must be hard for you. I didn't think. Do you want to go somewhere else? Somewhere quieter?'

Fiona was about to agree but checked herself and shook her head. 'No. I've got to get used to being out-and-about sometime.'

'So, how is it going? How *does* it feel to be out?' Teresa asked.

Fiona's frown deepened. She couldn't believe Teresa would ask that. But, looking around, everybody seemed to be engrossed in their own conversations. Anyway, she thought, I guess *out* could mean anything. She shrugged.

'It's okay. My room is pretty scungy but at least I've got the only key other than management.' She pulled it from around her neck. She'd found the chain in some kerbside rubbish waiting for collection.

'I already know some of the girls - women,' she corrected herself, almost smiling at her hypocrisy. 'Either from inside or just, you know, the streets. There's a couple of older ones I don't know. I keep to myself pretty much.'

'Have you met your Probation Officer yet?'

'Yeah. Bob Hasting. I reported in yesterday. He's alright.'

'I've heard he's one of the good ones.'

So there *are* bad ones Fiona thought. Great! She was about to say as much to Teresa but stopped herself.

'What do you want? My shout,' Teresa said as she got up to order. Fiona watched as she made her way confidently to the counter, nodding hello to a couple of people. She felt a wave of envy. Life was easy for Teresa.

Checking the crowd, she noticed a man she recognised. He was someone she'd met at a nightclub in the wealthy end of town. He'd offered her money for sex and she'd been desperate. He looked over at her from where he sat now with his wife and two kids. She met his gaze. He had more to lose than her. But he showed no signs of recognising her. She was from his other life. His secret life.

The music changed from a fast, lively piece to a slower one. It sounded a bit like her tune. She wondered if her grandmother had liked classical music. Other than her tune, she'd only heard Gran playing Scottish music.

'So, what are you going to do with yourself now?' Teresa asked as she put the coffees down. 'Is there anything specific you have to do for your probation order?'

'Usual stuff. Stay out of trouble, stay off drugs. Bob Hasting said he might be able to fast track me into a course of some sort.'

'Great. What about the music lessons you started inside – do you want to keep doing them?'

Fiona's heart raced. 'Yes, but I can't afford a-' Before she could finish Teresa dug into her bag and put the flute case on the table.

'It's yours for now if you want – until you can afford to get one of your own.'

Fiona's heart startled. Was Teresa really going to trust her with the flute? What if it got stolen? What if she got desperate?

As if reading her thoughts, Teresa continued. 'I bought the flute with a grant to teach music to disadvantaged...' Fiona saw her hesitate.

'Crims?'

'To people like you,' Teresa continued. 'People who are trying to get back on track. People who have not had a fair go.'

'Maybe I had a fair go and I just blew it,' Fiona replied sharply. She didn't want to believe her luck, because luck had never lasted long for her. Better for Teresa to take it back now than later. Better to have nothing than to have it taken away.

Teresa shrugged. 'Depends on what you mean by fair go I guess. Fiona, I won't bullshit you. We both know the flute is worth a fair bit and you could easily pawn it. But I've decided to take a gamble. I've seen how much playing means to you. I figure you won't risk losing it just to get wasted.'

Fiona couldn't look at her. Memories flooded in of all the things she and her mother had pawned over the years, even things that had belonged to her dad and grandmother. Inside her, the whirlpool grew. Jake had trusted her and look how she had treated him.

'Of course,' Teresa said 'I could be wrong. At the end of the day only you know if you can be trusted. It will all depend on what's important to you.'

Fiona felt the weight of the statement. Yes, she thought, it's up to me now. Can't blame Mum or Jake or the world any longer. It was both frightening and powerful. Teresa gave her a friendly kick under the table. 'Pawn it and I'll set Saint Paul on to you.'

Before she could stop herself, Fiona smiled. She opened the case and looked at the flute. The whirlpool stopped and her chest filled with joy. Her tune played loudly in her head.

'Thanks,' she muttered. She remembered her grandmother telling her to always look at people when you thank them. She looked up.

'Thanks Teresa. I really...' She couldn't finish.

'That's OK. You know, don't you, that I think you could be a really good player, Fiona. You understand music. More than most of the people I've taught.'

Fiona looked away. This was too much for her to take in. It had been a long time since anyone other than Jake had seen her as anything other than a thieving druggie.

The noise in the cafe was rising and covered up the silence between them as they drank their coffees. Teresa played peek-a-boo with the toddler sitting at the table next door, making them all, even Fiona, laugh as his little face lit up with anticipation and delight.

'I've got to go,' Teresa said eventually. 'Paul needs the car. So, let me know if you want lessons. A small group comes to my place on Saturday mornings. Oh, and I'll be at the Black Bull in North Adelaide next Tuesday night. A group of us have a ceilidh there. Come along if you want.'

As they left Teresa had a quick word to the man behind the counter. 'I was right,' she said giving Fiona an awkward hug, 'Vivaldi's Four Seasons.'

Fiona waved Teresa goodbye. She hadn't heard the word ceilidh since Vonnie had died. 'Just a party with live music,' her Mother had explained to one of her Australian boyfriends. But Fiona knew it was more than that. More like a gathering, a joining with others around the music they shared. She'd not been to one since she left Scotland.

Will I manage to not stuff up this time? Fiona thought, putting the flute in her backpack. Taking one more look at the sea she caught a bus home getting off two stops early to avoid being seen by the Wesley gang and questioned about her outing. As she walked home, she hummed her tune, the sad, happy, hopeful tune, and dared to believe that everything would turn out OK. She remembered the little boy's laugh and soon she too was laughing.

The tune was still in her head when she got back to Wesley. Going straight to her room she tried to play it but something about it eluded her, so instead she played the tunes she'd learned in prison and before she knew it, another day had passed. Another day clean. Another day safe.

***

Fiona was up early to go to Teresa's house. The whirlpool was strong inside her and she felt nauseous at the thought of having to meet the rest of the group. It was one thing to play in prison or in her room, quite another to play in front of people, straight people. She looked at her clothes and realised how shabby they were. What do normal people wear she wondered? She only had two pairs of jeans and three t-shirts. All of them second hand and pretty worn-out. She tried to recall what Teresa had worn when they met but couldn't. She did remember noticing the other women at the café all had crisp shirts and close-fitting pants. Most had been dripping in jewellery too. Fiona didn't want to look like them but still she felt again the chasm between her and *them*.

She still had Lanie's silk shirt and decided that would do, over her black jeans. In fact, she quite liked the contrast thing: soft and hard. Like me, she thought. Hard as rocks on the outside and marshmallow inside. She pulled on a denim jacket that she'd bought with her first dole payment. The silky shirt would attract attention if Angie saw her. It wouldn't do to be seen leaving looking different than usual.

Her fears were well-founded. Angie was just getting up as she locked her room. Fiona could see she was wasted. It didn't stop her making a comment about hearing Fiona playing the flute the day before. As much as Fiona wanted to keep the flute to herself, it was impossible if she wanted to play, so she said she'd stolen it from a pawn shop. Angie and the others seemed to believe that and had made jokes about how she had bored the pawnbroker to sleep with her playing. The insult was worth it.

Her flute fitted - only just - into her backpack. Nobody at Wesley knew about the lessons and she was determined they would never find out. She hated the lying. Not because it was wrong, but because it dragged her back to the days when she was using. Back to being a child. She felt like a schoolgirl, sneaking things behind her parent's backs. But the price of honesty would be too great.

'Off to join an orchestra are we, Sinclair?' Angie asked. Fiona startled and checked that her flute was concealed. Just a lucky guess, she thought. Despite her toughness, Angie also had an educated background. Her father was an army man and they'd travelled the world until, at the age of twelve, she was 'dumped', as she called it, in an elite private boarding school. She'd talked about it in drug treatment class, much to Fiona's surprise. Angie held her cards close. Loneliness and drugs soon followed and by fifteen she was expelled, rejected by her family and well on her way to the life she now lived.

Fiona had to admit there was a side to Angie that she found interesting. She had an honesty and an intellect Fiona admired. She'd once confessed that she wished she'd stayed at school. Fiona wasn't sure if she meant it or was trying to get Fiona to reveal something about herself. She'd decided it was the latter and said nothing.

'No, they wouldn't take me,' Fiona responded. 'Didn't pass the piss test.' Angie laughed as she stumbled down the corridor. Fiona hoped she wouldn't even remember the conversation tomorrow.

***

Fiona was the first to arrive at the lesson. She met Teresa in the studio at the back of the house, as arranged. A middle-aged husband and wife arrived after her and then a young Chinese man. They all said hello but, to Fiona's relief, nobody seemed interested in small talk. Teresa had taught them all some of the same tunes and for most of the lesson they played together. Then they each played a solo. Fiona's was Dark Isle. She went last and was glad she did. With each little mistake they made her nervousness decreased and her heart rate slowed. They were all better than her, but not by much.

The husband played a classical tune. 'Bach's Air on a G string,' he said, laughing. The tune was familiar and Fiona enjoyed its predictability. His wife's piece was a children's tune. 'I play it for my grandchildren,' she said and Fiona thought of the many hours her grandmother had played for her.

Li Wan's tune was very different; a strange oriental sound that grated at first but was soon strangely mesmerising. It helped her calm down. He bowed to Teresa when he finished, acknowledging her teaching. Fiona admired his humility. Teresa turned to her.

'Have you anyting to play?' Fiona took a deep breath. Her anxiety from the morning had gone down during the walk there and while playing. With all eyes on her, the whirlpool began spinning. She played slowly and only faltered a couple of times. When she got to the end she felt both relief and fear. What would they think?

'Oh, I remember my mother singing that,' said the wife. 'She was from Glasgow.'

Fiona, who had said nothing about herself so far, forced herself to reply. 'My Mum was born in Oban and I lived in Aberdeen until I was fourteen.' The couple went on to tell her about their recent trip to Scotland and how they'd been robbed at the train station in Glasgow. Fiona cringed thinking how she had done the same so many times at the Adelaide train station. She shot a glance to Teresa who had her head down, looking at music sheets. Teresa shook her head very slightly. A wave of gratitude filled Fiona and she gave Teresa a slight smile when she eventually looked up. It felt strange to have someone, *someone straight,* on her side.

The lesson finished with a new piece they all played together. All, except Li Wan, made a bit of a mess of it, laughing as they stumbled to the end.

'Hmm, that might take a little work. I'll see you all next week.' Teresa said as they packed up. Fiona noticed them putting money in a box and felt a sudden panic. She didn't need to look into her wallet to know she had barely enough for a coffee and the bus fare. Teresa came up behind her.

'The first lesson is always free. You can just pay me what you can until you get a job.' Fiona's relief was tinged with guilt at having not thought about payment. After years of having been forced into rehabilitation programs she didn't want to do she'd forgotten how the real world operated.

'I can pay,' she insisted, trying to work out what she would go without.

'Yes, once you get a job,' Teresa repeated. 'Now I'm gasping for a coffee. How about you? Come into the house and I'll just grab my bag.'

Fiona would rather have stayed outside but it had begun raining and Teresa insisted, holding the door open for her. She felt uneasy being in Teresa and Paul's home, like an intruder, lifting the covers on someone else's life. Looking around Fiona remembered the many houses that she'd broken into, taking whatever she could before the alarm roused the neighbours. Back then she'd told herself they deserved it for having such weak security. And anyway, she would tell herself, they'll just claim it on insurance. Now, here she was, an invited guest in just the type of house she used to prefer to rob. Cream brick and suburban. The type of house that usually had plenty to steal but no alarms.

Teresa left her in the lounge. A piano in the corner was laden with sheet music, and every surface had either books or magazines on it. A television seemed to be shoved aside, barely viewable from the large lounge strewn with cushions. There were a number of paintings on the walls, mostly of misty seascapes, and an antique sideboard had a number of pictures, all in different frames. Fiona had never asked Teresa if she had any children, but she guessed she didn't. There was no sign of any here.

A man's woollen jumper hung on the back of a chair. Paul's, she presumed. Fiona felt again an unwelcome twinge of attraction and resisted the urge to pick it up to feel its comforting folds.

'Paul's gone out for a run,' Teresa yelled from the bedroom, as if reading her thoughts. 'Make yourself at home.'

The radio was on. 'Turn that up,' Teresa called out. 'Sounds like a flute piece.'

Teresa's familiarity unnerved her. She wondered briefly what was in it for her. She certainly hadn't invited any of the others back. Well not that day anyway.

Fiona followed the sound and found the radio partly hidden by a stack of CDs. She adjusted the sound just as a new movement started. A soft but haunting melody. She turned it up again and frowned, astonished.

It was her tune. The tune Gran had played for her. The tune she kept hearing in her head. She'd never thought about it being a piece of classical music. Listening carefully, she began humming the tune unaware that Teresa had crept into the room. The next movement began and Fiona stopped humming. She didn't know this part.

'How do you know that?' Teresa asked.

'Shush,' Fiona snapped. Seeing the bemused look on Teresa's face, she blushed. 'I mean, can we just find out what it is?' They sat together listening to the last movement.

'That was a flute Concerto RV431 by Vivaldi,' the announcer said. 'Remarkable because it has only recently been discovered in archives in Edinburgh. It is thought to have been taken there by a local nobleman after his Grand Tour to Venice. You're listening to Notes to Music on ABC Classic FM. The next piece-'

Teresa turned off the radio and stared at Fiona, eyebrows raised. Fiona thought she was annoyed. 'I'm sorry. I thought I knew the tune,' she apologised. 'But I couldn't have. I've never listened to classical music and anyway if it's just been discovered…'

'But you *did* know it,' Teresa expounded. 'You were humming it!'

Fiona blushed again. 'Well, I think it's a tune my grandmother used to play to me.' Teresa's look of amazement confused her. She shrugged. 'I don't know. Perhaps I was just making it up, you know, by chance?'

'No, you knew it,' Teresa insisted. 'The second movement, you definitely knew it. You were right on note all the time in. Anyway, some "chance" that would be,' she exclaimed, 'channeling Vivaldi!'

Fiona's curiosity grew. 'I am sure my grandmother used to play it to me. She didn't play any other classical music that I can remember, and she had no formal training. Just music handed down to her through the family, I think. But if it has only recently been discovered?'

'And surely it can't be a coincidence, can it? That it was discovered in Scotland?' Teresa continued.

'But in Edinburgh. That's miles from where my Gran lived and it belonged to a nobleman. That definitely is nothing to do with our family.'

'Well,' Teresa said, ushering her out of the house, 'There's a mystery that needs solving. And I think you're just the person to do it, Fiona Sinclair.'

***

Teresa and Fiona chatted for about half an hour over coffee; about Wesley and the lesson. They were back outside when Fiona had a sudden thought. 'That radio station, does it replay programs at all?'

'Yes, of course. Brilliant!' said Teresa excitedly. 'I'm still in the dark ages with all that download and podcast stuff, but I'm sure you could find it. I think you go to Listen Again or something. Google the ABC *Notes to Music* program. That's what we were listening to. You could put in Vivaldi as well to see what else was on. I think they might have done a whole series on the great Red Priest not long ago. Paul listens to it.'

'What red priest?' Fiona asked.

'Vivaldi. That's what they called him, even back then I think, because of his red hair. He was a priest you know. You can come back and use our computer if you like?'

The image of Paul's jumper loomed, and Fiona gently declined. 'Thanks, but I'll use the library. I've been meaning to join anyway.'

'Good idea,' Teresa said waving goodbye beforeturning back. 'Oh yes and I meant to say, we're going to The Black Bull pub on Tuesday night. I join in with a small group of musos there most weeks. Bring your flute if you want. Everyone's welcome.'

***

The local library was at the back of the Town Hall. Fiona remembered going there on a school excursion. They'd been told how old it was. 1865 they'd said. She laughed, thinking of it now. Old by Adelaide standards maybe, but nothing compared to places in Scotland. Adelaide's old buildings were more like Edinburgh's New Town. She wondered as she approached it where in Edinburgh the manuscript of the concerto had been found.

She could still recall her first trip to Edinburgh to see the military concert, *The Tattoo*, when she was about six. It was one of her only good memories of the three of them together, her Mum and Gran. Perhaps it was being somewhere foreign to them all, but they'd all gotten on and had fun. She remembered walking up the Royal Mile to the Castle and looking down on the layers and layers of ancient buildings.

'They're medieval,' Vonnie had said, reading from a tour guidebook. 'There's been a settlement here since 900 BC and the St Margaret's chapel was built in the 1100s.'

They could see over to the New Town. 'They had to move people out of the old area in the eighteenth century because it was overcrowded and filthy. They still call it *Auld Reekie*,'Gran said. 'My own Grandmother used to tell me that one of her ancestors had come here when the New Town was being built. She said she'd worked as a lady's maid for one of the toffs somewhere near here. I seem to remember the family she worked for fought at Culloden for the Red Coats. Our family were Jacobites, you know.'

As the memory floated in her mind, Fiona began to hum her tune again. Did she imagine it or had Gran said that the lady's maid had once owned her flute? It was all such a long time ago. She did remember how cold it was that day and how warm Gran's hands had been.

Fiona shivered as she entered the library. *The Tattoo* had bad memories too. Vonnie had watched it every year since, on television. It was always on New Year's Day in Australia. She was usually hung over or getting drunk again. She'd get teary when the lone piper played *Amazing Grace* at the end.

'Oh Fi,' she'd say, 'I do miss Scotland sometimes.'

'Well let's go back then,' Fiona would plead. 'We could stay with Gran and visit Uncle Andy.'

'Aye. We'll do that,' Vonnie would say. 'One day.' But by the time she was old enough to know how much it would cost, Fiona knew they would never go. And now they were both gone, Vonnie and her grandmother, and Fiona didn't even have enough money for new underwear. She pushed the black thoughts from her mind. The tune had disappeared.

'Free for the first half hour,' the librarian said, 'two dollars an hour after that.' Fiona made her way to the computers. She hadn't been in a library since school days and that seemed like a lifetime away. She looked around her but nobody she knew was there and everyone else was just getting about their own business; mostly parents and children and some older people reading newspapers or using the computers. They all seemed to know what they were doing.

The whirlpool began to stir. She hadn't used a computer for anything other than emails for years. Her hands became sweaty and she felt nauseous. A dishevelled man smelling a little of something stale looked up as she sat down. She felt as if he was looking at her eyebrow piercings and a familiar anger rose in her. But he reached over towards her computer and gathered some papers.

'Sorry pet. I'll just tidy up my stuff.' His smile lit up his blue eyes and she thought of her Uncle Andy. He'd be about this man's age now. She hoped he smelt a little better though.

After a few false starts, she found the right program to replay. She pulled out her earphones and listened. By the end of the hour her head was spinning. The program had been about baroque music. She'd heard about different types of classical music but didn't really know which was which.

'Baroque comes from a Spanish word meaning an irregular pearl, or a pearl of imperfect shape' the program announcer said. 'It was different from the music that came before, which had balance and symmetry. Baroque is more unpredictable, complex and fanciful.'

About halfway through, Fiona's heart started to beat faster. 'The next piece is called Il Gran Mogol. It was recently discovered by Andrew Wooley, a musicologist, who found the manuscript in National Archives in Edinburgh. Scotland itself had a strong baroque scene but, after thorough research, Wooley has concluded it was definitely written by Vivaldi and may have been taken to Scotland by a Scottish nobleman, Lord Robert Kerr, after his Grand Tour in Venice.'

Fiona listened to the concerto twice. The second movement certainly sounded like her tune, but now she didn't know if it was because she'd listened to it so many times. She looked for a CD of it but there wasn't one, so she borrowed another Vivaldi CD and a couple of books about the baroque composers of Venice. There was nothing in them about *Il Gran Mogol* but plenty about Vivaldi and about an orphanage called *le Pietá*, where he'd taught.

'An orphanage,' she muttered to herself as she added another book to her pile. *Why would someone so famous teach at an orphanage?* She flicked through it. A chapter heading caught her eye *Vivaldi and the Giro Sisters.* Who were *they*, she wondered?

She walked home more excited than she had been for many years; the weight of the books and CD in her backpack offering her endless possibilities. She realised she'd not felt the whirlpool for a whole two hours. Nor had she thought about drugs or prison or Wesley, or even Paul's jumper!

She was walking so fast she nearly walked into a little boy on a push along bike. 'Sorry. Sorry,' she said to the mother, getting ready to be yelled at.

'No need, he went in front of you,' the mother said smiling. Fiona smiled back. A full smile. She caught her reflection in the woman's glasses.

Perhaps I'm not half crim any more, she dared to think, but an irregular pearl. Perhaps I'm just unpredictable, complex and fanciful.

***

Angie was standing in the passage talking to a young girl when Fiona arrived at Wesley. The girl greeted Fiona before she could escape to her room.

'Hi Fi, remember me?' Fiona wanted to get the books into her room before Angie saw them.

'Sure. Tahlia isn't it?' she opened her door, dropped her bag inside and went back to join the other two. 'Your Mum and mine were drinking buddies if I remember.'

'Yep. Sorry to hear about your Mum. Mine is still alive and kicking, unfortunately.'

Fiona tried to hide her scowl. As much as she had come to hate Vonnie, she would have given anything to have her alive. Fiona could feel Angie watching her.

'Tahlia's come here straight from juvey. She's on home detention.'

Tahlia lifted her leg to show off her band. Her skinny legs looked more like that of a fourteen-year-old than the eighteen she must have been to have been allowed into Wesley.

'I've been telling her that we are all like sisters here. That's right isn't it, Fi? We look out for each other.' Angie said putting her arms gently on Tahlia's shoulder and giving it a comforting squeeze. Tahlia smiled at Angie, grateful for the nurturing. Something about the look on Angie's face however sent a shiver down Fiona's spine. A flash of memory came back to her of Tahlia as a little girl watching Vonnie and her mother getting drunk with two men. Fiona had been about sixteen and Tahlia eight or so. One of the men had been making lewd jokes about the girls. Both their mothers had laughingly protested. 'They wouldn't know where to put it!' Vonnie had said. Fiona wondered how life had been for Tahlia since then.

'Yep we're all sisters here,' she said. Then, looking as nonchalant as she could manage, she said 'Let me know if you need anything, Tahlia. Any help or...' she chose her words carefully, 'Anything at all.'

Angie hugged Tahlia even tighter. 'Fi keeps to herself most of the time though. She leaves the Wesley House activities to me and the others. Isn't that right, Sinclair?'

Fiona shrugged. 'Yep. Angie's the one with all the smarts around here. I'll see you around Tahlia.'

She went into her room trying to shake off a creeping ominous feeling in her stomach. Tahlia's almost pre-pubescent looks kept coming back to her. But worse was Angie's proprietorial claim on her.

Picking up her books, she began to read about Vivaldi, the Giro sisters and the abandoned girls of the *Ospedale le Pieta*. The canals of Venice opened up and the mystery tune began once more.

CHAPTER 5

Venice 1737

A salty Adriatic squall menaced along the canal as Paolina Giro pressed against the rain-streaked window. She resisted the urge to lean out, seeking, as always, to see but not be seen as she watched impatiently for Antonio. She'd spent the early morning at *le Pieta* with him and a young man, a Lord of some sort, from Scotland. The man was eager to buy some music and Antonio had been unusually distracted. It wasn't the first time she'd noticed how tired he'd been looking so she'd stepped in and arranged for the young man to come to their home on *via Carbon* the following week.

But it was of none of this that she thought as she searched the canal path. She was eager to talk to Antonio about the gossip she'd overheard that morning at the fish market.

'He uttered profanities in front of the Bishop's messenger and ended the rehearsal early,' a woman had said to her friends there. 'The choir, the girls from the *Ospedale le Pieta*, were left in the hands of the assistant maestro,' she'd continued, the sound of contempt in her voice.

At first Paolina gave them only a passing interest, neither knowing nor caring about whom they were talking. It could have been any of

Venice's hundreds of music teachers and she was too busy for idle gossip. It was what came next, however, that caught her interest.

'Remember when, all those years ago, he fled from the morning service, leaving Bishop Xavier to finish the communion?'

Paolina listened more closely as she continued. 'Some said he was gasping for air as he left. He has been weakly since birth, you know. But others say he'd simply had an inspiration for a new composition and needed to write it down.'

Antonio, Paolina almost gasped. They were talking about Antonio. Pulling her hood up, Paolina moved closer as the conversation became more animated.

'*Le Pietá* should be his priority but it will surely suffer with the two new operas he is taking to Ferrara. And those sisters from Mantua, daughters of a common barber...'

The fishmonger's calls drowned out their words. 'Fresh from the ocean this very morning. Come Signoras open your purses and take home a feast to please your men and feed their desire.'

Paolina turned towards the women a little; she needed to hear what they had to say about her and Anna.

'They couldn't be less alike,' one of the women said. 'The older one, a drab spinster, is his housekeeper and the younger one, his much-favoured singer and his. . .' Overhead a gull screeched and the salty smell of the shining fish filled the air.

The women gathered closer, their eyebrows raised in excited concentration. Paolina sidled alongside, leaning forward, pretending to be closely inspecting the fish, her hood now fully obscuring her face.

'I've heard it said that he and the younger one are-' A gush of wind carried their words away as a wave of acerbic amusement rippled around the group. The oldest woman, as wide as she was tall, shook her head.

'Disgusting! He may not be administering communion anymore, but he is still a priest and must remain celibate. A live-in housekeeper he deserves but living with a singer! And she is young enough to be his daughter! Surely the Bishop wouldn't allow it.'

Paolina retreated, stunned. It did not surprise her that they were gossiping about Antonio. That day, twenty years ago, when he walked out of San Giovanni, renouncing forever his duties to administer the sacred rites, still remained the subject of curiosity and speculation among many of Venice's self-righteous citizens.

But this conversation was much more menacing.

Her thoughts raced. *What has happened to fuel this malicious gossip? Has somebody approached the Bishop about our living arrangement? Had someone objected to them moving in to Antonio's house?*

Yet, it was not the threat of their relationship being exposed that most concerned her. It was the suggestion that Antonio and Anna were, what? Lovers?

'Oh Anna. Sweet Anna,' she whispered to herself. You have done nothing to deserve this scandalous venom. If we are not careful they will ruin your reputation and your career.

Words of retort formed, like armed soldiers. At one time, back in Mantua, Paolina would not have hesitated to confront the women, demanding that they take back their dangerous words. Back then, she'd had nothing to lose. She'd learned quickly that, here in Venice, it was how you handle gossip that can either make or destroy fortunes and fame. Gossip was the currency that fed and excited Venetians. Rumours soon became fact, and, if posted to the Council of Ten through the *bocca de lione,* the lion's mouth, retribution would soon follow. Banishment from the city for petty indiscretions was common. Paolina knew she had to be cautious.

She walked to the canal edge where she was hidden from the women by a flapping canopy covering the tables of spices: red, yellow and brown. The smell of saffron and nutmeg surrounded her. She gathered her thoughts as she watched the chaos of the canal. Slender gondolas, some curtained for privacy, carried patricians and nobles to and from the

Doges Palace. They wove, like black swans, between the heavy barges, laden with wooden poles or stone slabs. Two men yelled their impatience as they guided one of the barges towards the building site of the new theatre, jostling through a crowd of smaller vessels laden with cabbage and turnips, apricots and apples, on their way to the market. Canal dogs yelped as if in agreement with the bargemen and cats sat watchful, anticipating the spillage from the baskets of fish being carried to the stalls, where their silvery bodies would be arranged with great care to please the eyes of the discerning housewife.

The heady aroma of the spices and the rhythmic bustle of the surroundings soothed and focused Paolina. This, she told herself, is the other face of Venice, *le Republica Serenissima,* where the elite mingle with workmen and merchants, where artisans live and love amongst nobles and courtesans. Venice, always the same, always on the move.

The ageless bells of *San Cassiano* heralded the hour and time slowed. Midday. As the last toll echoed across the water, Paolina recalled her mother's words.

'Don't let your temper rule you Paolina. Think before you act. You have a fine brain – use it!'

Perhaps, she told herself, it has nothing to do with our living arrangements. They could have no evidence of anything disreputable. Who were they anyway, to judge her and Anna; just the greedy wives of insignificant tradesmen, with too much time on their hands? Papa may have been a common barber, but he'd accumulated a goodly fortune making wigs for the wealthy of Mantua and Venice. And fortune, after all, is what counts, especially here along the Grand Canal.

And, Paolina thought as her confidence swelled, since I have taken over Antonio's bookkeeping, he's gained a reputation for being not only a fine musician but also a shrewd businessman. Why, just this morning hadn't he, at her insistence, finalised the sale of that flute concerto? His reputation for producing compositions at a high quality had reached into the well-bred homes and concert halls all over Europe and Britain.

Was it not him and his music that drew the wealthy young men from afar to vacation and spend their money in Venice?

Without Antonio Vivaldi, her thoughts continued, these spouses of merchants would be nothing but common housewives. It is malicious envy of Antonio's fame that fuels their petty gossip.

Pulling her hood back to rest on her shoulders, Paolina returned to the fish market. The women stopped their chatter. Her unusual height, for she stood a full head taller than any of the other women; and her steely grey hair, pulled tightly off her angular face, left them in no doubt that she was someone who would not shy away from a confrontation. They stepped aside, exchanging embarrassed glances.

Paolina nodded an acknowledgment to them. Yes, I have heard your scandalous accusations, it seemed to say. And one day, when Antonio soars to even greater heights, taking Anna and myself with him, you will regret your malicious words.

'Ciao Signor,' she said to the fishmonger, raising her voice just a little, signalling her authority. 'Show me the finest catch you have to offer. Father Vivaldi has important guests for dinner this evening and it would be a pity for Venice's best produce to go to waste,' she turned momentarily to the women, 'on those mewling cats.'

***

Paolina did not take the gondola back across the canal, preferring to walk across the bridge at Rialto, meandering amongst the crowds to *via Carbon* where she and Anna lived. The house had been rented for them by Antonio. Their bedrooms were on the third floor. A study, dining area, and galley kitchen were on the second. Like most houses in Venice, the ground floor, subject to regular flooding, was kept as a courtyard and storage area. Antonio maintained his official residence at his father's house at the *Campo Girocolomi* but used their study as a music room. A place to write and sometimes teach. He often met customers there too, and Paolina could immediately record the agreed price in her ledger and have the purchaser sign; a practice she'd learned from her father. Sometimes Antonio would spend the night, slipping away in the early hours in a covered gondola.

Paolina initially refused the arrangement. 'We cannot live in your house and from your means. I may well be seen as beyond an age where such things matter, but I have Anna's reputation and career to think of.'

But Antonio had been insistent. 'Do not concern yourself. Our companionship can be easily explained. Do we not share an interest in Anna's career? And anyway,' he said taking her hand, 'you are my nurse, my housekeeper and my bookkeeper, are you not? Even the Bishop has a live-in housekeeper, your cousin Maria.'

'Yes,' she said grabbing her hand back, 'and it is also common knowledge that Maria is not just his housekeeper. The good citizens of Venice may not question him, but you are not so well protected as a Bishop, Antonio. If we were to be reported to the Council of Ten, we would be thrown out of the city, just as your brother was for his indiscretion.'

'Be assured, my Paolina, Venice only chooses to see what is in her interests to see - *scegliere cosa vedere*. My music is drawing money into Venice from all over Europe; money that flows into all their purses. Why, young gentlemen come here from as far as Britain and France on their grand tour just to buy my concertos, attend my operas and marvel at the choir of le Pietá.'

'I doubt not your worth, Antonio, nor your fame, but is it enough to protect you against those that value gossip over profit?'

'You must realise, Paolina, nothing is more important to Venetians than profit. The money of those that come to Venice to see me and hear my music finds its way into every corner of our fair city. They flock to the warehouses for silk and wool, to the coffee houses for gossip and glory, and to the gambling tables for the excitement. And let us not forget the courtesans. Their doors are more often closed than open during the festival season when my music fills the churches and the theatres.'

'Why,' he continued, opening his arms wide and smiling at his exaggeration. 'If I were to be thrown out, the very fabric of Venice could collapse.'

As if to confirm his claims, a passer-by, wearing the red cape worn by only the most distinguished notaries, caught sight of Antonio at the window and called his greeting. 'Buongiorno, Don Vivaldi. May the day be good to you and bring you good fortune.'

Antonio waved his acknowledgment back, smiling knowingly at Paolina.

'Be in no doubt Paolina, all of Venice knows my hard work helps pay for their fancy wigs, their silks and furs. They may whisper and gossip, but no one will risk their luxuries just to expose us. Not in Venice, the most affluent and secretive of cities.'

***

These words came back to Paolina as she crossed the bridge. She remembered a favourite saying of her father's: *better to be known and gossiped about than be an insignificant member of the great unknown.* Yes, Papa was right, she thought. A few whispered rumours are a small price to pay for the fame that Antonio, and now Anna, are enjoying. Jealousy is rife in Venice and no more so than in the musical fraternity where Antonio's positions at the Church of *le Pietá* and the *Teatre san Angelo* is both celebrated and envied. And with envy comes gossip.

Arriving at *via Carbon* she pushed at the large wooden door that led into their courtyard. It clanged shut behind her and she climbed the sandstone steps to their apartment. Now, protected from inquiring eyes, Paolina smiled to herself, amused at the women's stupidity. *How typically foolish of them to assume it is Anna, not me, her "drab" sister, that Antonio is interested in bedding.*

Despite her restored optimism, Paolina found it difficult to settle to her housework, and so she sat down, waiting at the window overlooking the gondola landing where Antonio would normally alight. When he finally appeared it was along the canal path, walking rather than by gondola. Her earlier fears returned. He leaned into the wind, clutching his breviary. His hair, soaked, clung like tattered kelp, his cassock billowing, as if at any moment, he would take flight.

Ah, Antonio Lucio Vivaldi, she thought, always in a hurry, as if the whole world is waiting for you. As he neared, however, it was not his haste that alarmed her but the anger she could read in every step.

The courtyard door below banged open as he pushed against it, bringing with him the sounds of the canal, urgent and demanding. Paolina heard him struggling for breath as he came up the stairs. Barely greeting her, he collapsed onto a chair, his chest rising and falling in shallow, rapid waves. The commotion from below added to her anguish.

Leaving him to catch his breath, she went downstairs to close the door, regaining, again, a soothing calm, broken only by Antonio's subsiding gasps. As she climbed the steps, she could smell the coffee she'd brewed earlier; its bitter, earthy aroma strengthened her resolve. *Whatever has happened, nobody is going to destroy what I have worked so hard to build.*

She waited. Patience had never come easily to her, but she knew she would get no answers until he regained his composure. When his breathing settled a little, she walked to him. Resting a hand on his shoulder, she took up a towel, gently squeezing his hair dry, tenderly restoring its chestnut gloss. His breathing slowed, his shoulders relaxed, giving way to her petting. Despite her burning curiosity about the morning's events, her thoughts turned to Mary Magdalene. Against all the conventions of her times, she too had found the courage to administer love to a man who would never be hers entirely. Paolina's heart swelled with adoration for her man of God, whose musical genius filled her with hope and joy. How tempting it is, she thought, to believe that ours is a love that will transcend rules and avoid censure. She kissed his cheek and he took her hand to his lips. They stayed like this until finally, she could wait no longer.

'What has happened, Antonio? What troubles you? There was gossip today at the market.'

Antonio did not reply but simply shook his head. She feared the worst.

Pushing away from her, he stood at the window. 'So, the tongues have been wagging already have they? How quickly bad news spreads in this town. Even my copyists, my nephews, cannot be trusted to keep anything to themselves.'

He paused. Paolina frowned. What had his nephews to do with this? She knew he disliked sharing bad news with her. News that could cast him in a bad light. But his distracted mood was angering her.

'You must tell me, Antonio. I am sick with anticipation of bad news.'

'It is the Ferrara operas. I have received yet another letter from that wretched Reverend Bolani. He is now insisting that I send him a different score, the *Alessandro nell Indie*, after, just last week, requesting *L'Olimpiade*. Can these provincial imbeciles not make up their minds?'

Paolina said a quiet prayer of thanks. Business. Just business.

Antonio continued, animated now as if relieved to have someone to share the morning's frustrations. 'Nothing, not a thing, did he mention of the ten letters *I* have sent *him* reminding him of the money he already owes me. No. I cannot do it, Paolina! It is too much to ask! I have already invested in a copyist for the *L'Olimpiade* and work has begun. I have a mind to pull out of my commitment in Ferrara altogether. I have plenty of other work. I don't need their petty politics.'

Paolina, relieved of her greatest fear, planned her response. The Ferrara operas were critical to ensure their income for another year. They had invested significant monies already, too much to simply walk away. However, even more important to Paolina, was Anna's career. *L'Olimpiade* was to be a major role for her, a role that would guarantee her fame across Europe. She could not let Antonio's temper and stubborn pride throw it all away. The way forward was clear to her.

'You must contact your patron, the Marchese Bentivoglio, and tell him of these ridiculous demands and ask his assistance to attain the monies owed to you. It is him for whom you are working, not Bolani.'

Her face, flushed, showed a renewed animation. She thrived on the excitement of negotiations, the way other women flourished in matters of the heart. During her many years assisting her father she'd watched him assert his business acumen. Over time she developed a shrewd instinct for new opportunities and her ability to negotiate a good price had helped to make him a wealthy man.

She went to the writing desk. She'd often drafted Antonio's letters because his own were those of an artist, not a businessman, embellished with gratuities and claims about his own genius and worth. Paolina knew this was a sure way to bring upon him the ire of powerful men of business.

For the first time since arriving home, Antonio smiled. He cupped her face in his hands. 'Yes, yes, you are right, as always. Ah, where would I be without my Giro sisters?'

They kissed. Not a kiss of passion although Paolina could feel her body responding to his touch. No, it was a kiss of familiarity, of companionship, of thanks.

Antonio sighed. 'I sometimes fear Venice tires of me, Paolina, and perhaps I too tire of Venice. I rush from one event to another, trying to please. And they too rush about as if in a fever; looking everywhere for excitement and never really hearing or seeing what they already have. Look at how they flock to hear Hasse's opera.'

Paolina had heard that a new opera had arrived in the city, brought all the way from Naples.

'They say his songs are more to their taste than mine. More melodic,' Antonio continued, shaking his head. 'If that is what they want, well Paolina, I cannot do it. I cannot change what I have spent a whole lifetime building.'

Paolina looked into his eyes and saw tears. She remembered her father becoming more sentimental as he aged. A shudder of fear ran through her. Anna's career might survive without Antonio, but she had now come to depend on him.

'Your reputation will never be extinguished, Antonio,' she said, wondering if this was true or simply blind hope.

'But I am tired, Paolina. Perhaps the time has come for me to step aside.'

Paolina took his hand. 'What has brought this gloom upon you, Antonio? Just yesterday you were talking of contacting King Charles in Vienna. You seemed so sure about the future, for you and for Anna.' And for me, she thought.

Antonio pulled her to his lap and they kissed, now as lovers, and laughed at the continued surprise they both felt at the delight they took in each other, found so late in life for them both.

'I am sure you are right, Paolina. I am invincible and will be famous forever,' he joked, but they both knew this was indeed what he hoped for. Taking his hands, she kissed his soft, lined palms and a shiver ran through her. These magical hands, that could caress and rouse a violin like no other, hold also my dreams and longings, she thought. She felt the rush of desire, flamed as much by secrecy as by love. Perhaps Venice, the mistress of deception, is, after all, where I belong, she thought.

Pulling him closer, she could feel him against her. But Anna would soon be home, so she drew away, willing her body to wait. She went to the small walnut writing desk.

'Drink your coffee dear Antonio. I will write the letter and soon we will be on our way to Ferrara, and then, God willing, we will be invited to Dresden where we will show the whole world how truly great Antonio Vivaldi is.'

As she wrote, Paolina heard him humming the tune of the Concerto his student had played for the Scotsman that morning. Its sad but hopeful resonance echoed her thoughts.

'Oh, I forgot to ask, what was it you heard today that upset you?' Antonio said.

Paolina looked at his weary face and knew she could not burden him with their stupidities.

'Nothing. Just *pettogolezzi*- gossip!'

Outside the bells ushered in the afternoon *riposa*.

CHAPTER 6

Australia 2010

Fiona spotted Teresa and Paul in the small back room of The Black Bull. She'd walked there, trying to get rid of the anxiety she felt about going to a normal place doing normal things. The whirlpool had increased the closer she got. It'd been a long time since she'd ventured into a respectable pub. No deals happening here, she thought as she looked around, automatically casing the place for hand bags left open and spare change left on the table. *Old habits.*

'Oh! Here she is,' Paul called out, beckoning Fiona over. 'Welcome to the best pub in Adelaide, Fiona. What do you want to drink?'

She hadn't seen him since the day in court and she'd never been around both him and Teresa. She'd told herself that her feelings about him were ridiculous but seeing him in the flesh again, with his untidy hair and sleepy eyes, brought on a warm rush she'd rather not feel. She wanted to turn and run, but a big group of people came in behind her, some carrying instruments.

'A beer'll do – a light. Thanks'. She had no intention of getting drunk. As Paul went up to the bar, she sat down next to Teresa and near the door. Around her, chairs were being shifted to form a circle in the centre of the room and people started getting out their instruments. Soon the circle filled with violins, flutes and one accordion.

Teresa smiled a welcome but continued her conversation with the man beside her. Paul gave her the beer and went back to the bar to talk to the barman. Relieved not to have to make conversation, Fiona watched as three musicians began playing, tentatively at first, then with confidence as they glanced at each other, getting into each other's rhythm. Slowly, two others joined them – a woman on a tin whistle, and the man who had been talking to Teresa, on another violin. Conversations dropped to a whisper as the whole pub gathered to listen. Before long, Teresa joined them on her violin, or fiddle as she preferred to call it.

Fiona had only been to a few concerts in Australia where the bands had been on a stage facing the audience. This was very different, with the musicians facing each other and some with their backs to the audience. She noticed too, how they made eye contact with each other as they joined in or took a lead. It's just like the ceilidhs I went to as a child, she thought as she sipped her beer. The circle seems to protect them and they play for themselves and each other, not for the audience. She wondered how it would feel, that circle of protection.

A long-forgotten memory rose up of visiting the ancient stone circle called Temple Wood with her grandmother and Uncle Andy. It was the old people's church he'd said: 'Like a church without the hypocrites.'

Fiona hadn't known what he meant then, but she certainly knew she would feel safer in the music circle than with many of the church people she'd met.

The musicians played in unison mostly. At times, one person would take a lead and the others would either stop or play quietly in the background. Supportive and respectful. Backward and forwards they went in a never-ending spiral of music. One of them played a tabor, a small flat drum that he held sideways, patting with his hand. It had a Celtic Cross printed on it.

Fiona remembered asking her uncle about the circular carvings in the Celtic cross. He said the circle meant life goes on: 'When the leaves fall it makes way for new buds,' he explained.

Looking at its intricate circles she thought about how her mother's death had spurred her to get clean. Jake leaving had cast her into a backward spiral. And now, here she was again, emerging like a new bud. She wondered what had changed to allow her to grow this time and her eyes fell on Teresa. Was she the link?

As the music swirled around her, her memories rose and fell, soothing and smothering the whirlpool. Soon it totally enveloped her and she was back there with her family, a little girl again, safe and loved.

Paul broke her trance when he sat down next to her. She startled and moved so that he wasn't touching her at all. He smelt of soap and sandalwood, Jake's favourite aftershave. Paul didn't seem to notice her reaction.

'How's it going with your probation? Bob's a good bloke, if you do the right thing, that is.'

'OK,' Fiona shrugged not wanting the night to be tainted with the other Fiona, the criminal Fiona.

'Look,' he said, 'I'm not supposed to see clients out socially, you know professional boundaries and all that, but I cleared it with Bob, 'cos well, you're Teresa's friend and she thought it would be good for you to be here.'

Teresa's friend? Fiona didn't think of herself that way, but she nodded anyway. Other than Lanie, she'd not had a friend since high school. And Lanie's friendship was not what she would call steady. The people she'd been close to at school had all gone on to university, or overseas. Friendship was not something she counted on.

'Look at my lovely wife,' Paul went on, a little under the weather, Fiona realised. 'Isn't she the best?'

His adoration for Teresa was so obvious that Fiona almost laughed at her own childish attraction to him. She remembered Jake saying, only half joking, that she'd fallen for the first man who had been kind to her.

She realised then how much Paul reminded her of Jake, both physically and in temperament.

'You two are good together,' she said as the music finished, but Paul was already standing up to give Teresa back her seat.

'Good *craic* eh?' Teresa said, flushed with exhilaration, her Irish brogue stronger than ever. 'We'll have you up with us before you know it,' she said to Fiona with a conspiratorial smile. Fiona blushed. She would love to be good enough to join in but could never see herself as having the courage.

Before she could think of an answer, the room went suddenly quiet. All eyes were on a woman in her late fifties who had been playing a tin whistle. Overweight and frumpy, her long grey hair was pulled into an unruly loose roll. She looked at her feet for a few seconds and then slowly raised her head, gazing towards the back of the room, and began to sing. Her voice, crystal clear, was full of both sadness and passion.

Bheir mi oro bhan o
Bheir mi oro bhan i
'S mi th bonachs tu'm dhith
'Siom adh oidhche fliuch is fuar
Ghab mi Cuart is mi leam fin
Gus an d'rainig mi'n tait
Fai'n robh gradh geal mo chridh

Fiona only recognised a few of the Gaelic words but it didn't matter. Its pathos and longing were clear. When the song finished the room remained quiet, allowing the last notes to fade, as if people needed time to come back from another world. The applause was gentle but sincere. People nodded their appreciation to the woman as she went back to her table, back to where she looked like an average, unassuming housewife again. Fiona wondered how many people, other than those in the Black Bull, knew this woman and yet had no idea of her amazing gift. She remembered Susan Boyle, the woman who'd won the talent show in Britain and all the fuss about how plain she looked. How shallow people are, she thought.

One of the musicians had brought their little girl with them. She was sitting cuddled in her grandmother's lap. Fiona remembered sitting by her grandmother's fire listening to her softly singing in Gaelic, or playing her flute, as she fell asleep.

Behind the grandmother was a mirror. Seeing her reflection served as a sudden reminder to Fiona that she was still the person who had traumatised a young man, perhaps for life. That she had thrown away a good relationship rather than face Jake's anger.

The negative thoughts flooded in. The whirlpool spun. *What would Gran think of me now? A drug addict. A thieving criminal. A prisoner. A fraud.*

Her stomach lurched and she thought she would vomit. 'I've got to go,' she blurted, grabbing her bag, making for the door as a rowdy reel began playing.

Teresa frowned. 'Are you okay?'

Fiona didn't, *couldn't* answer.

As she reached the door, Fiona turned back. Teresa was staring after her, looking worried. Fiona fought off the urge to run. You owe this woman, she told herself. If you're going to start again you can't run away every time you're afraid.

'Thank you,' she mouthed. Teresa smiled and nodded just as Paul put his arm around her. They fit together without even trying, Fiona thought. A wave of jealousy ran through her, convinced she would never know that sort of love again.

That night Fiona went to sleep with the music from the Bull in her head. She dreamt she was with her mother in a small boat. They were going to an island where Teresa and Gran were waiting. As they got near to it a whirlpool started ahead of them. It began spinning faster and faster. Vonnie wanted to go closer.

'It will be exciting, Fiona. Come with me. We belong together,' she said. Fiona could hear the deafening whirl and see the bottomless hole.

'Sorry, I can't go Mum.' She jumped out of the boat just as it and her mother disappeared. She swam until she was on dry land.

Waking she could still hear the whir but now it was inside her. She gave into it and for the first time since her mother's death, she cried as if she wouldn't stop.

***

Sitting in the waiting room of the Probation Office, a room like so many she'd been in for most of her life, waiting for one public servant or another to decide her fate, Fiona had to fight hard to remember that she was building a new life. It was full of people that she either knew or could guess what they were about. Users or dealers, or both. Just seeing them triggered in her an urge to use. Her old rehab worker had warned her about this and recommended no contact. Now here she was sharing a small room where getting a fix was just a nod away.

Her hands began twitching and her skin prickled. The whirlpool, which had been stirring all day, began spinning and her breath came in shallow gulps.

She closed her eyes and forced herself to take a deep breath and slowly release it through her mouth. Once she would have been embarrassed to do this publicly but she no longer cared what she looked like to anyone in this waiting room.

The panic began to slow. Two older people came in. She saw the signs of their alcoholism. The whites of their eyes were turning yellow, their skin hung off their bones and their hands were shaking beyond control. The man, unshaven and smelling of urine, had given into despair. The woman tried to cover her situation with make-up and cheap perfume, just as Vonnie had done in the last years. The shame and humiliation that had haunted Fiona, stealing the joy from her youth, crowded her thoughts and the old familiar loneliness began to drag at her, like an ache. And with the ache, an anger rose. A nod to the dealer in the corner, a casual conversation over a cigarette in the car park would get her a taste that would chase the loneliness away.

'Fiona Sinclair?' Bob ushered her into a long corridor with rooms going off on either side. As she followed him to his room, Angie and Tahlia came out of the one adjoining. She nodded to them and wondered why they were there together. Tahlia had a defeated look about her and Angie met Fiona's inquiring look with a glare that converted to a smile. A false smile. Fiona put her head down. She had enough on her plate without worrying about Tahlia. A man came out of the room they had been in. Fiona thought that he rubbed his groin before he caught her watching him. He acknowledged Bob and smiled at Fiona.

Amongst the clutter on Bob's desk Fiona saw the bulging green government file with her name in large black handwriting: Fiona Morag Sinclair. The sight of it, her life put on record, started the whirring in her stomach and the tightness in her chest. The whirlpool raged, fast and strong.

Fiona had seen dozens of social workers over the year and had prepared what she would and wouldn't say to Bob. Even though Teresa and Paul had said he was trustworthy, they had never sat where she was. She had plenty of time to observe Bob while he tried to open up his computer. He muttered under his breath before picking up the phone and calling for help. Fiona noticed his tweed jacket, worn at the elbow, sat untidily on his shoulders. He wore a bow tie, slightly skew-whiff. The comforting smell of Butter Menthols reminded her of her uncle.

In her experience most social workers were either burnt-out middle-aged men and women, only working so they could build up their superannuation before they retired, or smartly dressed young women with trendy haircuts, just out of university, who thought they could save her life. The older ones were less easily fooled but they never followed up on their promises. She suspected Bob was one of those and was glad because the younger ones were the worst. One of them, in the juvenile system, had once told her to take up extreme sports.

'I've just been bungy jumping,' she said in her eastern suburbs accent with its long vowels and throaty effect. 'It's so good to face your fears.'

'You have no idea of how many fears I've faced,' Fiona had fumed grabbing her file and flinging it across the room. They'd swapped her to another worker cut from the same cloth. This time Fiona had decided to be agreeable, to please her. It worked a treat.

She noticed a large red sticker on her file and guessed it was probably a warning. "Aggressive Client. Be wary."

Bob mumbled to himself as he rummaged through the piles on his desk, groaning when he found her file right in front of him. For a moment Fiona wondered if he had dementia. She'd done work experience in an aged care home when she was at school, thinking at that time of going into nursing. The experience had cured her of that idea. But once Bob sat down she could see a bright alertness in his eyes.

He proceeded to ask her all the usual questions: where she was living, had she found work, what her plans were. But, unlike the others she'd dealt with, he seemed to really listen, as if he actually wanted to hear what she said. His calm focus and Butter Menthol smell made the whirlpool slow down. She answered his questions as honestly as she could. He seemed particularly interested in Wesley House.

'A few of my clients have lived there,' he said. 'Some found it a safe place to land when leaving prison, especially those who had been in for a long time. They say they like the curfew because it limits their choices. Some have gotten out as soon as they could. Others, and unfortunately this seems to be the majority have used it as a base to carry on doing exactly what got them into trouble in the first place.'

Fiona waited for him to ask which category she fitted into but, instead, he said 'You will probably be making decisions about which of those you fit into. If you are the second, and my guess is you are, we should start planning your next move.'

'That is my plan. I just need money to do that, and a rental record. The unit I shared with...' she hesitated, she didn't want any questions about Jake and what went wrong, 'a friend, was in his name.'

'If you agree for me to talk with him, I can send a letter to the Department of Housing to say you contributed to the rent.'

When she didn't answer him, Bob nodded. 'All in good time, Fiona. You are hopefully in a safe place at Wesley and there is no rush. But think about it and we can talk about it more next week.'

By the time she left, the urge to score had gone, although his words "hopefully in a safe place" stayed with her. Was she?

Tahlia was sitting in the garden when Fiona arrived home. She was totally wasted. One of the older women was there too.

'She came home like this. Angie said she demanded she score for her. It would have been on the house no doubt. Bastards!'

An emptiness opened up in Fiona that she hadn't felt since Vonnie had died. She wanted to enfold Tahlia in her arms, to squeeze some life back into her. She wanted to hit her too. To punish her. She did neither.

Back in her room she took out her flute. Teresa had found the score of her Vivaldi concerto and rewritten the second movement into a simplified version so that Fiona could follow it. She played until her sadness disappeared and told herself that Tahlia was just another junkie kid. There's nothing I can do to save her, she thought. Yet when she went to bed that night she wished it were otherwise.

The weekly lessons and trips to the library filled almost all of Fiona's time. She looked into some house sharing situations but hadn't found anything she was comfortable with. They were mostly students looking for someone to share the rent. She could imagine being left to do all the housework. A couple of adverts had been with older women. Fiona sensed their neediness before she went through the door. Mental health problems, mostly. She'd already been her mother's prop and this was not something she ever wanted to do again.

She kept to her room more and more at Wesley. Tahlia was becoming more dependent on Angie and Fiona had hardly seen her straight for weeks. It upset her to see Tahlia like that, but she knew she could do little for her.

Even her sessions with Bob were a relief from Wesley. As she'd predicted, he wanted to hear about what had led her back to using after a year of being clean. She gave him the condensed version.

'I had a relationship break up.'

'So, had it only been the relationship that kept you from using?'

Fiona had thought about this a lot since her arrest. 'I thought it was, but I've been clean for three months now, so maybe it wasn't.'

'Perhaps if we go back and look at how it all started you might get a better picture of why you used and what will stop it happening again. Are you happy to do that, Fiona?'

Slowly, cautiously, she began to offload her story.

'The stealing started before the drug use, when I was about fourteen. At first it was just to get by, for food mostly, and cigarettes for my mother. But then, later, I did it because I could. I was good at it. It felt good.'

'So it was a kind of revenge?'

'Yes,' she admitted, holding his gaze, awaiting his response. She expected a lecture. But Bob was not that sort of counsellor.

'Revenge for?'

'Every dumb fucker who's messed me around.'

Bob nodded, not bothered by her language. 'And the marijuana and amphetamine use? When did that start?' He asked.

'The marijuana when I was about thirteen. At first, it was just to get to sleep, especially if I was home alone when Mum was out drinking. But later, by the time I was fifteen, I would start as soon as I'd done my homework. On weekends, it was pretty much all day.'

She waited again for the lecture on the links between mental illness and heavy dope smoking. It didn't come.

'Sounds like the drugs served a purpose. At first to stop being scared and help you sleep, and then what? An escape?'

'Yeah, I guess. Escape from my shit life.'

'But only after you'd done your homework,' Bob said with a conspiratorial smile.

Fiona wasn't sure if it was a question or a statement. She thought about the many times she'd put off using to get an assignment done. Even she didn't understand how, or why, she kept up with her study. What use was it ever going to be now? Uni was out of the question. Employment a remote possibility.

'And the amphetamines?'

'Once I finished school it was like this big chasm opened up. Speed was there. Just to party with, at first, then I needed it daily.'

'Did it go with anything else? A relationship?'

'I mostly used speed when I was with a friend. It was more her thing than mine at first. I didn't like the whole bikie gang thing that went with it.'

She threw a glance at Bob, wondering if she had said too much. Surely everyone knew the links between speed and bikies.

'Is that who you would get it from? Bikies?' Bob asked. Fiona sat back in her chair as a wave of anger rose in her. He's just like all the others, she thought. She stood up, grabbing her bag.

'Don't think for one effing minute I'm going to grass my dealer - ex-dealer. It's more than my life's worth.'

Bob's face became animated and he vigorously shook his head. 'No. Sorry. I didn't mean that. Sorry.'

She glared at him.

'Sorry, Fiona,' he said with conviction. 'I'm just wondering how it impacted on you financially. Speed costs, and even dope isn't cheap. Sit down. Please. I won't ever ask you to be an informer. That's not my job.'

He seemed genuine. She sat back down on the edge of the chair, keeping hold of her bag.

'So, you had to pay for it?' Bob continued.

'I pawned stuff. Well, the stuff that my darling mother hadn't already pawned. Cow! And then I started stealing big time. House breaks and bottle shops.'

'Yes, I see that you had a few juvenile convictions and three as an adult. Then there is a break before this latest case of Aggravated Break and Enter.

'And that's just what I got caught for,' Fiona said before she could stop herself. For some reason, she was dropping her guard. 'I could talk the talk, you know? Not like the other girls who were foul-mouthed. When I took out my studs, people didn't watch me like they did the others.'

'So, you see yourself as different from the others? Better?' Bob asked.

Fiona hesitated. 'Not better. Most of them are OK, really. Most of them have had even more crap than me to deal with. Foster homes and abuse is all they know.'

'So, you have known a better life. One you want to get back to, perhaps?'

Fiona nodded. Talking to him about that was too much. He filled the gap. 'So, anything else? Heroin?'

Fiona sighed. She knew that coming clean about her drug use was the way to get help, but this was hard.

'Just once.' Fiona looked at her feet as she fought to keep at bay a memory she'd almost managed to forget. Bob waited.

'I mostly stayed away from that crowd. Well, until you fuckers put me inside. They were all over me then, when they knew I was probably going down. The dealers came out of the woodwork, harassing me to take stuff inside. Keeping it sweet in case they got grassed. I told them all to piss off.'

The memories of those last days before her court case and her first day inside flooded in. The whirring took over and her anger flared.

'Great fun that was. Strip searched twice. First the screws and then the fine genteel women of the Little Yatala Hotel.'

Bob smiled.

'What's so funny?' she snarled, staring him down. 'Don't suppose you've ever been strip searched and then bashed. It's no fun you know.'

Bob's face sank. 'Sorry. Again. It's this job; we get a bit blasé about prison. Yes, I appreciate it must have been very hard for you, Fiona. Your first time in adult prison and all. It's just, I've never heard it called that before.'

Fiona dropped her stare.

'Is that it then, just the bad crowd that kept you away from injecting heroin? You could have smoked it, I suppose?'

What game is he playing? she thought.

'Really? Didn't know that!' Sarcasm came easily when she was angry.

Bob continued, undeterred. 'I just wonder if that was all that kept you away from hard drugs? I'd guess there is plenty of pressure for you to use at Wesley, too. It must be difficult not to relapse. '

'Listen, I don't use heroin. OK?'

Bob met and gently held her stare. Despite her efforts, the scene with Richie came back like a tidal wave.

***

She was sixteen. It had been mid-week and she had an essay to finish. Vonnie had just received the letter from Andy that Gran had died. For Fiona, it seemed unreal, like a bad dream that she would wake up from. It had been eight years since they'd left and it was not easy to talk to Gran on the phone since her hearing had gone. There'd been letters, but they'd shifted so often that even those had been few and far between. Fiona couldn't feel anything much and just wanted to keep going with what she was doing. But for Vonnie, it had been an excuse to get pissed.

'Come on Fi, come out and have a drink with me. We have to have a wake of some sort.'

'What do you care,' Fiona had shouted at her mother. 'If you hadn't pissed all our money away at the pub we could've afforded to go back to see her before she died. Anyway, I've got work to do. I've got a history essay to hand up tomorrow. Go on your own. You know you just want to meet a new bloke, since Richie tossed you over.'

She could have left it at that but the anger rose in her and she knew where to hit where it hurt. 'Crutch happy you are? Can't do without a man for ten minutes, can you? Gran would be so ashamed of you.'

Her mother had grabbed her arm, almost pulling her off the chair. 'Don't you ever think that you knew her better than me you smug bitch. She was *my mother*, and she always loved me, no matter what.'

The door slammed behind her. Fiona welcomed the peace and quiet and tried to get on with her essay. She couldn't stop thinking about what Vonnie had said. She knew she was right. Gran had loved her only daughter, through all the drinking and the drama. It was hard to believe she wasn't there anymore, in Scotland, waiting for them. Going back there was all that had kept Fiona going some days.

'Fuck you, Mother,' she muttered to herself slamming her book shut. The French revolution didn't seem so important anymore.

She was rolling a joint when the doorbell rang. She could see Richie through the peephole.

'She's not in.'

'I know. I saw her at the pub. She said to come and get the stuff I left behind. She said it was in a box in the wardrobe in your room.'

That'd be right, thought Fiona, stash your hanger-on's shit in my room. She opened the door. She'd always quite liked Richie. He at least had a job and had read a book in the last ten years. They went into her room.

'Sorry to hear about your Gran. Your mum said she wanted to have a wake with you but you'd been a bitch to her. She always blames you for her problems you know.'

'No shit.'

He picked up her book. 'You're *so not* like your mother.'

Fiona smiled. She told him about the row. Digging into his pocket, he pulled out a small packet of white powder. 'This might help,' he said. She'd never used anything other than dope and she was pretty sure that heroin wasn't going to help with her homework.

'Yeah right!' she scoffed.

'No really. We can smoke it if you like. Roll it with that,' he said, pointing to the joint. 'You can have just enough to calm you down. You'll write a brilliant essay after this.'

What the fuck, who cares anyway? She thought. She knew Vonnie would hate that she used with Richie, and revenge was sweet.

'Yeah, it might help me to stop being so pissed off.'

The impact was immediate. She floated into a world of happiness where anything was possible. The whirlpool, which had been in overtime since the row, rippled out and she was surrounded by a soft blue lake. She looked at her essay lying on the desk and smiled. *Tomorrow.*

She noticed that Richie had not smoked any of the joint. He leaned over, kissed her roughly, and rubbed her nipple. She laughed thinking he was teasing and anyway, the stuff was making her feel horny. Part of her, the stoned part of her, was ready to go with it. She closed her eyes. Richie started tugging at her jeans.

She pushed his hand away. Even though every stoned cell in her body was telling her to go with it, she knew in some last remnant of her sensible self, that this was not how she wanted the first time to be. She struggled against the heroin. He'd already undone his fly and was trying to lie on her. She tried to scream and push him off, but she was too out of it and he was heavy.

She sank back under his weight. *Might as well give in. I'm just a slut. Just like her.*

Neither of them heard the apartment door open. Vonnie started screaming as soon as she came into the room. 'You prick! Get off her, she's just a kid.'

Richie laughed as he stood and pulled up his jeans.

'Thought it was like-mother-like-daughter,' he said, grabbing his bag and leaving.

The door slammed. Vonnie tried to stroke her hair but Fiona just stared at her from a world far away. Drunk and stoned, mother and daughter, they withdrew into their own worlds.

They never spoke of it again and Fiona hadn't used heroin since.

Fiona shuddered as the memory washed over her. She knew she wasn't to blame but somehow she still felt ashamed whenever she let herself think about it, which wasn't often. Bob was still watching. 'I don't and won't use heroin, alright!' She snapped.

Bob nodded. 'OK. So, what about marijuana? When are you most likely to use that again?' He asked. 'When would it seem like a good thing to use?'

Fiona looked up, surprised. She hadn't expected him to ask this. Most counsellors just lectured her on why she shouldn't use. Caught unawares, she answered honestly.

'When I think about my mum, mostly.' Her voice caught and tears began to well. She hadn't cried in public since the day she left Scotland and she wasn't going to do so today. She hated the way Bob made her feel. Really feel. Her anger flared. 'When I think about what a fucking selfish bitch she was,' she sneered.

Bob didn't bite.

'How would you feel about talking to me more about your mother? I gather she died just before you last got arrested?'

Fiona stared at her feet as the whirlpool spun faster.

'She seems to have left a big mark on you,' Bob ventured.

'What do you want to know?' Fiona spat. 'She was just a drunk. She didn't give a shit about me. She just wanted to have a good time, no responsibilities. She only ever looked after herself.'

'Yes, I've read Paul Kelty's report. Your mum had a pretty chaotic lifestyle once your dad died. Must have been tough for you growing up with that. Not much of a role model then?'

Hearing Bob criticise her mother made Fiona want to defend her. 'She wasn't all bad.'

'Oh,' said Bob feigning surprise. 'So, there was some good stuff too?'

Fiona knew she'd walked into his trap. She didn't mind but it was a while before she could answer.

'She was spoiled rotten when she was little, by my grandfather. Gran said he worshipped the ground she walked on. There hadn't been a girl in the family for years. Her brother adored her too, so she grew up getting everything her own way. Gran said she tried to discipline her but she would just go to Gramps and get what she wanted. He died when Mum was thirteen. That's when she started playing up, according to Gran. Mum said all she ever wanted was to have a good time. "Life's for living," she used to say. Then she got stuck with me when she was eighteen. She always said that I cramped her style.'

'That must have been tough on someone like her. A child to look after when all she wanted to do was have a good time?' Bob suggested. 'But it was tough on you too, if she didn't really want you and you felt like she thought she'd been stuck with you.'

Fiona nodded. Bob watched her and a silence filled the room. For a long time, she'd only felt anger at Vonnie. But as she got older she began to realise that her mother had done it tough too. Yet forgiving her was still something she couldn't do. It would be like letting go of a shield.

Bob broke the silence. 'Sometimes when we're angry at those close to us, it helps to put ourselves in their shoes. Take their part. Do you think you could do that? It's not easy, but I think you could manage it, Fiona.'

She shrugged.

'Perhaps you could write about it, rather than talk. Write to me as if it's from her. Get into her head.'

Fiona scoffed. 'Would that be the drunk head or the sober one?'

Bob ignored her sarcasm. 'Whichever is going to help you, Fiona. Sometimes writing from other people's perspective helps to get in touch with another side of them, the side that didn't make you so angry or hurt. Just, you know, see life from their perspective. Have you ever done that before?'

Fiona had learned about point of view in English classes. She shrugged.

'Take it slowly. Just do as much as you want. If you feel like it's getting too much, just stop.'

Fiona had a million thoughts in her head during the walk back to Wesley House. She'd done some writing over the years but had always thrown it away. At school, she'd received good marks for her short stories and poetry. One of her poems had even been in the school magazine.

The hostel was quiet and only Tahlia was around, sitting in the kitchen. She startled when Fiona sat next to her.

'Want a cuppa?'

'I guess, if you're having one,' Tahlia almost whispered.

Fiona watched her as she got the mugs out. She could see new track marks in her arms. The gaunt blackness around her eyes reminded Fiona of how she used to look before she met Jake.

'Are you doing OK?' she asked. 'Is Angie looking out for you like she said she would.'

Tahlia shrugged. 'You could call it that.'

Fiona knew then, in that comment, what was happening. 'You don't have to do it you know. You don't have to do what...' She knew that if she directly named Angie she would be targeted for a bashing or worse. 'You can make your own choices, Tahlia.'

'Will you help me then?' Tahlia pleaded. 'Will you score for me?'

Fiona shook her head. 'No but I will-' What, she asked herself? What can I do? I'm barely keeping my own head above water.

Tahlia laughed, a bitter sad laugh. 'See. I don't have any choice. Besides, the punters Angie lines me up with are all rich and clean. It's not so bad.'

Fiona remembered that day, many years ago at the pub. It was as if hers and Tahlia's lives had been decided for them then and there. She gave her a quick hug.

'If you change your mind, let me know.'

Taking her tea, she went to her room and locked the door. *My door, my key,* she thought. *When I get myself out of here I'll be better placed to help Tahlia.*

She took out the notebook and pen Bob had given her. 'A clean slate on which to make your mark,' he'd said. She agreed that if it got too much, she would ring him.

Turning on the tiny CD player she'd bought for five dollars, she chose the 'Four Stone Walls' track. On the good days, and there had been some, her and Vonnie would sing it together. She placed her tattered photo next to the CD player. The letter flowed easily.

Dear Bob

I am Fiona's mother, Vonnie. Veronica really, but that sounds way too serious, don't you think? As you know I'm dead now, but my life was great fun while it lasted, although my Mum and Fiona didn't think so. They are so alike – so serious.

I was just starting to really get out from under Mum's rules when I found out I was pregnant. I was only seventeen and I thought about getting rid of it, but Mum and Gregor, Fiona's father, talked me out of it. They would help, they said. Gregor even offered to marry me there and then, much to the horror of his stuck-up mother.

We never did get married but it was all OK for a while. I moved to Aberdeen and Gregor would come in off the rigs every two weeks and be home for two weeks. He was making plenty of money, so we had it pretty good really. Mum would come and stay once a month for a week, while Gregor was away. Sometimes I wished she wouldn't, she's so fussy. I could see her plotting how she would clean the flat up as soon as she walked in the door. She wouldn't say anything ye ken, just sort of sniff and look like she was picking out where to sit that was clean.

I used to go out as much as I could when she was there. That's fair, isn't it? I didn't have anybody to look after Fi any other time. Mum would say 'That's fine you go and enjoy yourself' but if I came home with the drink in me we would have a row and then she would talk about the 'state of the hoose, not fit for a wean to grow up in,' and that sort of shite.

We would always try to patch it up before she left, but we both knew that she thought I was doing a rubbish job of being a Mum. But I wasna'. Not then anyway. I'd play with Fiona and take her to the shops and buy her lots of toys. I never had any of that when I was growing up. One doll and a cradle that my brothers broke, that's all I got to play with.

I had good pals in Aberdeen. I was always good at making friends. Two of them had kids too, so we would go to each other's place. We'd get a bottle of Grants when we could afford it. The weans'd play together and we'd put the TV or a video on and get carry-out fish and chips for our tea.

Anyway, things were going OK until the accident. Gregor was flown by helicopter to the Aberdeen Infirmary, but he was dead on arrival. His Mum came up from Edinburgh and, I swear, she wouldn't even look at me or Fi, like it was my fault he was dead.

We got a payout right enough. Well it was for Fiona really seeing we weren't married. I went out and bought a brand-new pusher for her and a diamond ring for me. We deserved that. I took some of my pals to Majorca for a week, too. We all left the kids with our Mums. We had a ball. I suppose I should have been the grieving widow but I just didn't see the point in not enjoying myself while I had the chance.

We lived on the rest of the money for a time but then it ran out and I had to get out of the flat. I was on the move ever since, really. There were a few men that I've fallen for. I like the ones that can show me a good time and have a few drinks and a laugh. It always seems to end up the same though. They either get sick of me and leave with half my stuff or else they think they can smack me about and stop me from going out. I read somewhere that some women actually like being beaten up. Maybe I was one of those, although I don't really think so. I just wanted to have a good time. Life's for living, you know?

Don't get me wrong, I always made sure Fi didn't see anything – she was always in the other room when any violence happened. I would send her up to Mum's sometimes when it was getting bad, or if I just needed to party to get over a break-up or something.

She liked it up there – they could listen to all their chookta music; Jimmy Shand and Salmon Tails up the River, that sort of rubbish. Does my head in! I'm more of a disco queen type: ABBA and Michael Jackson. That's my music.

Anyway, when Fiona was six she said she wanted to live up with her Gran and go to school in Oban. I said it suited me fine but, really, I was pissed off. If I'm honest I was jealous of them, her and Mum. I'd always wanted to get on with Mum like Fi did, but it never happened.

It was about that time that I met Stewart, the man of my dreams - my soul mate - well that's what I thought anyway. He was tall, like Gregor, but he was an Aussie. He lived on a farm over there but was working on the rigs in Scotland for a year. We shacked up straight away and it was good. He loved a drink and he was always cashed up when he came back on shore. He got on with all my pals too. He only met Fi a couple of times, and we used to laugh at her being a swat. When it was time for him to go back to Australia I said I would go too. I think it took him by surprise, especially when I said I would be bringing Fi. He said it was OK by him.

His Aussie friends were great at first and his family thought I was a laugh. It's funny though, he sort of stopped drinking when he got back on the farm. It's like he was another person, more serious. I was going to stop drinking too but, well, I just couldn't, not totally. I used to have a little dram every day to get me through. Nothing wrong with that is there? I wrote myself off a couple of times at the club after the footy. One time I didn't make it home, slept at his mate's place in the town. Nothing happened but Stewart didn't believe me and that was that. He said he wasn't going to be Fi's father. He told me to pack our stuff and go. Just like that! There we were in a foreign country and nowhere to live.

Fi had to change schools 'cos we had to move to the city. I lied and said he'd been beating me up. He hadn't, but plenty of others had so I didn't think it was a real lie. Anyway, we got a house from the Women's Shelter, a *mob of lesos they were, and I got a job at the pub working late most nights. Fi was always in her room studying. I think that was when she started on the dope. She'd go out late some nights for about an hour and come home and straight to her room. She doesn't know that I know this but she started pinching things too- you know perfume, CDs and mobile phones that she could flog to her pals to get money for the dope, I guess. We never talked about it.*

There was the time that I found her with one of my exes. I booted him out and I tried to let her know that I would protect her, but she just looked at me like I was a piece of shit. Maybe I'd left it too late.

Soon after that I started having the blackouts and losing heaps of weight. Fi made me go and see a doctor. I was supposed to stop drinking but I just couldn't – I would feel crook if I didn't have it.

Och well. Life's for living and then, hey- you die!

Fiona put down the pen. That's enough, she thought. The CD was up to her other favourite track and she sat and listened until it finished.

The heat wave of a thousand fears, rainbows from a million tears
Echoes of a symphony playing on your mind.

She wasn't sure what it all meant but she knew what the heat wave of a thousand fears felt like. She pictured herself as that little girl and, for the first time, realised that she probably wasn't to blame.

Christ Mum, I wish you'd told me it wasn't my fault, she thought and a huge weight that she'd not even been conscious of lifted from her. She stared at her reflection in the mirror and saw the woman she had become, not the child she'd been avoiding.

***

Sleep evaded Fiona. The relief that came from letting go of her long-held sense that she was somehow to blame for her mother's drinking, came with a price; a deep and profound regret that she hadn't talked - really talked - to her mother while she was alive. She picked up one of the books from the library and began to read.

These four ospedali, or 'hospitals' were charitable institutions for orphaned, abandoned, illegitimate or indigent children. Since one of them, the Pietà, deserves our especial attention, being not only the most famous (and most thoroughly researched), but also the one with which our composer (Vivaldi) was closely associated during most of his life, it will be useful to describe it in some detail. Founded in 1346... the Pietà, like its sister institutions, was supported by the state and run by a board of governors appointed by the Senate. Its population was reported in 1663 to lie between 400 and 500; by 1738 it held 1000. The girls were divided into two categories: the figlie di comun, or commoners, who received a general education, and the figlie di coro, whose education was specifically musical.

As Fiona read about the glorious music made by the girls in red at *le Pieta,* she couldn't help but compare it with the juvenile detention centre and the women's prison. How different it was for the unwanted girls abandoned in Venice. She wondered what would have happened if all the neglected, abused and abandoned girls she knew had been treated with such respect. Where would Tahlia and I be now if our mothers had lived in Venice back in Vivaldi's time, she wondered. Instead of being offered a safe home and music tuition we've been thrown into a system where we're treated little better than society's rubbish. She wondered why nobody else could see that their bad behaviour was the result of years of ill treatment. First by parents too broken themselves to parent, then passed about to homeless shelters or foster carers or residential-care homes. Fiona had heard horror stories about foster parents, ill-equipped for the job, many driven by money, not concern, who would turf the kids out once the going got hard. Was the whole social system too blind to see the pain behind their anger, she wondered?

She wondered how different she would be if she had been given music instead of shame.

From the kitchen Fiona could hear shouting as a few of the women arrived back home for curfew. She wondered if Angie was amongst them and if Tahlia would tell her about their conversation. The voices got louder and coarser as they argued over some petty dispute, their language reflecting their world and reinforcing all that everyone thought of them. She picked up her flute and gave thanks for her grandmother, Teresa and even her mum. At least she had something to go back to. Something that wasn't hard and angry and bitter.

CHAPTER 7

Venice 1737

Nothing Robert had read or heard prepared him for Venice's splendour. His own Scottish home, Newbattle Abbey, once the home of Cistercian monks, was grand beyond most establishments that he'd visited. But its grandeur paled in comparison to what he saw before him. It was as if a hundred architects had clamoured to fill every space with a building of his own design, each carrying on from the next but determined to be different. Each as splendid as it was serene.

Wrapping himself in the red silk gown, that his ciccroni, his guide and confidante, Paulo, had laid out for him, he threw open the shutters to watch the evening light as it began to slowly transform the canal from a loud and bustling trade metropolis, to an elegant theatre; the cradle of the world's art and music, the home of the world's greatest composers and performers. He could hear beneath him the clatter of a dozen or so gondolas tied to the pier, bumping in the tide against wooden pylons. Several skiffs lay anchored along the waterway, their sails lying piled on decks, awaiting the morning when boatmen would hoist them and sail out into the ocean where they would carry cargo to and from all parts of the city and beyond.

His senses were both excited and confronted. He saw chaos and order. Each fairy tale building exuded magic and mystery as Venice's normal, everyday life ensued, as if her inhabitants knew not the mystical enchantment surrounding them.

A group of girls wearing red, scurried past. They were from the *ospedali le Pieta* Paulo had said, out on a rare visit to a sister church. Their subdued laughter reminded Robert of that of his childhood friend Elspeth. She'd been forbidden to laugh in the presence of the members of the Kerr family, especially when Robert's father was at home. But sometimes she was unable to stop herself. He recalled one such occasion when it had taken his mother's pleas to prevent his father from whipping her.

Robert shuddered, remembering how close he'd come to being tied forever to the isolated loneliness of Scotland and the brutality of his father. Paulo came up behind him and rubbed his shoulders.

'What is it, Robbie. You look so sad.'

'I was just remembering the last time I spoke to my father.'

'Tell me, Robbie. It will seem not so bad if you share it with me.'

The two men, one impetuous, young and wealthy, the other an older, wiser courtier, sat down together on the low lounge, sipping the wine Paulo had bought.'

'I was in the walled garden, playing my flute, when I heard Father and my brother, William preparing to leave for a gathering at Dunbar. I remember seeing Mother looking down on me from her first-floor window. I waved but she didn't wave back. I should have known then that she was not on my side in this latest dilemma.

'I'd hardly been able to concentrate enough to practice. I was in such a state, tryingto escape the dark thoughts that filled me. Just that day I learned that my cousin, Donald would not accompany me on my Grand Tour and yet I was still being sent abroad.'

Paulo pulled a comical face and Robert smiled.

'Yes, yes, I know now it was the best thing to have ever happened to me but back then I was frightened.'

'Tell me what it was like for my frightened wee Robbie?' Paulo said taking his hand. Robert laughed at Paulo's adoption of his country's quirky words. They sounded strange in his Latin accent.

'Well, as I said, I'd been practicing my flute as I often did in our small walled garden. From there I could see Father and William's horses; massive creatures, stomping and fuming, their saliva spraying all those around them. They only ride the biggest and the most excitable of stallions, you understand. I could see the poor groomsmen too. They were trying to settle the horses. But they would not calm down. It seemed they had picked up on the atmosphere around them. You see, Paulo, this was to be an important day for the Kerr family.'

Paulo nodded but Robert could see the amused disbelief in his eyes. He was not a man to be impressed by men and large horses. He smiled too remembering his feeble grovelling that day. How long ago it all seemed now.

'I heard my brother bellow as he pulled himself onto his horse, 'Robert, you Jessie, come out of your hiding place. We are soon to depart.' He came charging towards the garden and I put down my flute, afraid he would catch me with it and berate me even more.

'I take it a Jessie is not a kind name to be called?' Paulo said. 'I have heard that a soft man is not taken to kindly in your country, let alone men who love each other. What would they make of us?' He asked.

'It would never be spoken of for if it were, I would be cast out, or worse, I would be forced to marry some poor woman. That is why I must stay always here in Venice.'

'So, what happened next? Did your father and brother ride off to their rally?'

'Not right away. My father began calling out to Mother, as if she were his prize hound. 'Come bid us farewell woman, for today we will witness one of the biggest rallies in Scotland's history.' Robert mimicked his father's baritone voice and coarse accent. They laughed until Robert recalled his mother's face as she joined them. 'Poor Mother. How could she put up with him?'

'It must have been a relief when they finally left.'

'Yes, and I could have simply bid them farewell, but I'd resolved to make one last bid to escape being sent away. Can you imagine if I had succeeded?' He said with a shiver.

'"Why are you wearing the clothes of a pansy, Robert?" William scorned as I appeared from within the garden walls. "You should be coming with us. Are you not eighteen and a man?" He laughed but there was no joy in his face, just disgust. "Look at how he dresses and wears his hair, Father. I do believe you have a daughter, not a son."'

'What was wrong with your hair?' Paulo asked twirling a lock that had fallen across Robert's brow.

Robert shrugged. 'I was wearing it as it is now - long and tied behind my neck. It was the fashion with my music society friends.'

Recounting the story to Paulo, Robert felt again the utter humiliation of William's words. His lips, red and fulsome, quivered just as they had done that day. He hung his head until Paulo gently patted his leg.

'Is it so bad? They are just words and he is just a man like you, with all his own secrets and fears, no doubt. What did you do next?'

'I tried to stand up to him but the stutter that has riddled me since I was a child took hold. Anyway, William was not interested in anything I had to say. "What kind of Kerr are you?" He said. "Do you not realise, brother, that Father will be addressing the entire assembly on behalf of King George? We hope to double the number of men and arms dedicated to his support."

'"Leave him, William," Father shouted. "According to your mother, he is still too much a boy, a mother's boy at that, to be concerned with affairs of the country."

'Mother had by now arrived at the gathering and stood beside me. I felt her stiffen at Father's snide remarks. I felt so guilty, Paulo. I know I am the greatest source of friction between them.'

'They are adults Robert. They choose their loyalties. You are fortunate to have such a strong mother. What happened next? Did she rebuff his remarks?'

'No, she remained silent as she often does. William and Father went on, praising each other, saying that Father had already been declared Marquis of all Lothian at my age and how William had been to battle and spilled blood for our King.'

Paulo topped up their wine glasses. His gentle encouragement over the weeks Robert had been in Venice had been all that Robert needed to finally explore his sexual desires.

Robert began feeling dizzy from the wine. He closed his eyes and remembered his father's parting words.

'"God help us if we had to rely on the likes of him to defeat the papist rebels. We can only pray, William, that the mewling's departure to the Continent will rouse his manhood. Stir his loins and stiffen his resolve."'

Their scathing laughter as they galloped across the bridge still pierced him. But even more upsetting was that when he looked to his mother for compassion, her eyes were cast down and she remained silent as the men disappeared across the bridge.

Pushing Paulo gently away and pulling the gown tighter around his shoulders, Robert smiled at the irony of it all. He had certainly discovered the type of man he was, and he had found his true loves. Paulo and music. It was here in Venice that he belonged.

Paulo's services had been arranged by his father's friend, Mr. Smith, the British Consul in Venice. He was known as one of the best *ciceroni* in Venice; his ability to move between worlds was renown. They were introduced when Robert first arrived. He'd met with Smith to cash in his travel bonds.

'I would advise that you take up the services of a *ciceroni*,' Smith counselled. 'He will show you the sights and keep you out of trouble. Venice is beautiful but there is a sinister undercurrent that can trap the uninitiated.'

Since that time Paulo had met with Robert every day and together they had visited the many churches and museums for which Venice was famous. Paulo explained to Robert the history of the city and the meaning behind the artworks he viewed. He introduced him into the homes of the wealthy patrician families who, excited by Robert's title, invited him to salon concerts and vast feasts. It was at one of these that Robert first met Vivaldi. They'd only exchanged a few words before Vivaldi was ushered off to meet another nobleman from France. He'd met the playwright Goldoni too. He'd entertained Robert with his tales of the eccentricities of the rich and famous Venetians.

'I do not have to go far to find the stories for my *comedia*,' Goldoni said. 'My plays and puppet shows are about the very people I meet every day.' He drew Robert closer and whispered, 'I have just written one about the red priest. It will probably upset him but will no doubt highly amuse even his greatest admirers.' Robert wondered if he too would make it into a play and what eccentricity of his Goldoni would satirise.

Although the exchange with Vivaldi had been short, Paulo managed to arrange for them to meet again at the *Ospedale le Pieta* to hear a Concerto that the composer was selling.

'Signora Giro, my assistant, will contact you,' Vivaldi said. 'She will arrange for a special recital for you by one of Venice's finest young flautists, one of the girls from the *Ospedale le Pieta*.

And true to his word an invitation for a recital arrived two days later for the following day. Robert had hoped to spend time alone with the composer but he'd been met at the door of the institution by Signora Giro. Her manner was brusque and Robert found himself wondering at her age. Her appearance was one of an aging spinster yet there was an energy about her that befitted a younger woman. A woman more his mother's age.

'This way Lord Kerr,' she said as she escorted him through a hall into a small alcove. In the hall about twenty young girls were gathered, each holding an instrument, mostly strings. He caught sight of Vivaldi who was in deep conversation with one of the girls. He made to go towards him but was prevented by the firm hand of Signora Giro. Her steely grey eyes left no doubt in Robert's mind that he was to stay with her and that she would guard the time of her employer jealously.

She approached one of the girls, a flautist, and brought her to where he stood. She played a lively, intricate piece and Robert marvelled at her musicianship.

'She is playing the first movement of the Concerto *Il Gran Mogul*,' Signora Giro said. 'Father Vivaldi said you may be interested in buying the manuscript. It is one of four that he has written to celebrate Venice's extensive influence across the seas and into the world. I expect you will want the whole set?'

The young flautist was dressed in red, as were all the girls from the institution. Her sweet countenance in the rather austere setting triggered in Robert a childlike longing for all that is simple. Again, he thought of Elspeth, for it was this naivety and simplicity that he'd valued in her when they played as children.

As he listened, he noticed that Vivaldi stopped what he was doing to listen too. He nodded to him, as if, Robert hoped, recognising in him the rapture which his music inspired. Robert raised his hand and began to move toward him, to thank him and hopefully gain some insight into the famous composer, but he turned to attend to some other distraction and Signora Giro's hand landed firmly on his arm, again.

'Are you ready to make the purchase, Signor Kerr? She asked.

'Yes. I will purchase the entire set.' Robert said, establishing he hoped, his status as a wealthy man.

'It will be Father Vivaldi's honour to provide them.' She said, her sternness giving way to a softness he had not expected. 'You can complete the transaction at Father Vivaldi's rooms at *via Carbon* in two weeks' time. In the meantime, you might want for your ciceroni to arrange an attendance at a service at *le Pietá* to hear Father Vivaldi's sacred music being played and sung. You will not be disappointed.'

Paulo secured a seat for Robert at an evening of sacred music at the church of *le Pietà*. Robert had initially dismissed the idea of attending there when he had seen the church's austere façade. It was so unlike that of most of the churches he'd visited. But having heard the Concerto and been encouraged by Signora Giro, he agreed. His interest was piqued even more when, at Florian's, the infamous house of coffee and gaming, he'd overheard whispers about Vivaldi.

'Is it true, Paulo that he is having an illicit liaison with one of his students?' Paulo had shrugged, a little annoyed.

'Antonio Vivaldi has devoted his life to his work, giving up his right to say communion so he can focus on his gift,' he said. 'It is jealousy of what he has achieved that fuels the gossip. As far as I can see he lives a very frugal life, working all hours that God sends. Some say he is a shrewd businessman and should be very wealthy by now, but others believe he is rash with his money, often buying expensive instruments for his favourite students.'

That evening, inside the church, Robert was again struck by how sparsely decorated it was. There was no gold panelling above the altar as he had seen in *San Rocco* and other more renowned churches. And only two simple paintings: one of the crucifixion, the other of the Madonna and Child. The white walls looked like large sheets of ice, as if to remind the worshipper that God had no time for frivolity, only honesty.

Finding a place in the centre of the large rectangular nave, Robert looked up to the balcony on either side at the choir stalls, where a strange metal grill covered the area where the choir would sit. Some said the grill was to protect the girls from licentious eyes. Others said that many of the girls were pock-marked and the grill saved them from shame. Robert wondered how the gentle female voices could penetrate such a barrier, and his hopes for a fine musical experience faltered. He had not expected such exclusion from the choir. How am I to hear their true sound, he wondered.

Movement behind the grill indicated that the choir was arriving. Paulo had said that girls sang even the base parts, but Robert could not even distinguish how many choristers there were, let alone whether there were any male voices amongst them.

A number of older patrons settled near him. Their loud, confident remarks reminded Robert that he was an innocent when it came to attending concerts. Again, he thought to leave, anxious not to be seen as a voyeur, come only to stare at souls less fortunate than himself. For the first time in several weeks, he wanted to be home with his mother at Newbattle where all was safe and certain. However, the church was filling fast; leaving now would make him conspicuous.

He caught sight of Signora Giro sitting with a young woman. She too was surveying the people gathered. Their eyes met. She smiled at him before lowering her gaze, but soon raised her head again and nodded to him. A man sitting next to Robert saw the exchange and leant in to whisper to him. 'That is the famous Anna Giro, Vivaldi's protégé. You seem to have caught her eye.'

Robert blushed. He was about to respond when a chord from the organ reverberated around the church and all murmurs fell away. Then, as the organ ended with a grand flourish, an excited silence was suddenly ended as the voices behind the grill burst forth as one. They soared and then sank into a chant like insistence before rushing forward again, the harmonies piercing and then conciliatory, taking their listeners on a spiritual journey. First a Gloria then a Magnificat. Robert's anxiety turned to excitement and wonder. Closing his eyes, he gave himself up to the sound that filled the church. It was as if his head were filled with molten gold. As if they were no longer human voices but ethereal echoes, resounding from Heaven, reverberating from the stars, soaring from the mountains, filling the rivers. Robert's thoughts and emotions were swept up and carried away and he wondered if this was what heaven was like.

The music entered his soul.

As the final notes faded, Robert opened his eyes, his cheeks wet with silent tears, his emotion extreme and conflicting. He felt fulfilled yet empty, overjoyed yet melancholy, as if he had discovered something that he'd not known he was missing. He stared at the painting of the Madonna and yearned for the peace he saw in her gaze. He looked then at the Crucifixion. Christ's body spoke not of pain but of supplication, of a giving over to destiny. Robert filled with a longing for his life to be more meaningful; a longing to be someone more than he was.

His mother's words flooded back to him. 'The tour will change you Robert. You will not want to come back.' He made his decision.

He would stay in Venice forever.

CHAPTER 8

Australia 2010

Fiona re-read the letter she'd written. Bob had been right; taking her mother's perspective had given her another way of looking at her life. Somehow the ever-present uncertainty and crippling humiliation now felt further away. Manageable. In fact, Fiona found "being her mother" surprisingly liberating. She even found herself wishing she had some of Vonnie's ability to laugh when there was nothing to laugh about. She smiled, imagining her mother's reaction if she were alive. She'd have been furious with her. 'You dinna ken what I think!' she would have said. 'Don't think you can read my mind, Miss Smarty Pants!'

Fiona picked up the pen and wrote some more – this time a poem. She knew it wasn't great but the physical act of putting words on paper comforted her. I must be weird, she laughed to herself. She practiced her flute for an hour, experimenting with some tunes of her own. And last of all she played, as best she could, the tune of the mystery concerto.

It was almost dark when she heard some of the women coming in the front door. Angie and Tahlia's voices, louder than usual, and a man's voice. Stupid bitches, she thought, they'll get kicked out if they're found out. She knew that a couple of the residents were sex workers, but their clients usually rented a hotel room. Their work meant they stayed away from crime, at least for a while. Her instincts told her there would be trouble from bringing a man to Wesley. Her whirlpool began spinning and she moved to the door, pressing her ear to it, hoping for some clue about who it was and why he was there.

Their noise faded. Soon she could hear the man grunting. It seemed to be coming from Angie's room. He let out a loud groan and the house fell silent.

Fiona desperately needed to go to the toilet but she waited for almost an hour, until the pain in her bladder became too great. Creeping into the corridor she almost collided with the man as he stumbled from Angie's room; his expensive suit askew, his tie in his pocket. He looked familiar. The smell of stale aftershave mingled with the salty smell of semen. His bulk filled the passage and he stared straight through her, his pupils like slits.

He's wasted, she thought as she sidled past him. Angie came into the corridor from her room just as Fiona went into the bathroom. She was fully dressed. Perhaps it hadn't been her he'd been with? From the toilet she could hear Angie and the man whispering. She was locking the front door behind him as Fiona tried to slip back into her room.

'Guess who Tahlia and I just fleeced?' Angie laughed, waving two one-hundred-dollar notes. 'Harvey Brown, my fat Provo. Can't get it up with his wife, he says. Didn't have any trouble with Tahlia it seems. All over in minutes though. Not a bad afternoon's work, I reckon.'

Fiona remembered then where she'd seen him. He worked at the Correction's Office. Her pulse raced and she opened her door, muttering something about being tired. But two of the other girls came in the front door laughing and making lewd actions.

'Just saw that creep, Harvey down the street. So is it party time Angie?'

Fiona was outnumbered and would have to feign interest. She tried to smile while her whole body was screaming at her to go into her room and lock the door.

'Yeah, but Tahlia and I get the biggest hit,' Angie replied. 'I did the organising and she did the rest. I'll bring some back for her. She said she's feeling sick.'

Fiona's stomach turned imagining him on top of tiny Tahlia. Just then, Tahlia crept out of the bedroom. She looked skinnier than ever, her eyes black with fatigue. She'd had a shower and her hair hung lank. She looked at the floor and Fiona wondered again how she could protect her. She tried to make eye contact, but Tahlia did not look at her.

'Come on,' Angie said putting the money in her bag, 'we'll go see Joe at the Mall. You coming Fiona?'

'Nah, you're right.' Fiona managed to say. 'I'll stick to my weed tonight.'

Locking her door, she realised she was shaking. She didn't care what Angie did with her own life. Sex work and drug use had been part of her existence for a very long time. But pimping? And Tahlia was still a child in so many ways.

Even worse for Fiona was seeing a Probation Officer at Wesley. It frightened her. She didn't much care for rules but right now she was trying to obey them. If he was corrupt enough to use one of his charges, what else was he capable of?

Checking that she'd locked her door Fiona promised herself to find a place of her own as soon as she could.

***

The following week passed without incident. The other women were quiet, having scored enough from Joe to keep them happy and out of it. She'd had another flute lesson and read some more about Venice, this time about the Grand Tour and the young noblemen who went to Venice in the eighteenth century. She remembered the mention of one of them, Robert Kerr, in the radio program about her tune.

On the day she was due to report to Bob again she considered not going, for fear of seeing Harvey Brown. It wasn't really an option though.

A warrant would be issued for her arrest for breaching her conditions and they knew where to find her. Besides, she reasoned, I'm pretty sure he was too out of it to remember me seeing him.

She pulled up the hood of her windcheater as she approached the reception counter. She couldn't see Harvey, but she knew he was around; she could smell his aftershave.

'Fiona Sinclair, to see Bob Hastings,' she said quietly through the grill, to the woman at reception.

'Bob's running a bit late,' she said. 'You can see Mr. Brown, the duty officer, if you want?'

'No thanks. I'll wait for Bob.'

She chose the seat furthest away from the front counter and adjacent to the door leading to the counselling rooms. She'd be hidden from view there when the door opened.

Two young boys, men really, although neither looked it, sat opposite her. She knew them from the streets. The taller of them nodded to her and patted his pocket, raising his eyebrows. She knew what he meant and shook her head. *Jesus, he's dealing in here. Idiot!*

The door opened and a sickening waft of the familiar aftershave filled the room. Her stomach turned and the whirlpool spun. She bent forward. Elbows on her knees. The hood fell over her face. Fear turned to resentment, then anger. *Even though it's him breaking the rules, it's me having to hide. It's all so wrong!*

Harvey came into the room, talking to the receptionist before calling in one of the boys. Fiona felt his eyes rest on her. She didn't look up until he'd gone. She was still there when the boy came out. He gave his mate a lazy high five, bumping shoulders, as the second young man went in. Fiona knew they'd just transferred drugs. They might be stupid but they're good, she thought. Fast and cool. Like I used to be. It felt like a very long time ago.

It was another twenty minutes before Bob finally called her through. After a few routine questions, he asked if she'd managed to write the letter.

Fiona pulled the pages out of her backpack, relieved, somehow, to be passing it over. As she watched him read, the whirlpool stirred. It was primarily about Vonnie, but it said a lot about her, too. She stared hard at the floor trying to calm herself.

Bob read slowly, as if taking in every word. When he finished he gave it back. 'You've been through a lot.'

Fiona shrugged, unable to look at him. 'Not really. Nothing compared to some.' She'd heard plenty of stories from the other girls. Her story didn't compare.

'Everyone's story counts,' Bob said. 'How did it feel writing it?'

'Strange,' Fiona said, finally making eye contact. 'It was as if she was watching me. I wanted to write it as if she was a complete cow, but...' Her face fell. It was hard to say. 'Maybe she did the best she could.'

'Maybe, but you have a right to be angry by the look of it,' Bob said pointing to the letter.

'Who says I'm angry?' Fiona snapped.

Bob waited. Fiona shrugged again. 'Yeah, alright I am pretty pissed off at her, but if I stay angry all the time it means she's still in control of my life. Now she's-' The unsaid words hung in the air for a moment. 'She's gone. She's dead.' The words went around in her head. *She's dead and I'm alive. I'm in charge now.* Something shifted inside of her.

I'm in charge now.

It seemed like an age before Bob spoke again. 'So, if she was here now, what would you say to her?'

Fiona laughed. 'That's a weird question. Dunno, probably – what's it like being dead?' Bob smiled and waited. Fiona realised he was not going to be so easily distracted.

'I guess I would want to...' Fiona couldn't find the words. She gulped back a sob and stared at the floor.

'So you do miss her?'

Fiona's anger burst through her tears. 'Of course I fucking miss her. She is- was- my Mum.' She reached over to grab some tissues.

Bob waited in silence.

'Sorry.'

'No need for sorry Fiona. It's a big thing for you. Love and hate sit pretty close at times. Most people have stuff they hate their parents for but most of us get a chance to work things through with them, one way or another. You didn't get that chance.'

'So, what? You hate your parents too?' She blurted out before she could stop herself.

'I think everyone does at times, even if they have no real justification. It's part of growing up. I do know some of how it feels Fiona. My father was alcoholic too,' Bob said.

Fiona looked up, surprised. She'd always imagined that people like Bob, with a university education and a career, would have come from perfect homes.

'So, where does all this leave you, Fiona?' Bob continued, pointing to the letter. 'Is it better to be talking about your mum or do you want to put it all away again?'

'No, it's better,' said Fiona quickly, nodding.

'Do you talk to anyone else about her? It might help sometimes to offload.'

'No. All the people I know have enough shit of their own.'

Teresa had once asked about her family, but she couldn't talk to her about Vonnie.

'There's nobody?' Bob asked.

Fiona shrugged again. 'I talk about some stuff with Teresa Kelty. She's my music teacher.'

'Teresa Kelty? Paul's wife? Yes, she'd be a good person to talk to, as a friend.'

There was that word again. Was Teresa a friend? Fiona wondered.

As she signed the attendance record Bob shifted in his chair. 'Fiona, before you go, there's something I need to tell you.'

The whirlpool lurched.

'I'm going to be away for two months. I'm taking some unexpected leave. My brother in England is very sick. You'll have to see someone else,' Bob continued, looking at a list. 'I think it will be Harvey Brown.'

Fiona froze. Her heart raced and the image of Harvey in the corridor and the sounds of him rutting filled her head. Her stomach heaved. Bob was staring at her.

'Is there something wrong Fiona?

She fought to get some words out. 'Do I get a say in that? He-' She began.

'He seems to be the only one with any capacity,' Bob said looking again at the list. 'Two months isn't long. Harvey is very experienced, especially with drug addiction.'

Yeah, Fiona thought, experienced is right. If she told Bob what she knew she'd have to make an official complaint. The other women at Wesley would be investigated. The memory of her first night in prison flooded back.

Bob was beginning to write his notes, as if nothing had happened. Fiona's fear turned to blind anger. *He's just like all the rest. None of them give a shit.* It was all she could do to stop herself from grabbing the file from under his nose.

'Fine. Whatever. You just go and enjoy yourself,' she snarled, making for the door.

Bob looked up, startled. 'Sorry, Fiona. I appreciate it's hard for you...'

She didn't look back. Fuck them, she thought. What's the bloody use of trying? Fuck you Bob. Fuck you Teresa. Fuck you Vonnie.

Fiona kept walking until she found herself at the mall. It was as if every cell in her body was screaming. She went to the ATM and took out all her meagre savings. Thoughts flooded in: of her loneliness and humiliation, of her fear at being pregnant and the sadness after it was gone, of Jake's rage, of the beating in prison and Lis's threats.

All the strategies she'd used so far to stay straight, disappeared. Getting out of it was all she could think about.

She found Joe easily enough. He greeted her with his usual charm.

'Look who's here. Haven't seen you for ages, *Thievin' Fi*,' he said. 'Lookin' good, girl. Plenty of work around for a looker like you if you need it?'

'Fuck off. Just give me a packet. I've got the money.'

They went to a deserted lane where she knew there were no CCTV cameras. She stood close to him, putting the money in his hand. With a final look around, he pulled a small bag out of his jacket. Fiona slid it through a hole in her pocket, into her jacket lining.

Deal done. Her heart pounded as she felt again the thrill and the terror of scoring.

'It's pretty good stuff Fi, baby. Don't share it with those other sluts at Wesley. Come back to me when you want some more.'

How the fuck does he know where I live? Adelaide is too small.

She pulled her hood up and headed back into the mall. It was all she could do not to run, but that would attract attention. She was walking so fast that she nearly collided with Teresa and Paul. *Adelaide!* No hiding here.

'Hi. Out shopping?' She mumbled.

'Yeah, just heading home,' said Teresa. 'Are you OK? You look a bit-'

'Yeah, fine. Just in a rush. See ya.'

'See you tomorrow,' Teresa called as Fiona broke into a run.

She went straight to her room and rolled the joint, her first for months. It felt good. Fat and soft. All the old talk started in her head. *I deserve it. It's only dope. I'll only have one and give the rest away.*

She lit up, inhaled and swallowed. At first nothing, then slowly, slowly that old delicious feeling. Here but not here. Sitting but floating. I'll just demand not to see Harvey, she thought. Bob's right, two months will go quickly. She got the letter out of her backpack and read it and began to laugh. It was hilarious.

What a joke you were, Mum, she thought as she sank into a haze. You were a nobody. You don't count anymore. You're dead.

She drew hard on the joint. Then again. She looked at the flute and smiled as she floated away. *My only friend is a flute.* She imagined the girls in red at *le Pietá* and wondered if they had ever played her tune.

CHAPTER 9

Venice 1737

Robert knocked at the entrance of the house on *via Carbon*. He was surprised at how modest a dwelling it was. He'd imagined that someone as famous as Vivaldi would have owned one of the many grand establishments that lined the Grand Canal. It did face the main canal, but its façade was plain and unadorned. There was no balcony and the yellow paint was peeling. It was three stories high, the third sitting oddly, as if it had been added, an afterthought. He imagined he saw a young woman's face at the window of the second story, but it disappeared before he could focus.

A group of youths jostled past him, speaking the local tongue, laughing and nudging each other as they walked. They were younger than him, but not by much and he envied them their companionship, their sense of belonging. Robert thought of his cousin, Donald and their days spent roaming the hills around the Abbey and fishing in the river that ran through the nearby woodlands. He was more like a brother to him than William had ever been. Once, after reading a book about the Norse Gods, they swapped blood and swore eternal kinship to each other. He wondered what Donald was doing now and if he would miss him now that he had decided to stay in Venice. He was still thinking about his family when the door opened. Signora Giro greeted him. He bowed to her.

'Signora Giro. I am-'

'Lord Kerr, yes I remember,' she said abruptly, standing aside to let him enter before leading the way up a stone staircase. 'Come, Father Vivaldi is waiting for you. He is saying that you want to hear more of the Concerto before you buy. I told him you have already committed to a purchase, but he is insisting. I trust you have brought your promissory note?'

She did not wait for an answer before they entered a room on the next level, clearly used as a music room. Piles of paper, he assumed to be manuscripts, lay on a large table, and several instruments, violins, violas and a single flute, on top of them. A worn carpet covered the floorboards and on the walls were three large tapestries of faded reds and yellow. Two paintings hung over the fireplace, the larger one of the Resurrection and a smaller one of St Cecilia who Robert knew to be the patron saint of music. Dozens of books lay in ordered piles around the edge of the floor. Despite the muted colours and untidiness, the room had a welcoming vibrancy.

Robert glanced around hoping that the girl from the church would be there, but it was only Vivaldi, who sat at a small table near the window, working on a large manuscript. His hair, faded to a dull orange like the leaves in late autumn, framed his lined face. Robert realised that he was older than he had initially thought. Older, by far, than his father and certainly frailer. The composer's breathing was laboured, a wheeze followed each inhale.

Signora Giro showed him to a chair in the centre of the room. Father Vivaldi did not look up for some time, immersed in his task. From across the canal, church bells tolled and the significance of the meeting settled upon Robert. He had never thought he would be in the company of such a great man let alone to hear him play his own work. Robert thought of his mother and how proud she would be. He thought too of his father and wondered if he would ever share with him this momentous event.

Vivaldi sat back and gazed for some time at the music before him, as if he were hearing it in his head by reading the notes. His breathing steadied and Robert thought he saw tears well. Finally, he looked up and nodded, a sad smile signalled his welcome. Without waiting for an introduction he addressed Robert as if they were long-time acquaintances.

'You are very young, Lord Kerr, to be venturing away from your family. I was younger too when I wrote this piece,' he said, indicating to the manuscript that lay before him. 'It was originally commissioned to celebrate the life of the daughter of a merchant from the land of the Moguls. She died while he was on the sea, far from home. With no mosque of his own faith to comfort him, he came to *le Pietá* to pray for her soul. I prayed with him. Some would say it was heretical to pray with a heathen, but his love for his daughter was profound and his grief, almost unbearable.'

He looked up then at Signora Giro before casting his eyes to the canal. 'Such is God's gift of love to all men,' he continued. 'It has the power to lift us to great heights, but when it is lost, we are all dashed to great depths. The wealthy fall as heavily as the poor.'

The words, so heartfelt and profound, left Robert feeling as if he was eavesdropping on the great man's thoughts. He wondered what loves the priest had known and lost. He thought too of the pain he felt at not ever having his father's love and wondered if that was the same pain as having lost love.

Unsure whether he was meant to say something in response and unable to think of any fitting remark, he shuffled his feet until behind him, Signora Giro gave a small cough. The composer turned back to the room and smiled at Robert.

'Signora Giro would like us to continue with the business at hand. And as always, she is quite right. You are no doubt keen, Signor Kerr, to be on your way.'

'I have nowhere to be Father Vivaldi, but I understand your time is precious.'

Vivaldi picked up the flute, then placed it back down. 'Unlike yourself, Lord Kerr, I am not proficient at the flute. I shall play the second movement on the violin. It is a simple tune, but many find it quite enchanting.'

'I would be pleased to hear it, Father. An enchanting tune befits the occasion.'

'You have read my mood well young man,' said Vivaldi as he positioned the instrument on his shoulder. Signora Giro took a seat at the far side of the room.

The tune transported him. It lifted him from the room and his heart filled his chest. Its melancholy beauty, although written here in vibrant Venice, reminded him much more of his homeland, where beauty and sadness were fated companions. He heard in it the softly swirling mists on the lochs and the pitiful cry of a laverack gliding between purple hills. He thought of his mother's soothing voice and lamented the loneliness of his father's aloofness. He felt again, listening to the tune, written to commemorate a father's love of his child, his own childhood; longing to be held in his father's powerful arms. He thought too of Paulo, sweet gentle Paulo, and the safety he felt in his arms.

As the final notes melted and a silence fell, the eyes of the composer met Robert's. Years and history divided them, but for this brief moment, they were united.

Such is the mystery and power of music.

Vivaldi was the first to speak. 'So, Lord Kerr, what do you think? Is it to your liking? Does it meet your requirements?'

Robert swallowed his rapture. 'I have no clever words of praise to give you, Father. I cannot say what it is, in technical terms, that impresses me so, only that the music moves me beyond myself. It reminds me of my home and of people I love. It takes my loneliness and turns it into a sweet joy, grateful for the life I have been given.'

The priest continued to gaze at him. The muscles in his cheeks quivered and his mouth fell. Tears filled his eyes. He gasped a little before taking his time to put the violin back in its case. Signora Giro came to his side. He gently brushed her away, before turning back to Robert.

'Your simple words of praise mean much to me, Signor Kerr. You have experienced the quintessence of music; it's ability to help us escape our flawed, human condition and connect with our eternal soul.'

He took Robert's hands in his own and stared deep into his eyes.

'I am an old man, Signor Kerr and I fear will not see many more years. The fate of this music is in your hands now. Take good care of it. Protect it for the future generations.'

Robert squeezed his hands as a sign of agreement, for he was unable to find the words to express his admiration. They stood like this for some time before Signora Giro gestured that she was about to usher him to the door. He was about to leave , when the young woman he had seen at the church burst into the room.

CHAPTER 10

Venice 1737

Paolina usually made a point of disappearing while Antonio played to a potential buyer. She would then re-appear only at the point of sale. But there was something about Antonio this day that triggered a wariness in her. And this rather strange young man added to the spell. He had about him an intensity that worried her, for Antonio too was intense and sad lately. It was as if an influence outside her control was upon him. Her logical brain tried to convince her otherwise, but the power of this inexplicable mood would not shift, so she stayed, taking a seat at the far end of the room.

She'd heard a young flautist playing this second movement at *le Pietá* the week before and thought no more of it. Now listening to Antonio playing, and seeing the enchantment on the Scotsman's face, she realised that something much more than a recital was happening; something outside of her knowledge. She felt excluded, as if she were witnessing a secret ritual.

When the music finished, she saw a look on Antonio's face that she had never seen before. At first, she thought it was just sadness. When he looked up she saw something more like remorse, as if he were thinking of something long forgotten. A shiver of fear ran through her.

115

It was at that moment that Anna came into the room, setting them all askew. Antonio smiled, for he loved Anna too much to be cross. The Scotsman startled and flushed, overawed as most men were by Anna's blossoming beauty, made all the more remarkable by her naïveté about her effect on them. Paolina, whilst infuriated at her for disobeying the demand that she stay upstairs, was, in fact, relieved by the intrusion. The spell, if that's what it was, had been broken and she was free to resume her role as assistant to the composer.

She'd prepared a receipt before the Scotsman came. He had agreed to bring a promissory note that she would exchange for cash with the British Consul, Mr Smith. She strode between the two men and retrieved the manuscript from the pile on the desk. She was about to pass it to Signor Kerr, hoping her boldness would detract his attention from Anna. She had been taking much more of an interest in Antonio's male customers lately, and this young man with his crooked smile and strange accent would no doubt catch her eye.

Anna walked to Antonio's side and stood looking playfully at the young man. Antonio, oblivious to Anna's impudence, drew her closer.

'Signor Kerr, may I introduce to you, my prima donna, Anna Giro.'

Anna curtsied to him. Rather than keep her eyes down, as Paolina had trained her to do, she smiled flirtatiously with the stranger.

'It is an honour to have a nobleman in this house. Should we not be offering wine?' She asked turning to Paolina.

'Yes, yes.' Antonio agreed. 'And you must join us, Signora Giro.' Paolina fetched the wine and poured them all a glass; a small one for herself and an even smaller one for Anna.

They exchanged pleasantries over the wine and Paolina discreetly gave the invoice she had prepared to their guest, who in turn gave her the agreed promissory note.

'Do you play yourself, Signor Kerr?' Anna asked.

'I play flute, but rather poorly. I intend to stay on in Venice to take further lessons.'

'Oh, yes you must,' Anna said. 'And you must come to see me in my next role as Griselda.'

Paolina could tolerate no more. 'I am sure the gentleman has plenty of offers of entertainment.' Taking his empty glass from him she continued, 'May I see you to the door, Signor?'

'No, I shall see our guest out for I must go too,' Antonio said. 'The plans for the new church, the new *le Pieta,* have arrived and I must view them. The Board have agreed to engage Tiepolo to paint the ceiling!'

Paolina watched from the top of the stairs as the two men exchanged further pleasantries before heading in different directions. Anna was slumped in a chair when Paolina returned.

'Why must you spoil all my fun? It is not often we have such a well born man in our house.'

'And why are you interested in a man, Anna? Marriage will ruin the career that you have worked so hard for.'

'I might as well become one of the common *le Pieta* girls then, if I am to be cloistered so.'

'You are hardly cloistered. And never for one minute let Antonio, or indeed me, hear you disparage those girls. As you know, Antonio holds them in high regard. You, however, as he says, are his prima donna. You must value that above all else. Once we get to Ferrara you will attract interest from far and wide and then you will be more than Venice's prima donna. You will be Europe's prima donna.'

'So, what did he buy then, the good-looking Signor?' Anna asked, her annoyance at Paolina dissipating in the light of such high praise.

'A flute concerto. Antonio has finally realised that he must focus more on writing concertos for the wealthy. He is having them printed in Amsterdam and can now sell copy after copy.'

'You sound like Papa, Paolina. Money, money, money.'

'I'll take that as a compliment,' Paolina smiled at her little sister. 'He did, after all, teach me all he knew about trade.'

As she tidied away the refreshments Paolina hummed to herself the tune she had just heard played. She remembered the look on Antonio's face and wondered what had been on his mind.

Antonio returned later that evening. He did not often spend the night with her, their intimacy usually a daytime delight. But she was not surprised to see him. Indeed she was pleased, for she knew in her heart something was worrying him.

'I cannot stop thinking about the young Lord Kerr,' Antonio said. 'When I saw how the music affected him, I was reminded of all that I have lost. At first, I thought him just one more of the many rich young men that explore and devour our city, only to return unchanged to their homelands. But when I started playing for him, I noticed something different. I saw in him a youthful innocence. I saw his raw, untrammelled vitality. Paolina, I saw in him the man I once was, a young man ready for life.'

She took his hand. 'We cannot escape aging Antonio. Would you really want to once again be so naïve, so fragile as you were at his age? I certainly would not.'

Antonio sighed. 'Maybe you are right. There is a season for all things. I should know,' he smiled, 'my *Quattro Stagioni* is played far and wide they tell me. I am winter and you, autumn, my Paolina.'

'And Anna, glorious spring,' Paolina laughed. Antonio picked up his violin and he played the autumn movement from his already famous composition. Its fulsome melody, strong and energetic, did indeed seem to reflect who she was. She was glad he had not played winter, for she found it far too icy, brittle even, and she did not want to think of Antonio that way. When he finished bringing the movement to its glorious resolution, she thought he would return to his work. Instead he played the second movement from *Il Gran Mogul*. The notes, pure and simple, filled the room.

'Do you know Paolina,' he said putting down the violin, 'this piece, it is not my best, far from it. It is so very simple and unadorned. I wrote it some time ago for a man I met, a man from the East. He had lost his daughter to disease. I remember when I was writing it thinking of all the lost opportunities when a child dies; of the pain for a parent who must keep on living after such a trauma. He told me he'd come to Venice on business hoping that by leaving his hometown he would forget. But, he said, he found no solace until he came to *le Pietá* and heard the choir. He approached me after the service and asked me to create something that would immortalise his daughter. Such was the faith he had in me. And when I played it for that young man, Kerr, I remembered again the power of music and gave thanks for the gift of music that God has given to me.'

'Your music is certainly a gift from God, Antonio. Everybody knows that. Perhaps it is time for you to move beyond Venice?'

'I don't know if I can leave Venice. It has been my home all my life. I just want to go back to a time when my music was a celebration of God's glory. Not a business for personal fame and money.' He looked at her searchingly. 'Do you understand?'

'But a new city will bring back the vibrancy of your younger days. Vienna is fast taking over from Venice as the centre for music. Perhaps Vienna is the place for you?'

'And Anna?' Antonio added. Paolina flushed. She tried to keep her ambitions for Anna in check, but Antonio could see through her.

'And Anna,' she conceded.

'When I played for Kerr I felt as if a spirit had come into the room and carried us both to a new place. A good place, where time and money and fame meant nothing. A place where I could be at peace and rest. Paolina, that is what music should be about.'

'There will be time enough for peace and rest after Ferrara,' she said, hoping to instil in him a renewed vigour. But the very mention of Ferrara seemed to overwhelm him and he gave way to despair. Paolina held his narrow shoulders and stood quietly, waiting for his silent sobs to subside. Shutting her own pain and fear away, a chill went through her. What would happen to them all if he could not go on?

Outside the bells chimed.

'You are tired Antonio. I am sorry. I sometimes forget that you are unwell. Your energy, once boundless, needs to be conserved. Tomorrow I will write again to Bogliana to have our arrangements in Ferrara confirmed.'

As they climbed the stairs, Paolina realised that no matter what they heard from Ferrara, she must move forward and trust her future to God.

CHAPTER 11

Venice 1737

The manuscript of *Il Gran Mogul* arrived at Robert's apartment just two weeks after his visit at *via Carbon*. A note was attached promising the imminent delivery of the other manuscripts, signed by Paolina Giro. Slipped into the wrapping paper, as if added at a later time, was a card with Anna Giro's name and two tickets to the opera *Griselda*. Robert's heart raced at the memory of her and he wondered if he would ever feel for women as other men did. Paulo had told him some men could love both. He was certainly attracted to Anna, but not like he was to Paulo. It was more a curiosity about their nature, an admiration of their quiet confidence. Much as he had once felt for Elspeth.

When Paulo arrived a little later, he tried to hide his excitement, but Paulo was wise. 'Anna Giro is the talk of the town. She must have an eye for you,' he teased.

'She reminds me of my childhood friend Elspeth. But I have no thoughts other than being a friend with either of them.'

'And who is this Elspeth? Should I be jealous?' Paulo asked as he pushed a stray lock behind Robert's ear and caressed his cheek.

Robert explained how Elspeth and her brother Calum had grown up with him. 'When my father was away from the Abbey my mother would allow me to play with them. She even made sure they attended the small school she'd established at the Abbey. She said she wanted to give me extra support to learn my numbers and alphabet, but I knew it was to get me away from my father, who wanted me to be outside with him and William. Mother knew that my stutter became much worse when I was with them. She was right. With her caring lessons in the company of Elspeth and Calum, the stutter all but disappeared.'

'In fact it was Elspeth who noticed I did not stutter when I sang. She taught me to try singing my words when the stutter was upon me. We spent many happy hours in the classroom and on cold wintry days, the three of us, me Elspeth and Calum, could be found huddled around the kitchen fireside telling stories.'

Paulo pushed him playfully onto the bed. 'Tell me more of this enchanted child, Elspeth,' he said as he lay beside him.

'She was good at creating other worlds with her stories about selkies and wood nymphs. I remember one about a black dwarf who protected the small animals of the highlands.'

'Was that your favourite?' At first, Robert thought Paulo was mocking him, but he could see the genuine interest in his eyes, so he continued.

'No, my favourite was the one she told of her great-grandparents. They'd been brought to Newbattle from the north when my great-grandfather destroyed their clan home at Red Castle. Her grandfather was a ghillie of some repute and he had refused to leave without his fiancée.

'Elspeth told of how they'd walked south for weeks on end, under the charge of the very men who had attacked their home. They tracked south then east, through the glens, along shepherd tracks, hearing the ghosts of those who had gone before them in those vast and lonely mountains. They arrived at Newbattle hungry and cold. Three weeks later they were married under our great sycamore tree. The tree is still there, and Elspeth's family have remained at Newbattle too.'

'Did you stay close friends with Elspeth and her brother?' Paulo asked.

'For many years we did, but once I began my formal education, first with tutors and then in Edinburgh, I rarely saw them. I suppose I began to see them as servants, no longer as friends. I think they too became wary of any informal interactions, fearful perhaps that Father would disapprove and banish them back to the highlands. But on the day of my departure, Elspeth broke the rules and spoke to me in a stolen moment alone. "You must remember me, Robbie," she said using her childhood name for me. She gave me a rabbit's foot for good luck. "I will pray for your safe return." She said.'

The memory of Elspeth and her kindness brought a tear to Robert's eyes. He realised he may never see her again. He got out of the bed and took out the rabbit's foot which he kept with his jewellery. He laid it alongside the Vivaldi manuscript. Then, picking up his flute, he turned to the second movement of *Il Gran Mogul* and began to play. He faltered and began again, this time playing it through with hardly a slip.

'If I do ever return to Scotland, I will play this for you, Elspeth,' he said quietly, making a promise to himself.

Remembering the tickets, he turned to Paulo. 'You must come with me to the opera!'

Paulo shook his head. 'No, no, my Lord that would not be right. I am your *ciceroni*. It would not be proper. One day you'll be with a person, maybe a man maybe woman, who you can take to the opera with you. But it will not be me.'

Robert's face fell. He could not think of a life without Paulo. Paulo was his first love and he could not imagine loving another.

As if reading his mind, Paulo took his hands. 'I am long practiced in reading men's nature, Robert. You think that this between us will last forever. But you are like a new sapling, you are bendable and green, full of the juice of life. But soon you will be a tall tree. There will be many more lovers in your life. I am delighted to have been the first, but one day you will move on.'

Robert was about to protest when Paulo kissed him. A lingering kiss, warm and tender. 'But there is no hurry, Robert. For now, we are happy.'

The tickets still lay on the table when Paulo prepared to leave several hours later.

'Perhaps you could ask your friend, Alistair to the opera,' Paulo said. Robert had recently met up with a man about his own age. His estate bordered that of Newbattle Abbey. Robert soon realised they were opposites in their tastes and desires, Alistair spending much of his time gambling and with the courtesans. But Alistair's amicable nature and their common history drew them together, often over a card game at *Florian's.*

Alistair had taken some persuading to go to an opera, until Robert mentioned Anna Giro's name. 'I have heard she is very beautiful,' he said. 'If I must go we will travel there by gondola, like true Venetians.'

The light began to fade and a fine mist flowed up the canal as Robert and Alistair climbed into their gondola. Venice had already put on her veil of intrigue and excitement for the evening. As they glided towards the theatre, Robert thought he could hear her proud, crumbling buildings whispering their stories about the men and women who lived there. Stories of how they exchanged their spices and coffee for cloth and wine; tales of the ships that sailed to her harbour across dangerous pirate-ridden seas, carrying their exotic cargo, joining west with east.

As Alistair spoke of his latest conquest, Robert reflected on how he'd opened his heart to this enigmatic city he now called home. He'd learned to embrace Venice's ambiguities, where rumours were encouraged, and tolerance overcame prejudice. Where Christians met and bartered, unhindered, with both Jews and Muslims. Where trade itself was like a religion, blessed by Gods and prophets, and music and art are held in the highest esteem.

Alistair's chatter turned to news from home. He told Robert that he'd met up with William just before he left and how he'd been bragging about a recent skirmish he quashed at the border. Rather than make him homesick, his stories tightened Robert's resolve to stay in Venice. He knew he would miss Scotland's rivers and glens but in Venice, he was free, at last. Free from his father's wrath, free from his brother's disdain and free even, from his mother's smothering love. Free, too, from Scotland's unsettled Union with England and the brewing battles that would pitch countrymen against each other in the name of religion and politics.

As they alighted from the gondola, Robert and Alistair donned their masks and entered the *Teatre de Angelo*. At the door they were provided with a small book of lyrics and a candle to read by. Excitement filled the dark theatre and candles flickered, like fireflies. They took their box seats on the second level, the higher boxes reserved for the very rich. Magnificent fans hovered, like elegant butterflies, over whispered scandal. Leaning forward, Robert could see the orchestra, gathered around a small harpsichord, lit by smoking torches; violins, viola, cellos, lutes and basses at the front, flutes, oboes and trumpets behind. Below them men and women, too poor to buy seats, mingled, admitted free, ensuring a full theatre and thunderous applause.

'I had not thought opera would be so well attended by all levels of society,' said Alistair. 'I thought it just for noblemen and their delicate women.'

'You forget,' said Robert, trying not to sound superior, 'that this is the birthplace of opera. Venetians have been listening to opera since the time of Monteverdi.'

'You sound as if you are in love with the place. Soon you will be telling me you are not leaving.'

'Indeed, dear friend.' Robert began but could not finish before the overture began. The larger flaring candles were snuffed, and the hum of the audience subdued. A young woman walked onto the stage.

Robert thought that Anna was to be the lead and his book of lyrics confirmed this. But surely this could not be her, the sweet-faced girl who had teased him with her smile? The singer's face, framed by a snow-white wig, was heavily powdered, her eyes accentuated with dark lining, her lips painted bright red. Her dress, as vibrant as her lips, was pulled tightly into her tiny waist pressing and lifting her delicate, fleshy breast. Her bustle, threaded with silver, drew the eye, alluring and licentious.

Robert leaned further forward and, just for a second, the singer seemed to turn and look at him directly. Finally, he recognised her. Those eyes, that had startled him with their playful innocence, now lured him into the passion of the opera. Sweet Anna Giro had become Queen Griselda.

She waited until all noise ceased. Opening out her slender shoulders, she tilted her face to the upper tiers, like a flower opening to the sun. Basking in the moment, she looked not at the audience, but to a place just above them, as if awaiting her annunciation; a virgin at her moment of conquer, a queen at her coronation.

A tremor of excitement ran through the theatre. She nodded to her audience now, a faint smile, that same smile Robert had imagined was for him alone, acknowledging their adoration. With a wave of her delicate hands, Anna Giro filled her lungs and began. By the end of the first Act, she'd won the hearts of all. Everyone was in love with Griselda and felt her pain.

Ho il cor già lacero da mille affanni,
gl'empi congiurano tutti a'miei danni,
vorrei nascondermi, fugir vorrei
del cielo i fulmini mi fan tremar.
Divengo stupida nel colpo atroce
non ho più lagrime, non ho più voce,
non posso piangere, non so parlar.
Ho il cor già lacero

My heart already torn to pieces
By innumerable pains, pitiless people
All conspire against me.
I wish I could hide.
I wish I could flee.
The lightening sky frightens me.
I am becoming numb
By this excruciating pain.
I have no more tears.
I have no more voice.
I cannot even cry.
I cannot even talk.

When the curtain finally fell Robert dared not turn to Alistair, for he too had no voice, could not cry, could not talk. He'd hardly dared breathe for the whole performance. The world outside had dropped away. He'd lived every moment of the tale of love denied, trust betrayed and justice triumphant, as if it were written especially for him. He joined in the deafening applause. Below him the common folk stamped their feet and shouted '*Bravo, bella donna. Bravo.*' She had given them her all. They loved her as their own. They no longer cared about scandalous rumours. She belonged to them all.

As flowers were strewn across the stage, Anna swept her arm above her and bowed in acknowledgment towards a box on the second tier where two elderly men sat. Goldoni, the stouter of the men, rose and bowed to the audience. Robert remembered having been introduced to him at *Florian's*. The other man remained partially hidden and gestured with open hands back to the stage where Anna bowed again; this time to him, alone it seemed. She blew him a kiss and the audience gasped as he leant forward as if to receive it. Robert gasped too, for it was indeed Antonio Vivaldi.

With applause still resounding through the theatre, Anna, her arms now full of flowers, waved her farewell. As she reached the curtained end of the stage, she pulled several of the flowers from the bunch, turned back slightly and raised them smiling, towards where Robert and Alistair sat. *Could she possibly recognise me?* Robert thought, before admonishing his vanity.

'She is indeed as beautiful as they say,' Alistair said as they left the theatre.

'She is everything,' Robert replied. 'Pretty and magnificent. Young and old. Innocent and experienced. She is all I love about Venice. She is music itself.'

'You have been smitten, my friend,' Alistair teased.

'Yes, smitten by Venice. I am staying here, Alistair.'

Alistair took some time to comprehend what he had heard. 'You can't. What will you do? Where will you live?'

They had reached *Florian's*. A veil of tobacco smoke, mixed with the intoxicating aroma of the roasting coffee beans greeted them. Mirrors, gilded with gold and silver, covered each side of the long narrow room. The high wooden ceiling arched overhead, like a shield. Glittering glass chandeliers, *ciocca,* holding dozens of flickering candles, cast a comforting glow, offering warmth and solace. Robert felt both anonymous and included. All things are possible in Venice, he thought.

An Englishman he'd met at various venues on his travels greeted them with a wave. He was playing *biribisso*. Robert and Alistair stood watching. Robert could tell Alistair was keen to try his hand.

He was surprised to see that many of the patrons were women. Already seated at a far table was Goldoni, surrounded by admirers, praising him for the play on which the opera was based.

'For all our petty squabbles, Father Vivaldi and I make a powerful alliance when we put our creative talents together,' Robert heard him say.

At another table, a group of men, local merchants Robert guessed, argued over the outcome of a game of dice. His coffee, thick and pungent was served in an elaborately decorated porcelain cup. It sent his head spinning.

'Now before you go any further with this nonsense about staying,' Alistair said 'I was waiting to tell you that William also said to let you know that a Commission has been found for you with Lord Barrell. It is time for all Scots, loyal to the King, to come home,' he said.

'To do what, Alistair?' Robert said in disbelief, that he could talk of such ridiculous things after the magnificence of what he had just seen. 'To kill our fellow countrymen?'

Alistair shrugged. 'To lead others into battle and of course to kill, if it is needed.'

Robert had heard this all before, from his father and his brother. Duty to the King over-riding loyalty to their highland countrymen. He thought again of Elspeth and her stories of clans and their devotion to the mountains and rivers. He wondered what his cousin, Donald Dunbar would make of this call to duty. He was an adventurer by nature and Robert feared that under the Marquis's influence he would readily take up arms. But he was also a romantic and had spent many years in the company of highlanders. He'd been born a low-lander but he'd become well versed in the Gaelic and the music of the highlands. Robert recalled that Donald and Elspeth would often speak to each other in Gaelic if the Marquis was absent from the Abbey.

He turned to Alistair and shook his head. 'I will not kill, Alistair. Not for King or country. Not for God or the Devil. I have found my love in Venice. Music is my sovereign and my creed, my ruler and my saviour.'

CHAPTER 12

Australia 2010

The late morning light filtered through the thin curtains. Its rays caught the flute, creating a cheerful dance on the wall. Fiona lay still, eyes barely open, following its playful movements, the memory of the previous day slowly returning. She looked at the torn letter and remembered Bob's news. What she couldn't remember was why she'd been so angry.

I don't need him, she told herself. I'll make my own way, just as I've always done.

She checked that she'd stashed the rest of the dope in the cavity of her reading lamp, safe from any random room inspection. When the time was right, she'd get rid of it. The used roach, she put in her pocket ready to flush down the toilet.

Glancing at the clock she realised that she was already late for her lesson with Teresa. She considered what lie she would invent and then checked herself.

Slept in, she wrote. *C U at the Bull maybe*. Send.

She stayed in the shower for longer than usual. The water felt good, cleansing. Drying herself, she stared in the steamed mirror. There but not there, like a mirage. Mirrors speak the truth. She wiped it dry.

Older yes, and something else. Calmer? Saner? Her hair, once cropped short with a blunt razor, had begun to grow out into soft irregular tufts. She had her mother's high cheekbones but her eyes, under that pronounced brow, reminded her of what she remembered of her father, intense and questioning. Lips, thin like a neat edge, held on tight to her secrets. Removing her earrings and tongue stud she'd put in in anger the day before, she remembered again the beating in prison and the horror of the image reflected in the cell toilet.

At least you're no longer that half person, she thought. 'But who are you now, Fiona Sinclair?' she quietly asked the image.

Back in her room she pulled on jeans and a t-shirt. Shouts from the kitchen area set her anxiety off. She thought about the dope hidden in the lamp and felt the familiar pull to spend the day stoned with no whirlpool, no memories. She picked up the flute, felt its pleasing weight and gently rubbed its dents. *Poor flute. You've been through it too.* She shut the thought of the drugs out of her mind and started playing. She'd had plenty of stick from the others about the flute but she couldn't hide the sound of it and she wasn't going to stop playing. Not for anyone.

After the noise in the kitchen had died down and a few doors had been slammed, Fiona heard a gentle tap on her door. It was one of the older women.

'Evie and I were wondering if you would play for us? In the garden perhaps. We like listening to you, but it's a bit muffled.'

Fiona's first thought was that she was being sarcastic. But she seemed genuine enough.

'Sure,' she said following her to the garden, making sure her door locked behind her. Fiona had never quite worked out where the older women stood with the others. She was pretty sure they didn't use - they certainly claimed not to. But they didn't kowtow to Angie and the others either. She guessed their age protected them a bit.

She played for a while and then they each had a go.

'It's harder than you think,' Evie said. 'You must have been learning before you came here.'

Fiona nodded but was not willing to tell them more. Even still, they opened up about themselves.

'I got done for fraud of the welfare system,' Evie the oldest one said. 'I'd been claiming, and my old man was working. He was a truckie and away most of the time, but he must have put me down as a dependent with the tax or somewhere. Anyway, I had no idea and I didn't consider us as a couple. He was hardly ever there and I sure as shit never saw his money. They said I'd been fraudulently claiming for three years. I went inside and he got off scot free.'

'But he wasn't even supporting you?' Fiona asked.

'Nope, but I couldn't prove it and he wasn't going to take the blame. Fraud is fraud they said.'

The other woman, Kathy, had been addicted to the pokies and she'd stolen from her boss. She didn't say much more than that.

'You should get out of here,' Evie said, out of the blue. 'You're too good for this lot. You're different.'

Fiona stiffened. Talk like this usually had a double edge. She was tempted to take the compliment, but fearful of a trap.

'I'll leave sometime. But not because I'm different. I'm not,' she said. 'We're all the same here. We've all been fucked over one way or another.'

'That's true, but believe us Fiona,' Kathy said, 'you are not like most of them. You've got a better chance than most of leaving it all behind. Don't wait till you get to my age to sort your shit out.'

Back in her room, Fiona thought about their advice. She wanted to move out but had no idea where to begin. Change was hard. No private landlord would take her on without a job. She might find a share house somewhere but not if they knew she'd been inside.

She picked up one of the library books. It had a whole chapter on the *Ospedale le Pieta*, the orphanage where Vivaldi's students lived. She read that many of them stayed on there even once they were sixteen and no longer considered orphans. Many preferred to keep on with their music and become a nun rather than face the alternatives. They were forbidden to play once they left, and marriage was often out of the question. *Most (Venetian) men,* she read, *required a woman to have a dowry. For those girls that didn't stay at le Pieta and did not marry, there was only one job available.*

Yes, just like Wesley house, she thought, Venice was famous for its courtesans. Girls and women with no or few options. Some things never change, she thought.

Her thoughts wandered to Tahlia. She hadn't seen her for a few days and she hoped she was OK. I think I would stay at the orphanage too if it meant I could keep on with my music.

***

A text from Teresa had given Fiona the courage to go to the Bull again. Checking that the corridor was empty and the key was around her neck, she slipped a piece of paper into the door jamb before pulling it shut. It was a trick Lanie had taught her at the shelters, to check if anyone went into their room. It had been a useful tip because the shelters were pretty lax about getting keys back when people left. She hadn't bothered before at Wesley; security was the one thing she thought they got right and besides, she never took her key off.

She'd just shut the door when, turning, she walked into Angie. 'Jees, you scared me,' she said.

'Always was good at surprising people, Fi. So where are you off to with your backpack and running shoes?'

Fiona had long since planned an answer in case someone saw her leave for her lessons or the Bull. 'Going to the pub to find Lanie's Mum. It's visitation day tomorrow for kids.'

She hoped it was a good enough lie. Enough to convince Angie.

'Bit dressed up aren't you? No rings tonight?' Angie said moving in closer to Fiona and almost pinning her to the door.

'Might hang out in the lounge bar for a while. It's always good there for a stray handbag.'

Angie nodded. 'So, you wouldn't be meeting that Kelty woman and her cute hubby that I saw you talking with at the Mall?'

Fiona fought the urge to push her away. She summoned all her survival resources. Angie was no dummy.

'Why would I meet them? They know me from inside, that's all. He did my report. You know what they're like, they think they're your friend. They wanted a chat. I pissed them off as quick as I could. Anyway,' she said inching out from the door, 'what's it to you?'

Angie grabbed her arm and pulled it above her head, pushing hard against her now. Fiona could smell the cheap perfume and stale cigarette smoke on her breath.

'Wouldn't want to think you might be spilling the beans about someone you might have seen here. I'd hate to have to go back to working the streets, because of some snivelling grass.'

Fiona made a decision not to resist. She relaxed against Angie and smiled. There was a time, when she was experimenting with her sexuality, she would have found Angie's muscular presence exciting, even attractive. She knew a submission here would be trouble, resistance a waste of time. She met Angie as her equal.

'None of my business, Angie. I just want to keep my head down, smoke my dope and finish my court order so I can get out of this place.'

Angie released her. 'Just so we understand each other, Fi. Harvey Brown might even come in handy for you too, if you do the right thing by him.'

Fiona was about to leave but turned back. 'Where's Tahlia? I haven't seen her for days.' Anger returned to Angie's eyes, like a snake striking

'She's gone.'

'Gone where?'

'Her mother's, or so she said.'

'So, she's still alive then – her mother?' Fiona heard herself ask.

'Yep. Got religion or something. Buddhism, Tahlia said. She's living in some commune in New South Wales. She came down and got her last week. Cleared it with the cops and off she went.'

Fiona barely kept the smile off her face as she almost ran out of the door. Well at least someone's mum came good, she thought.

***

She took the long way to the Bull, going by bus towards the pub where Lanie's mum would be, in case Angie had someone following her. She even went in and looked around. Her heart was pounding and the whirlpool stirring. Memories of hauling Vonnie from countless pubs almost engulfed her. She spotted Lanie's mum, waved, barely taking her eyes off the machine. Fiona leant down as if putting something in her bag. The chances of anyone watching were slim, but she had to go through with the charade.

Leaving the pub, she checked around for anyone she knew and then ran the rest of the way to the Bull via the back streets. She'd found that running, the pounding rhythm of her feet meeting the pavement, worked better than a drug to move the dark shadows of the encroaching whirlpool.

Arriving at the Bull earlier than planned she bought a beer and watched the musicians arrive. Their cheerful confidence made her nervous. Shoving her wallet back into her backpack she noticed her flute case protruding. She hoped that it had been covered back at Wesley and convinced herself that it must have been. Angie would not have let that go.

She'd decided to bring it to the Bull at the last minute, thinking she might just join in. But seeing the other musos, she changed her mind. She was not in their league.

A young man carrying a fiddle case came in, calling some joke over his shoulder. He bumped her table, upending her glass.

'Jesus, Mary and Joseph! Sorry, sorry' he said grabbing a beer mat, attempting to mop it up. 'Here now, let me buy you another one.'

'No. It's all right. I was just…' Fiona jolted backwards as he pushed the puddle of beer off the table onto her jeans. She felt the eyes of everyone in the vicinity on her. Her nervousness turned to anger. Anger at having beer spilt on her but even more, anger at feeling singled out. Exposed.

'Jesus, Mary and Joseph,' he exclaimed again. 'I'm an idjit, so I am.'

'Leave it!' Fiona yelled. She looked up, fists clenched, ready defend herself, but halted. All she could see on his face was pure remorse. He looked genuinely horrified at what he had done.

'I'm so, so sorry Miss. Let me clean it up.' Anticipating a repeat of the damage Fiona grabbed hold of his wrist to stop the next deluge. He's like a clumsy, comedic clown, she thought and, inexplicably, she began to laugh. 'Calm down man,' she said, still laughing. 'I'm *drookit* enough already!'

He looked at her and relaxed. A smile slowly spread across his face. '*Drookit* is it? I've not heard that since I went to Glasgow to see Dublin play Celtic.'

'Celtic was my dad's team. I guess you got a drubbing then?' The barmaid appeared with a cloth for the table and a tea towel for Fiona. She smiled and thanked her.

'No worries, love. We're always cleaning up after young Paddy here. I'll get you another one,' she said, clearing away the near empty glass. 'Yours a Guinness, Paddy? I'll put them both on your tab shall I?' She disappeared behind the bar before Fiona could protest. With soaking jeans, she had no intention of staying.

'Do you mind if I sit?' Paddy asked, indicating to the chair beside her. 'You know Paul and Teresa don't you?'

Fiona stiffened, remembering her earlier confrontation with Angie. *Was it possible she'd known all along where she was going and sent someone to spy on her?*

'Who's asking?' She snapped.

Patrick's grin widened. 'Keep your tartan knickers on. I've not been stalking you. I saw you with them last time.'

Fiona reddened trying to control her paranoia. If Patrick noticed, he didn't let on. 'They'll be here soon enough to be sure.'

She bit her lip realising he was just making small talk. It had been a long time since she'd chatted in a pub with a stranger. Pubs had always been for scamming. She glanced at Paddy, fearful he could read her mind. She still felt as if she had "Crim" written on her forehead. Clenching her fist, she scowled, and the whirlpool started spinning. She picked up her backpack, ready to leave.

'Should be good crack here tonight,' Paddy continued quickly. She wondered if he was deliberately talking just to keep her there. 'Do you play?' He asked nodding towards her bag. She pushed the flute case down.

'No, not really.'

He put his hand out to her. 'You might not believe this but my name's Patrick. Patrick Daniel Thomas Doyle. Can't get much more Irish than that I reckon. Of course, the Aussies call me Paddy.'

She put the bag down and awkwardly took his hand. 'Fiona, Fiona Sinclair.'

He laughed. 'That's as Scottish as mine is Irish. I reckon we've both got a touch of the Celt then.'

The barmaid arrived with their beers. 'Come on, sit back down. There's no one here going to notice the state of your jeans. And if they do just say it was my fault. They'll all believe you.'

Fiona looked around. He was right. No one was looking any more, busy as they were with their own friends. She reminded herself that part of being straight was being unnoticeable, anonymous even, and she liked the idea. She looked down at her jeans. The tea towel had done a good job of drying her off. Maybe she could do this. Maybe she could do normal things. Maybe she could stay.

Pushing herself to make conversation she was about to ask where in Ireland he was from when Patrick stood up. 'Ah, here's your mates.' He nodded to Paul and Teresa as they came towards them. 'I'll be leaving you to it then. Enjoy your night and try not to spill anymore beer on yourself' he said, winking at Fiona as he joined the music circle where some others had started tuning their instruments.

'I see you've met our Patrick,' said Paul, taking the chair opposite her. 'Talked the proverbial pants off you, no doubt.'

'No, just soaked them,' she said pointing to the cloth still on her lap. Teresa slid in next to her on the bench seat just as two women crammed in the other side.

Fiona startled. No escape routes. The whirlpool took off. She stood up.

'Can I get through' she said, trying to push past a confused Teresa just as the room filled with a resounding chord from an accordian. The musicians launched into a reel, lively and infectious. People started clapping in time. Patrick, who was one of the players, looked over at her and smiled. Teresa stood to let her out, looking concerned. Fiona's head began to spin and the music seemed to join with her whirlpool, twirling it in a dance as if taking her into its control. As if assuring her that all was well She sat down again. Teresa was still looking at her. Fiona took a deep breath.

'Can we swap seats?' She asked. 'Since being inside I hate feeling trapped.'

A wave of understanding and relief swept across Teresa's face. 'Yes. Of course. Sorry, I should have realised,' she said.

As they sat again, Fiona checked that she now had a clear path to the door. The reel got faster and her whirlpool slowed, as if bowing out of the dance. As the audience clapped in time, the players dropped out one by one as the pace increased. Soon it was just Patrick and another fiddler in a frantic race to the finish. The crowd laughed as the players finally nodded to each other and, with a final flourish, ended the number together. Brothers in the moment.

Fiona laughed too. The whirlpool had gone, and she felt as if she'd been carried to another world; a world where good people lived; a safe world.

***

The evening went quickly. She forced herself to talk to Teresa and Paul during the breaks but mostly just listened to all that was going on around her. Snippets of conversations about work and kids, laughter from an adjoining bar and the music of her childhood flowing over it all.

By ten o'clock most of the musos had left, leaving only Teresa, Patrick and the old man with his flute sitting in the circle. Paul was in the front bar.

The three musicians played a slow song that Fiona recognised from times past. It wrapped around her like a blanket and she wished the night could go on. When Patrick and the old man started packing their instruments away she picked up her bag, ready to leave. It was only then that Teresa spotted the flute case.

'Oh, you brought your flute, Fiona? How about we play one of the pieces we've been practicing? How about Loch Lomond?'

'I couldn't. Not with...' She looked around.

'Go on, Fi,' Patrick said gently. 'We all started somewhere. There's just us here now.'

Her mother and the girls from prison were the only people in Australia that called her Fi and usually she hated it, but coming from Patrick, it was OK.

She took her flute out. Teresa began, just as she did at lessons. Fiona took up the tune a few bars in. She played softly at first, becoming louder as her confidence grew. She made a couple of mistakes, but Teresa carried her along. She didn't notice that Patrick and the old man had come beside them. At the next chorus, they joined in. It felt like being carried along in a stream where nothing could harm her, as if she had jumped out of that boat in her dream and was being carried on the tide, safely, to the island.

As they finished they smiled and nodded to each other. There was no need for applause. They all knew what they'd done.

Getting up to leave, the old man patted Fiona on the shoulder. 'Well done, lass,' he whispered in his raspy voice.

'You've broken the ice,' said Teresa as they packed their instruments away. 'The first time in public is always the hardest.'

'Well, well, Fi Sinclair,' Patrick said, coming up behind her. 'For someone who "doesn't play, not really" you did pretty well!'

'Thanks.' Fiona nodded, stumbling to find words. 'It was good, you know, playing together with-'

'Friends?' Patrick finished for her.

'Yes. With friends,' Fiona smiled.

She was about to say more but Teresa interrupted. 'Fiona, we'll drop you home if you like?' Paul was saying goodbye to some other people from the pub leaving Fiona alone in the car with Teresa.

'You were great tonight, Fiona. It's good to see you relaxed again. You seemed a bit stressed when we saw you yesterday.'

Fiona shook her head, trying to shake away the shame of using again.. *How could she have been so stupid?* Looking at Teresa she wondered if she'd guessed why she'd been in the mall. Perhaps she'd heard about her outburst at Bob. But Teresa's face showed nothing but friendly interest. Fiona wondered if, some day, she would be able to confide in Teresa. Really confide in her. Instead she said, 'Bob's going away for a while and I have to see Harvey Brown now.'

She watched for Teresa's response, noticing a slight grimace in her expression. Fiona went on. ' Don't know him but I think I might have seen him before. Somewhere else,' she finished.

'Not just at the office then?' Teresa asked, almost prying, Fiona thought, but trying not to seem too interested.

Fiona took a chance. 'Maybe at Wesley one time.'

Teresa's eyebrows furrowed. 'Really? I wouldn't have thought,' she hesitated. 'Perhaps doing a home visit? Probation Officer's have to do that sometimes.'

'At night,' Fiona continued. 'At midnight.' There it was, said. Fiona held her breath, watching closely for Teresa's response. Passing on this information was dangerous and put her firmly in the "them" camp.

Teresa bit her lip and stared straight ahead, eventually looking around meeting Fiona's gaze. 'Fiona, if you have any concerns about him, you should speak to someone in authority. Paul perhaps?'

Fiona shook her head. She wasn't ready to do that. 'Perhaps it wasn't him. I probably got it wrong,' she said. She could tell Teresa didn't believe her.

'If it was him and he knows you saw him things could get tricky. Maybe you could ask for a change of Probation Officer.. You'd have to give them a reason though'

'I'll be alright, Teresa. I don't think he knows I saw him.'

Teresa looked worried. 'Perhaps see how you get on and if anything happens just let me know. If there's anything you're not comfortable with, anything unprofessional, I could probably have a word with his Manager. I've heard she won't tolerate inappropriate behaviour of any sort..'

Fiona nodded. At least someone else knows now, she thought.

Paul joined them and started the car and they both knew that the discussion had come to an end, at least for now.

'Teresa was telling me about the Vivaldi tune that you know, Fiona. She tells me you're doing some research to try and work out how you know it?'

Although pleased to be talking about something other than Harvey, Fiona hesitated, still nervous and unused to having normal conversations with Paul. Conversations about something other than scoring and scamming. Conversations that didn't focus on her homeless status or worse, on the past. Even Teresa would always check with her about the bad stuff. Paul just treated her like a normal adult.

She cleared her throat and told herself off for being so scared. 'Yep. Just books I can get from the library. They even got hold of the article written by the bloke who discovered the lost Concerto. He reckons nobody really knows how the Concerto came to be lost for so long.'

'But it was found in Scotland? Is that right?'

'Yeah. Edinburgh.'

'So is that just a coincidence then? You knowing it and being Scottish?'

Fiona shrugged. 'The bloke who discovered it thinks that this Lord Kerr, whose archives it was in, probably bought it in Venice while on a tour. But he lived on the east coast and my mother's family is from the highlands.'

'It's not so far away though, is it? Not compared to Australian distances.'

'No. But the East coast is like another country to them.'

'It sure is a mystery,' Teresa joined in. 'You'd think if you went to all the bother of buying it you would make sure it was passed down to your children or relatives. Vivaldi is very famous, after all. Although I do remember hearing somewhere that his music wasn't played for almost two hundred years. Even the *Four Seasons* that we hear everywhere now was unknown in that time.'

'I know,' said Fiona, totally absorbed in the conversation now. 'That's so weird because from what I've read he was pretty famous when he wrote all his Concertos. Even Kings and Popes bought music from him.' The tremor had gone from her voice and she could hear her adult self.

She was so engrossed in the conversation that she forgot to ask to be dropped off on the main road. By the time she realised her mistake they were already pulling up in front of Wesley House. She looked around. The house was in darkness and nobody was around. She jumped out. Teresa was saying something about studying Music History but she closed the door on her. Paul pulled the car away quickly, maybe realising her dilemma. As the car disappeared she smiled to herself, remembering what it felt like to be happy. Really happy. Not stoned happy.

It was past curfew and the doors were locked. Fiona went to the laundry window, being as quiet as she could. She held the window open just enough to hoist herself in. She was tall enough that her hands reached the floor while her feet were still in between the window and the frame. She slowly withdrew each leg, making sure the window didn't bang shut. The street light helped her to see the obstacles in her way – a bucket and mop and a crate of tinned fruit. The laundry was meant to be locked but the lock on the window had been faulty for some time and no one had come to repair it. They knew better than to make a fuss; the window was a common curfew entry for those who were agile and skinny enough to use it.

She knew something was wrong as soon as she approached her room. The small slip of paper was on the floor and the door slightly ajar. Her hand flew to her neck. Her own key was there. Opening the door, she saw that all of her books had been thrown off the shelf and her drawers wrenched open. She turned to the lamp. It had been upended; the packet of dope gone.

Bitches! Thank God I had my flute with me, they would have pawned that for sure. Then she laughed. Have the dope, she thought, I don't want it. She had something they would never have. She had her flute and her music, and she even had friends – real friends.

Fiona double checked the locked on the door, pulled the chain latch across and wedged a chair against the door handle. She would phone management tomorrow and demand they change the lock. As she cleaned up the mess, she resolved to start looking for somewhere else to live immediately.

Soon I'll be free of all this shit, she thought.

CHAPTER 13

Venice 1737

Paolina wrapped the *biscotti* ready to take to share with her cousin Maria. Her mother had taught her how to bake even though they'd had servants to do their cooking and cleaning.

'A woman always needs to know how to cook, Paolina. Your future will depend on it.' But Paolina had known from a very young age that it was her love of numbers and the cut and thrust of her father's business that would be her future. Working beside him had given her a role and status that not even her mother shared. And it was her fiscal talents that had initially ingratiated her with Antonio. The love came later.

It had not been the same for Maria and Bishop Xavier. They had fallen in love when Maria was just twenty and they'd lived secretly as husband and wife for the last sixteen years. It was from Maria that Paolina had sought counsel before she moved into Antonio's house.

'Of course you should Paolina, but first get approval from Bishop Xavier,' Maria had advised. 'Once you have his blessing, let it be known to the gossips at the market. They will spread the word that you have his permission to move into Father Vivaldi's house as his housekeeper. It is not unusual for a cleric to have a live-in housekeeper.'

'What if they suspect that there is more between us? If the other priests turn against both Antonio and the Bishop, we will all be reported to the Council of Ten. We will all be banished!'

'It will not happen, Paolina.' Maria had said. 'Many of the clergy already know that I am more than a housekeeper to the Bishop, but none have reported us because they too have their secrets. Besides, you want Anna to have recognition, do you not? How better than to be so closely associated with Antonio Vivaldi!'

'So,' Paolina asked, 'for Anna to have success I must partake in this dance of deception. Is that what you are saying Maria?'

Maria smiled and patted her hand. 'All life in Venice is like a dance, Paolina, a *tarantella*, keeping us protected from the spiteful poison of envy.'

Paolina nodded. 'Yes, I am beginning to understand how the dance works. Antonio too is sure the Bishop will protect him. He says his recent audience with the Pope has brought the Bishop many advantages from Rome. It seems that even your Bishop Xavier is part of Venice's dance, Maria.'

Paolina met with Bishop Xavier the following day. He greeted her warmly and, not standing on ceremony, ushered her into his private rooms. After brief pleasantries she came to the point.

'Your Excellency may have heard that I am working as Father Vivaldi's secretary and housekeeper. In exchange he will provide me with a small wage and tutoring for my sister, Anna. He has recently rented a property at *via Carbon* where Anna and I will reside.'

'Yes, yes, Signora Paolina. But this is an arrangement that does not need my approval.'

'I am concerned that the arrangement will be misconstrued and that our reputation, mine and Anna's, and even Father Vivaldi's will be tainted. I cannot risk harming Anna's career.'

The Bishop nodded and smiled. 'Ah, I see. Be assured Signora, all Venice knows that Father Antonio is a busy man. The governors of *le Pietá* have put many demands on him. He must come up with a new oratorio every Saints Day, I am told. And since the success of his *Quattro Stagioni,* his Four Seasons, he has achieved much acclaim, here and abroad.

'Everyone will understand that he needs someone to arrange his affairs and look after his home, and who better than you, who has for many years provided just such a service to your late Father. And of course,' he concluded opening his arms, palms upturned, as if inviting opposition, 'no one will question that he is by far the best teacher for your talented and tantalizing sister, Anna.'

'So, we have your blessing to reside in his house?' Paolina asked wanting no loose ends.

'Rest assured Signora Giro, I will do all I can to make sure no one misrepresents you.'

Paolina and Anna moved into *via Carbon* the following week.

It was not only their similar living arrangements that Maria and Paolina shared. They were cousins with a long-buried secret. A secret so dark Paolina had not allowed it to surface for many years. Once she had tried to talk to Maria about it, but she changed the subject and they had gone forward with their lives. Paolina had even convinced herself that maybe she had imagined it – their dark secret.

Arriving at the Bishop's home, Paolina adjusted the basket with the *biscotti* and rapped her knuckles on the door. She was surprised to find it was the kitchen maid, not Maria, who came to greet her.

'*Buena sera* Signora Giro. Signora Maria said to tell you the Bishop has asked that you join them in the upstairs drawing room. She instructed that I inform you of another man with them, a Cardinal.'

Paolina frowned. She had not changed her dress since the morning's baking and was unprepared for meeting the Bishop, let alone a Cardinal. Passing the basket to the maid, she brushed crumbs off her dress and tidied a stray hair into her headscarf. She wondered what the Bishop could possibly want with her. Perhaps he had a message for Antonio, she thought, straightening her scarf again as she climbed the stairs. She knocked and entered, remaining close to the door; the smell of tobacco and wine escalated her apprehension.

Bishop Xavier came to greet her and, taking her hand, led her into the centre of the room. Unlike Antonio he had a palatial villa. Marble frescos lined the walls and a giant chandelier hung from the ceiling. A balcony opened out to sweeping views along the canal. Paolina had been here once before and knew you could see San Marco from there. Today she stayed as close to the exit as she could.

'Come in, come in my dear Signora Giro,' the Bishop slurred. 'Your visit is very timely. We require a special favour from you.'

Looking around the room, Paolina noticed that Maria too stood back from the men. She was staring at Paolina, her eyes strangely focussed, as if trying to alert her to something. Paolina turned to the Cardinal, wondering what possible favour she could grant him.

Her body recognised him before her memory. She began trembling uncontrollably and her stomach turned to stone. She grasped the back of a chair, her knees almost collapsing beneath her.

The Eminent *Cardinal Ruffo*. Older, but still those granite cold eyes.

Ruffo, taking her faint as an act of reverence, came forward extending his hand for her to kiss his gold and turquoise ring. Bile filled her mouth at the sight of his swollen red fingers. She swallowed as a wave of revulsion ran through her. The memories of his loathsome touching, his vile invasions, his sadistic threats overwhelmed her.

'Come, come Signorina Giro,' the Bishop said, his judgement clearly affected by the alcohol. 'There is no need to tremble so. He is not the Pope, well not *yet*,' he laughed. 'Cardinal Ruffo and I have been friends since the seminary. Rome has honoured him since his early days when he was your parish priest in Mantua. Maybe you do not recognise him?'

Maria came to her side, giving her arm a gentle squeeze of support as Paolina struggled to regain her balance.

'The Bishop and his Eminence were discussing Anna,' she said.

The sound of Anna's name broke through her shock. Paolina pulled herself to her full height. 'What of Anna? Why would you be concerned with her?' She asked as she gathered her thoughts; a lioness in fear for her cub.

The Bishop laughed, still oblivious to Paolina's reaction. 'Signora Anna is becoming quite famous you know. You must expect some interest in her, even from the clergy. The Cardinal has asked me to arrange a private concert for him with Anna. I suggested it could be arranged when you are in Ferraro. He is a good friend, Marchese Bentivoglio, your patron there.'

Paolina forced herself to look at Ruffo. He met her gaze but showed no sign of recognising her. *He does not remember,* she thought, unsure if she was relieved or angered. *But we remember you,* she thought, gripping Maria's hand. *We will never forget.* She wanted to spit in his flabby face.

'Yes Signora, I have heard that your famous Vivaldi greatly favours Anna,' the Cardinal said turning slightly to Bishop Xavier and raising his eyebrows. The Bishop dropped his head. Paolina thought she saw a small grimace as he did so.

She hesitated, unsure how to respond. She dug deep within herself to control her shaking. She needed to manage her response carefully. 'Father Vivaldi is yet to receive confirmation that we are to go to Ferraro. There are some disputes and decisions yet to be made. He is waiting to hear back from Marchese Bentivoglio.'

Ruffo faced her, wringing his hands. Paolina stared at him, willing him to remember her. His face contorted momentarily. Did the long-buried memory creep up on him? It was a fleeting response; a tiny chink in his powerful armour before it disappeared and he regained his loathsome impenetrability.

Paolina took strength in his silence. Pulling away from Maria's grip, she raised her voice. 'Even if the opera should come to fruition, Anna will be under the Marchese's patronage while we are in Mantua and will have no capacity for private concerts.'

Bishop Xavier cleared his throat and gave a weak laugh, anxiously anticipating the Cardinal's response. 'Come now, Signora, you must remember who you are addressing,' he said, his censorial tone not lost on Paolina. But she was not to be silenced. Not this time.

She raised her voice further. 'Father Vivaldi and my sister will be greatly honoured by Your Eminence's presence at the scheduled productions, but my sister will, at all other times, be within the confines of the court.'

Ruffo clenched his fists and Paolina could see the vein in his neck pulsing. His already ruddy face turned a darker crimson. He turned his back on the women and gestured to the Bishop to be rid of them.

***

Without a word between them Paolina and Maria walked together into the icy mid autumn air. Rather than cooling her emotions, Paolina's anger flared and she gasped for breath. Maria held her arm tightly, drawing her forward, as if removing her from danger. Once they were well away from the Bishop's house they stopped and clung to each other, like the two frightened girls of their past. Maria recovered first.

'It was a long time ago cousin. I am sure he does not remember us. There were so many of us.' She gently cradled Paolina's face in her hands. 'You will do well to let it pass, Paolina.'

Paolina pulled away, tears of rage streaming down her cheeks. 'Why? Why should we let it pass? We had to let it pass back then; we had no choice. Even Sister Judith was silenced when she tried to tell the Abbess. We could do nothing then and he got away with it. But we are grown women now. It's not right, Maria. We are left to suffer, and he goes on. Maybe he even still…' The sentence was too painful to complete.

They walked on in silence, arm in arm, neither of them knowing nor caring where they were going. Paolina was surprised when she looked up and saw they'd walked as far as the *Fonde menta Nuova* and were looking across the sea to the island of Murano. The wide stretch of water, expansive and rhythmic, helped to calm her a little.

'It's strange, Maria but I thought I'd forgotten. Not *what he did*,' she paused. 'But I thought the feelings had gone. Until I saw him. Those hands. Those fingers.' Paolina shuddered.

Maria put her arm around Paolina's waist and hugged her close. She need not say more. Words only made it worse; made it real again.

They stood watching the boats coming and going from the garden island. Gradually Paolina's anger turned to resolve. 'One thing I know, dear cousin, I will never let him near Anna. I will do everything within my power to prevent him even breathing the same air as her. He shall never rest his filthy hands anywhere near her. Nothing is more important to me.'

A gull screeched overhead, a witness to her statement.

CHAPTER 14

Australia 2010

Harvey called Fiona in from the waiting area at the Probation Office. She'd lain awake the previous night planning how to approach the appointment with him. She decided she would fake a doctor's appointment to leave quickly. She'd be pushy and demand to sign the attendance form and go. If he asked any questions she'd give him token answers. Yes and no. He couldn't make her talk.

'Can I just sign on? I've got a doctor's appointment?' She asked, sitting on the edge of her chair. Harvey ignored her and spent time reading her file, before speaking to her. A photo of him with a woman, his wife perhaps, sat on a shelf nearby. She felt nervous. Just being in a room with him made her skin crawl. When he looked up she avoided eye contact, but she could sense he was closely observing her. She began to fidget and the whirlpool inside her would not be quieted. The smell of his aftershave made her feel like gagging.

'So, Ms Sinclair, Mr Hasting seems to think all is going well with you: stable accommodation, doing some lessons of some sort, no further offending.'

He waited as if expecting her to respond. She did not.

'What have you to say to that, Ms Sinclair? Have you anything to add?' He made no attempt to keep the sneer from his voice. Fiona remained calm although she wanted to scratch his ugly face.

'No. All good,' she said as lightly as she could, relieved that Bob had left such thorough case notes giving Harvey no reason to enquire further about any aspect of her life.

'Can I just sign now, please?' she asked. 'I have a doctor's appointment.'

'Do you indeed?' He asked, passing the form to her. 'Nothing serious I hope. Nothing contagious?'

Her anger flared almost beyond her control. *Just do what it takes to get out of here,* she told herself. She signed the attendance sheet and was about to leave when Harvey spoke again.

'You live at Wesley House, don't you? Must be hard to avoid the influence of some of the other women there, I imagine.'

Fiona flinched at the mention of Wesley. She knew better than to agree with him. She recognised the trap. 'It's OK. I keep to myself.'

'So, nothing unusual happened there recently?' Harvey probed. She could smell his sour breath. Every part of her wanted to run but she forced herself to stay cool. Meeting his stare, she managed a smile. 'No, all good there. As I said, I keep to myself and what the others do is their business. Can I go now? I have an appointment.'

'Yes, so you said. With the doctor. Not one of your music lessons with Mrs Kelty then? She's Paul Kelty's wife, isn't she?'

Fiona's heart heaved. He knows too much about me. She smelled his threat. 'Yes, but I never see him. Just Mrs Kelty.'

'Of course. Paul Kelty is beyond reproach I am sure. I see from Bob's notes that you've been urine tested three times since you've been out and that you're clean. Even of cannabis. That is a surprise.'

She knew then, in that instance, in that barb, that Angie had spoken to him about her.

'Yes. I want to stay clean. No drugs.' She turned to leave but he moved between her and the door. It was only then that she noticed the venetian blinds were closed. Bob never had them closed. Her stomach lurched.

'Would you be clean now, Fiona?' He asked, his voice low and insinuating.

'Yes.' She stared at the floor and prayed.

She could feel his breath on her, long and raspy. His hand went to his groin before he grabbed her wrist. A woman's voice, just centimetres away, in the corridor on the other side of the glass divide, broke her terror. He dropped her hand and reached behind her for a sample container. He was tall and his armpit was level with her nose. She could smell old sweat.

'You won't be worried about another test then, Miss Sinclair?'

She knew for certain that whoever had taken her dope had told him about it. Her hands shook as she took the container. She could hear the woman's voice further down the corridor.

'There may be no need for this, of course,' he whispered. 'I could make a home visit to you at Wesley House instead. I'm sure we can come to an arrangement.' He lifted her face up with a finger.

The smell of his sweat, his aftershave, of his stinking nasty treachery, overwhelmed her. She dropped the container and pulled away. The whirlpool spun but she forced herself to think.

'Really, you've got to believe me,' she pleaded. 'I don't care what goes on at Wesley. I know how to keep my mouth shut. Anyway, I won't be staying there much longer. I'm moving in with a friend.'

'Oh really? What friend is that? Teresa or someone else from that pub you go to?' He asked, bending to pick up the container and brushing himself against her.

Prick, she thought. He knows everything I do. Angie's face flashed before her but for now she just needed to get away from him. Her mind raced. She grabbed at a name.

'Yes. With Patrick Doyle.' Any name to get him away from her.

Harvey shrugged. 'What a pity. Well,' he said giving her the container again 'looks like I will be needing this after all.'

Fiona's mind rushed to all the tricks she'd heard about substituting a sample urine, but she knew it was useless. She was gone. Her plans, her music, her freedom. All gone.

She walked into the corridor ahead of him. Two women were at the other end and Harvey called for one of them to take her to the toilets.

She did it as quickly as possible, hoping that the woman would stay outside but it was Harvey waiting when she came out. She handed the ziplock bag with her sample inside back to him and signed the label.

'Nice and warm,' he smirked. 'Good girl.'

Raising her head, she met his insidious smile. 'It'll be dirty for cannabis. I had a toke last week.'

Harvey looked to see that no one else was around. 'One toke? Word is you use all the time there at Wesley House. Word is that you're a dope head. Not even your new friends can save you now, Miss Sinclair.'

As he escorted her back to the waiting room his voice returned to normal. 'The results will be back in two days, Miss Sinclair. If it is positive the court will be notified of the breach of your suspended sentence conditions. They may decide to revoke the suspension. In short, you're likely to be returned to prison. *If* it comes back positive, of course.'

A female officer passed them. Fiona thought she saw a querying look flash across her face. Her mind raced and the whirlpool churned, dragging her down and down.

As she walked out of the office, black thoughts, dangerous words rushed in and took hold of her. *Back inside. One mistake. Criminal. Stupid. No better and no smarter than the bitches I live with. No better than my slag of a mother.*

Fuck, fuck fuck.

***

Two days later Fiona sat slumped into the chair opposite Teresa at the back of the coffee shop. They were the only customers. She put the flute in its case on the table.

'Here, take it back. I'm not going to need it anymore.'

'What's happened?' Teresa demanded.

'Just the usual shit. I've been urined. It'll be dirty. I'm going back inside. That bastard wants to put me back in, for sure!'

'Who do you mean? Harvey Brown?'

Fiona nodded. 'He offered me an out, but I'm not interested.'

Teresa frowned. 'What do you mean *an out*? Like do a program or something?'

Fiona let out a bitter laugh. 'Yeah, that's right,' she snarled, 'a program that runs at Wesley at midnight. Teresa, you have no fucking idea.'

Teresa reached out to take her hand. Fiona ached to be held by her; to be told that she would look after her. That everything would be all right. But she pulled away.

'Don't pretend that you're my friend, Teresa. Friends share things and you know nothing about me.'

Fiona felt the silence between them; a wall of stone she could not, *would not* climb.

When Teresa finally spoke, Fiona could hear the sadness in her voice. 'You're right Fiona, we aren't friends. But I do care about you, and other women like you who just need a chance.'

The wall began to crumble. Teresa went on, choosing her words as if stepping through a minefield.

'If I understand you rightly, then you've made the right decision. Harvey,' she hesitated and drew a breath. When she continued, it was as if she had retreated a little. 'Harvey doesn't decide who goes back to jail. That's the Court's decision.'

'But he will write the report. He will get a say and I won't. That's the bottom line for people like me, Teresa. That's why the other girls give up and keep fucking up. They don't see any hope because there is no hope.'

'And what if there was hope Fiona? What if Harvey didn't have the power any longer? What if he were to be investigated?'

Fiona looked up to meet Teresa's questioning stare. 'What are you saying? What do you know?'

'I don't *know* anything. Just rumours. I've heard Paul say things about Harvey.'

Fiona's mind raced and her stomach clenched. *What can she know? If people know about Harvey's corruption - people like Teresa and Paul - surely something can be done about him.* The wall crumbled some more.

'Fiona, tell me what happened. If you were propositioned by Harvey, someone needs to know. You can tell me, or someone at the Corrections Office, at least. Do you have someone else you can trust? Would you tell Paul?'

Fiona took a deep breath and shook her head. 'You've got to promise not to tell Paul. If it gets out that I grassed on Harvey, my life will be shit at Wesley and when I'm back inside. '

'I don't like having secrets from Paul but, yes, OK, I promise.'

'It was him, Harvey, at Wesley that night. I hoped he was too out of it to know I saw him, but he knows, for sure. Probably from Angie. He's going to make me pay Teresa. He's offered to bury the urinalysis results in return for sex.'

Fiona could tell from the look on Teresa's face that she was not surprised. At first, Fiona was relieved at being believed and then the enormity of what that meant hit her. She pulled away.

'You know, don't you? You already know what's happening and you've done nothing! You and Paul just let me and other girls deal with him.'

'I don't *know* anything, Fiona. Honest. Paul and I,' Teresa hesitated. 'We've heard rumours. Let's leave it at that. But if someone was to give me evidence, even vague evidence, then perhaps I could do something.'

'Do what?'

'Report him, I guess.'

The lameness of her response shocked and defeated Fiona. The chasm between their two worlds opened before her. 'You really have no fucking idea, do you. They would all just pull together. The police, the court, Corrections. I'd be just a thieving junkie whingeing 'cos I got caught using and he'd come out squeaky clean. I'd be back inside, but this time I'd be everyone's enemy.'

It was only the look of helplessness on Teresa's face that kept Fiona from running.

'I know how risky it is, Fiona, but if nobody says anything this will go on and there will be more girls just like you. Caught in the middle. At least think about it?'

Fiona shook her head. Teresa's kindness became unbearable. Trust, so easily given, so cruelly broken, lay in front of Fiona, like a shattered crystal chalice.

Maybe it was Teresa's pathetic pleading eyes, her funky earrings, or the cheery music in the cafe but, in that moment, Fiona hated everything about her. Her cool life, her cosy home, her cute husband.

She grabbed the flute. 'Don't bother trying to rescue me, Teresa. Don't think you have any idea what we go through, us *thieving, whoring junkies.* Go back to your fairy tale world with your prince charming husband.'

She waved the flute in Teresa's face and rammed it into her backpack 'Let's see who can be trusted now,' she sneered as she pushed her chair back and fled.

***

Fiona went straight to the Mall. Visions of her mother flashed in front of her. Feelings of betrayal and abandonment, her lifelong friends egged her on. The whirlpool spun out of existence and a cold, hardness grew inside her.

The pawn broker was reluctant to take the flute at first, but he finally relented. She got just enough.

Joe was at his usual spot. This time the packet was white powder.

CHAPTER 15

Australia 2010

Fiona peeled off her t-shirt. But there was no breeze and the sweat clung to her. Midnight and still 30 degrees. The stifling air filled the room like a blanket. The syringe lay on the bedside cupboard. Full but unused.

The belt she'd used as a tourniquet fell to the floor. Her pulsing vein had been ready, waiting. But the image of her mother's wasted yellow body came to her. Wasted body, wasted years, wasted life. Releasing the tourniquet, she'd stared at the syringe for a very long time.

It represented all she hated. Behind it, the empty shelf. No flute, no music.

Wasted. The word ran through her like a knife piercing her pain. *I am not her,* she thought. *I am not wasted. Not yet.*

Checking her jeans pocket she found the pawn shop receipt. Next dole payment she would get her flute back. Nobody need ever know how close she'd come.

Dropping, finally, into a fitful sleep, Fiona dreamed she was back in her cell, the walls closing in on her. She tried to call out but no sound came. She heard keys jangling. The screws were coming to take her flute. She tried to run but couldn't.

The sound of keys continued, even as she pulled herself awake. No longer a dream. Her door creaked opened. She lay dead still, her mind snapped into full consciousness.

The dim light from the passage outlined his towering shape: the loathsome reek of his aftershave intermingled with the smell of stale whiskey.

Fiona's heart pounded. Pretending to sleep, she forced her mind to race ahead of the paralysing fear. *Think Fiona, think.*

Harvey's bulk came towards her. She leapt out of bed, flicking on the bedside light. In her hand, the full syringe.

Harvey staggered slightly as he came towards her, unzipping his jeans.

'Well, well, princess. Caught you in the act have I? Just a junkie after all I see. You won't mind taking care of this then,' he said rubbing his erect penis. 'This can be our secret.'

Fiona could see that he was drunk. Drunk enough to make a bad decision. She took a chance.

'Anything it takes, Harvey. But let's have a hit first. It'll be twice as good. You'll last longer.' She saw his eyes widen and knew she almost had him.

'Not my usual poison, princess. Well, not by syringe. But I've heard-'

'You've heard right. Your cock will feel like it has reached paradise.'

His erection pulsed. 'Half each,' she suggested.

'That's more like it, princess,' he said. 'And if you're a very good girl I might just lose that nasty test result, too.'

'You'd better, big boy,' Fiona heard herself say. It was her voice, but not her. She wrapped her belt around his upper arm and passed him the syringe. 'You go first – don't want you to get any nasty junkie germs.'

Harvey's hands shook as he took the syringe. 'You do it,' he said. 'I can't find a vein.' Fiona flicked his arm. It appeared, blue and pulsing.

Everything slowed down as the cold hard truth of what she was about to do swept over her. There was no whirlpool. No fear. Just a wall of anger. Her heart went deathly still.

Taking the syringe, she emptied the entire contents into him, and with it, all her rage. A wave of triumph washed over her as she thought of every man who had taken advantage of her and her sad, lonely mother. Of every dealer who had gotten women hooked with kindness then watched them crawl with greed. Of every do-gooder who had ignored their despair in the name of justice.

Harvey dropped to the floor, his pupils dilated, his weapon flaccid.

Fiona froze. Panic replaced her triumph. She'd never seen anyone drop like that before. She remembered, too late, Joe saying something about a strong batch. She'd taken no notice at the time. Adrenalin raced through her veins and scrambled her thoughts. All she could hear was the prison door slamming.

Teresa's words came back to her. "You have to trust someone Fiona." She picked up her phone. Its repetitive ring tone seemed to last a lifetime before Teresa answered.

'I think I've killed him. Harvey Brown.'

'Who? Fiona? What do you mean? Killed? Where are you?' Teresa's sleepy words tumbled together.

'At Wesley. He tried. He was going to…'

'Jesus. Fiona. Are you OK? What happened?'

'I had a full syringe.' Fiona knew that what she said next could determine the rest of her life. 'I gave it to him. He used it all. I told him not to. And then he dropped.'

'Shit. Shit,' Teresa cursed quietly. Fiona heard a muffled conversation with Paul. 'Just a friend, a bit drunk. Go back to sleep.'

Then: 'Hang on. I'm going into the kitchen.'

Fiona hung on because it was all she had. Teresa's voice returned, steady now and fully audible. 'Are you sure he's dead?'

'He dropped like a sack. I've never seen anyone do that before.'

'Put him in the recovery position then get out of there, Fiona. I'll phone an ambulance.'

'I'll go back inside. He was going to rape me, Teresa. And now he's dead.'

Teresa fell silent.

'Oh Fiona, I'm so sorry. I should have done something. I will make it up to you but for now, do as I say, put him in the recovery position then get out of there. Do you hear me, Fiona?'

'Yes but–'

'Leave the front door wide open,' Teresa interrupted 'so the ambos can get in. I'll meet you in the alley at the back.'

Fiona did as she was told grabbing her T-shirt and backpack as she left. She heard the ambulance arrive just before Teresa's car pulled into the lane. Her legs trembled despite the heat. By the time lights were switched on in the house, Teresa had turned off her lights and cruised towards Fiona. They drove off towards the beach, neither saying a word. Teresa's phone rang. She looked at the screen.

'Paul. I'll have to answer it.'

She pulled over. Fiona could hear the panic in Paul's voice.

'I'm fine,' Teresa replied. 'I can't say where I am right now. You're going to have to trust me. I'll ring you later.' She hung up.

The roads were empty but there were about twenty cars in the seaside car park. Others looking for respite from the heat. They pulled in further along the esplanade.

'Okay, Fiona. Tell me what happened.' And she did. About the attack and much, much more. Teresa listened without saying a word. Her story exhausted, Fiona looked out across the bay. Pale pink streaks ushered in the dawn. Her whole body shook, as if it had emptied itself of a toxic substance. A police car drove past, and Teresa waved as if she knew them.

'I know you'll hate me now, but I didn't mean to kill him, Teresa. I just wanted him out of it enough so he couldn't rape me.'

Teresa took her hand. 'I believe you. I wouldn't be here if I didn't.' They watched as the sea slowly embraced the new day.

'Right,' Teresa said. 'What I'm going to do now is wrong. Legally wrong. Professionally wrong, and maybe ethically wrong. But morally, I know I'm right.'

Turning to Fiona she spoke with decision. 'You'll come back to our place and get some track pants, then I'll drop you back near Wesley House. It'll be crawling with Police by now. You'll have to pull out the acting job of a lifetime, Fiona. Say that you've been with me at the beach trying to get some sleep where it was cool.

'Tell them I dropped you off here on my way to the gym. When you need to, and not before, tell them that Harvey must have let himself into your room. He'll have the key that he used on him as proof of that. You'll have to own up to the syringe –it's got your prints all over it. Tell them you were going to use it but changed your mind and rang me instead.'

Fiona nodded. Her surprise at Teresa's cunning was overridden by her fear. 'I'll go back inside, won't I?'

'I don't know, Fiona. If they believe you about being with me, you stand a chance. Hopefully those cops remember me waving to them to corroborate your alibi. I'll bet they did a rego check to see who was waving to them.'

'To be honest, Fiona,' Teresa continued, 'I think they're going to be a lot more concerned about why Harvey, a Probation Officer was at Wesley full of smack and with his pants down.. You possessing a Class A drug will come second as far as they're concerned. There's nothing to involve you in this accident. He administered his own dose, right?'

Fiona stared ahead and didn't answer.

Teresa breathed out. 'Jesus.' She turned from Fiona and stared at the rising sun.

'OK. In my mind, it doesn't change anything. He would have raped you. It was self-defence. So, let's get your... Our story straight.'

***

The house was silent and Paul still asleep when they arrived. Teresa went in to see him after finding a pair of track pants and a clean T-shirt for Fiona. She could hear their raised voices.

'I thought we'd agreed never to bring any Corrections clients in here! I agreed to them being in the studio for lessons, but you said they wouldn't come into the house.'

'That's why I'm going to find her somewhere else to stay. Anyway, Fiona's not my *client*. She's a friend and she can't stay at Wesley anymore.'

'Why. What's happened?'

Fiona's stomach tightened and began to whirl. *Please, please, don't tell him Teresa.*

'She saw Harvey there last week. After hours.'

Fiona couldn't hear what Paul said next, but she could guess from Teresa's response.

'Oh, come on Paul, she's not like the rest. She knows right from wrong. Even you said that.'

'But what if she's not as different as we think. Most of the offenders I deal with know right from wrong. But it comes down to how desperate they get.'

Fiona had heard enough. She needed to get out of these people's lives. The door slammed as she left.

All the way back to Wesley House she went over the story she'd agreed on with Teresa. As she rounded the last corner, she saw three police cars. Teresa's words came back to her. "You'll have to pull off the acting job of your career."

A female officer met her at the door and asked for her name. Fiona could see a male officer questioning Angie and the older women at the end of the corridor and another taking prints from her door.

'Fiona Sinclair. I live here. I broke curfew. I've been at the beach.'

'Really? Is there anyone that can verify that?'

'Teresa Kelty. Why? What's happened?'

A detective joined them and flashed his warrant card. 'There's been a serious incident here. Do you know anything about that?

'No. Should I?'

'He was found unconscious in your room.'

'Unconscious!' Fiona fought hard to keep the relief from her voice before she quickly added 'My room? How did he get in?

'We thought you might be able to tell us that. He had a key on him that fits your lock. He might have died if someone hadn't put him in the recovery position and phoned the ambulance. 'The officers were watching her closely. 'Do you know anything about how he came to be in your room?'

Fiona shook her head. 'No. I told you I wasn't here. Who was it?'

'A Mr Harvey Brown. Do you know him?'

Fiona frowned. 'Really? He's a Probation Officer. I met him once at the office and,' she deliberately hesitated, pretending to be careful about what to say next.

'And?' The female officer prompted, watching her closely.

'Well, I thought I saw him here once before. But it couldn't have been. It was after curfew. I thought it strange because men aren't allowed without management permission and never after curfew.'

The two officers exchanged looks. 'So how did he get a key to your room?'

'Fucked if I know. Sorry. I don't know. I always keep mine around my neck.' She pulled her key out to show them. 'The manager told me that the keys get changed every time someone new comes in. The only other key is meant to be with management, for emergencies.'

The police officers scribbled some notes. 'OK Ms Sinclair. We'll need you to come to the station with us to make a formal statement. You'll be finger printed and urine tested. Any problems with that?'

Fiona shook her head. 'I'll be dirty for cannabis. I had a joint last week. That should be on the Departments records.'

'Nothing more? No speed? No heroin?'

'No. I've been staying clean since I came out. The joint was a one off and I don't usually use heroin. Ask anybody. But I did score some yesterday. I even bought a clean syringe. I was pissed off for getting caught out for cannabis. But I decided not to use. I left it in my room.'

'So you bought it but didn't use it?'

'That's right. I pawned my... Something precious to me to get it. But it's not my scene, heroin. Check your records. I changed my mind, and I rang Teresa Kelty instead. She's my music teacher.'

The officers shrugged. 'Come with us and make a statement.'

'Can I get some clean clothes first? I don't think I'll be staying here any longer.'

The female officer watched as Fiona changed and threw a few things into her backpack. She had no idea where she was going but she knew she wouldn't go back to Wesley.

She spent the next three hours at the police station, most of it waiting in a small interview room. Finally, the officers who had been at Wesley came in.

'Do you require a solicitor, Miss Sinclair?

'Am I being charged with anything?'

'From your own admission possession of a Class A drug for personal use and equipment.'

'Then no, I don't need one. I'm guilty of that.'

'I see you're on a good behaviour bond with a suspended sentence, Miss Sinclair.

'Ms.'

'What?'

'Ms. As in not Miss and not Mrs. And yes, I'm on Probation.'

Fiona felt as if she had slipped into a role. She knew her best chance here was to differentiate herself from being just a druggie. She needed to show them she was reformed.

'Ms Sinclair, where did you get the heroin from?

'Some bloke in the Mall. Don't know his name.'

The sergeant pulled at his thinning hair and shifted his considerable weight in the undersized chair. Fiona took her chance.

'I want to have him, Harvey Brown, charged with trespassing. He was in my room without my permission. What is he saying about why he was there?'

The female officer stepped forward. 'You are entitled to make a complaint. That's up to you, Fiona. You probably should let the managers of the hostel know what you intend to do too. It is their property, but you have rights as the tenant. As to why Mr. Brown was there, he's not well enough for us to interview him at this stage. But for now, we need to clear up this heroin use situation.'

They asked a few more questions about the identity of the person she'd bought the heroin from and asked again how she thought Harvey got into her room. They urine tested her before she left, and she signed an affidavit to appear in court in a month. She gave them the address of a women's shelter she knew of as her next residence. By the time they found out she wasn't there, she'd hopefully have somewhere to stay. She picked up the backpack and headed into the street. She should have felt exhausted from all the stress and lack of sleep, but somehow, she felt as if she could fly.

Fiona didn't see Teresa until she was next to her car. 'Come on, get in,' Teresa said through the open window.

'No. I've caused you and Paul enough grief.'

'Get in, Fiona. It's going to be OK. Anyway, we're in this together now. I hope you stuck to our story because I've been questioned too. I said you were with me. That we're friends.'

There was that word again. She got into the car. Teresa continued. 'I also told them that I'd heard rumours about Harvey using Wesley as a place to get sex.'

Did they say if he's said anything yet?'

'I asked but they weren't forthcoming. He's still in hospital which is unusual. Most overdosers are released within a few hours of coming around. My guess is he won't say a word until he has a lawyer. He's going to have a hard time explaining what he was doing there.'

'Did they believe you, about me?'

Teresa shrugged. 'Hard to say. They seemed to. I asked Paul to contact the office for you and tell them you can't stay at Wesley anymore, because of the crime scene in your room. They agreed. He went there and got the rest of your stuff. I hope that's OK. There were a couple of letters for you. He put them in the bag. And here – this is yours, too.'

She reached over to the back seat and passed Fiona the flute. 'I found the pawn slip in your jeans pocket and got it back.'

Fiona laughed with both relief and disbelief. 'You have been busy! But what am I going to do with a flute? I haven't even got anywhere to live!'

'You could stay with us.'

'No. No way. I heard you arguing this morning. Paul's right. How do you know I won't get desperate enough to rip you off big time?'

Teresa shrugged. 'Fiona, you spilled your story to me last night. I think I'm a good enough judge of people to know when they're faking it. Anyway, if you really don't want to stay with us, then how about with Patrick?'

'You told Patrick?' Fiona gasped.

'No, just that you needed a place to stay. He's offered for you to live at the back of his house in his mum's granny flat. It can only be for a month or two while she's in Ireland, but he said he would be glad of the company.'

'Does he know I'm a thieving druggie capable of murder?'

Teresa ignored the bait. 'Like I said, I haven't told him anything, just that you need somewhere to stay for a bit. He's got a bit of a chequered history himself. He knows what it means to be homeless.'

Fiona stared out the window. Through their silence, they could hear the dimmed radio. It was on ABC Classic FM. Vivaldi's Four Seasons was playing.

'He can't leave you alone,' Teresa said half laughing, half crying. 'The red priest seems to pop up in your life quite a bit lately. Perhaps you need to find out more about him, and his orphaned girls, of course.'

They drove to Patrick's house listening to Vivaldi. As they pulled to the curb Fiona turned to Teresa.

'What if Harvey tells them what I did? What if he convinces them that I tried to kill him?'

'I'm not a lawyer, Fiona, but I expect you'll be advised by a lawyer to plead not guilty. When Paul went to get your belongings Angie told him they had all been asleep and didn't hear a thing. Anyway, Harvey hasn't any excuse for being in your room, even if you had invited him. Let's wait and see what happens next.'

That night as Fiona lay in Patrick's mum's bed, images of Harvey lying on the floor plagued her. She could still smell him and hear the thud as he dropped.

He would have raped you, she told herself. *But you could have killed him,* another voice inside her answered.

She tossed and turned. Surrounded by old-lady cushions and paintings of gardens, she almost laughed at the absurdity of it all. I bet Patrick's mum has never nearly killed someone, she thought.

Teresa's reassurance about Harvey's unethical actions came back to her, but Fiona was still worried. He'll no doubt have a story to tell that will get him off the hook, she thought. Men like him always worm their way out of things. It'll be his word against mine. And Teresa's, she remembered.

When sleep finally came, she dreamt again of being in the boat heading towards the black hole, the whirlpool. This time it was Harvey in the boat. He was holding her down. She struggled and pushed him off her. He hit the deck. Thud. She dived into the sea and watched the boat and Harvey disappear into the whirlpool's vortex.

She woke to the sounds of birds outside her window and a radio on next door. Pulling herself out of sleep she looked around. The unit was decorated in soft pinks and greys. Adjoining the bedroom was a kitchenette and a lounge area overlooking a small enclosed garden. She ached to stay in bed all day but knew she should get up and thank Patrick properly. She showered and pulled some clothes out of the two garbage bags that held all her belongings. Patrick had cleared some shelf space, but she wouldn't be staying long.

With her hair still wet, she knocked timidly at Patrick's back door.

'Top o' the morning to you,' he said in an exaggerated Irish accent. Behind his smiling eyes, Fiona saw a look of concern.

'I just wanted to say thank you for - you know - letting me crash here. I won't stay long and I'll pay you rent out of my next dole.'

'You can pay if you want but it's not costing me anything. You could always pay in kind.'

Fiona stiffened. Patrick went on, shaking his head. 'No, no! Jesus, I didn't mean *that*. Cooking. I meant cooking. Mum always does it. Sausages and mash is about my limit, so if you want, you could cook for us both. Instead of paying rent.'

'Sure. I can do curries and roasts and pizza. Oh, and fish and chips.'

'No fried Mars Bar then?'

Fiona smiled and then laughed. She'd not heard that stupid joke about the infamous Glasgow diet for a long time. It felt good to laugh.

Later that day they went grocery shopping together. Patrick paid but Fiona kept a record, so she could pay him back. They called in at the Salvos. Patrick said he was looking for a book, but he encouraged Fiona to pick out some clothes. She told him she would pay him back for those, too.

'All in good time. I do know what it's like being on the bones of your arse.'

'When was that?' She asked as they walked home.

'When I first came to Australia. I was working up North in the mines. Too much time off. Nothing to do. Too much drinking. Too many drugs.'

'What got you out of it?' Fiona asked.

'Friends that weren't into that shit. And a half a dozen big brothers back home threatening to come over here if I didn't sort myself out.'

'Well,' said Fiona, 'that's me buggered. I've got no friends and no family back home. None that I know of, anyway.'

'You've friends if you want them, Fi. Can't do anything about the family I'm afraid.'

Teresa was waiting for them when they got home. Patrick took the shopping from Fiona and she went with Teresa to the flat. The door had barely closed when Teresa burst out, 'Fiona, Harvey's dead!'

Fiona began to shake. Teresa guided her into a chair.

'Shit. Shit. I did kill him. I killed him.'

'No, Fiona,' Teresa said. 'It wasn't the heroin. He'd recovered from the overdose. They gave him narcan when they found him, remember. Paul said he'd been discharged to go home when he started to get a blinding headache and blurred vision. They did an MRI and he had a massive tumour. He died as they were preparing to operate.'

Fiona tried to understand what this meant. 'Did he speak to the police at all?'

'I don't think so. According to Paul before they knew about the tumour his wife had been at the hospital and they had a massive row. Also, the Manager from Corrections had been in. He suspended Harvey, pending an inquiry into his unprofessional conduct. Paul said word is he told them both he had no recollection of how he got into your room and remembered nothing about using.'

Fiona's mind was racing. 'So, he's dead and he didn't tell anybody what I did?'

Teresa nodded. 'It might be true that he didn't remember. The tumour and all. Anyway, it was what he'd been doing, and was about to do to you, that was wrong. I think we're in the clear, Fiona.'

'We? You'd only go for aiding and abetting; I'd go for murder.'

Teresa didn't respond. Fiona paced the room. Finally, she turned to Teresa.

'I know I should be punished, but he was going to rape me, Teresa. He was going to rape me and take away my freedom, my life. I'm glad he's dead.' There, the words were out.

Teresa came to her and they hugged until their tears stopped.

***

A brief article appeared in the local newspaper the following week.

The man found collapsed at a Correctional hostel, was that of 57-year-old Harvey Brown. Mr Brown has since died of an unrelated condition. An inquest concluded that he died from a brain haemorrhage. There were no suspicious circumstances surrounding his death. The 24-year-old woman, in whose room he was found, could not be interviewed for legal reasons, however another resident at the hostel said that Mr Brown had been a frequent visitor and was well liked by the girls. The hostel is a post release house for women exiting prison. A spokesperson for the Department for Correctional Services said that the women who live there have committed a variety of offences including home invasion, break and enter, larceny, and shoplifting. An anonymous source also indicated that many of the women were sex workers. The Department for Corrections said that they maintain a strict curfew and have released a statement that Mr Brown did not have Departmental approval to be at the hostel.

As her court day drew near, Fiona tried to withdraw from the life she'd started to create for herself; she thought that she would miss it less that way. But she couldn't. It was, at last, the life she wanted for herself.

She went to Teresa's once a week for lessons and a couple of times a month, to the Bull where she'd become a regular participant. She asked Corrections to urine test her weekly. She said it was to stop her using, but she knew she wasn't going to use and wanted the proof.

Each day she walked or ran, practiced flute and spent time in the library. Her research into the tune, her tune, hadn't gone far.

Although there was only the one article about the tune, there was much more in the library about Vivaldi. The Librarian had downloaded an e-book for her. Fiona asked her to print off a letter Vivaldi had written, to show Teresa.

'Did you know he'd been accused of having it off with his favourite singer?'

'No!'

They read the letter together. 'He was pretty pissed off at being accused of it,' Teresa said. 'Listen to this.' She read an excerpt:

"I have been teaching at le Pietá for thirty years without any scandal. I never stayed at the Giro house. Let wicked tongues say what they wish. Your Excellency must know I have a house in Venice for which I pay two hundred ducats and the Giro's live in a house of their own very far from mine. I will stop here for I am going to humiliate myself."

'Hard to imagine a composer having to write that. The Giro sisters sound interesting too. Maybe you could find out about them? They might lead you to an answer about your mystery tune.'

Fiona applied for a lot of jobs but nothing had turned up. As soon as they knew she'd been inside, nobody wanted her.

'Don't tell them,' Teresa advised. 'Just say you were looking after a dying aunt or something?'

'I know I could, but I'm done with lying, no matter what.'

'What about at court?'

'Well I've only been charged with possession and of course breach of my original suspended sentence. I'm pleading guilty so I'm counting on them to not cross examine me.'

'What about the trespassing charge against Harvey.'

'I didn't pursue it and I never heard anymore about him being in my room. It's all been hushed up. I just feel sorry for his wife and kids, really.'

When the court day arrived, Fiona steeled herself to do another stint inside. Her new Probation Officer, the woman who'd given Harvey a look that day in the corridor, was optimistic that she wouldn't get jail time.

'You've had only one dirty urine for cannabis in all that time and the new offence is not major. After Mr Brown's death, the Department examined his whole case load. They decided that all his reports that hadn't gone to court already, be redone. I've made sure they know about your new accommodation and the support you have from Mrs Kelty and Mr Doyle.'

Patrick went with her on the day of the court case. She gave him her backpack before they went in.

'You might have to look after this for me if I go down.'

'I'll guard it with my life. If you walk, the first beer is on you. *Again.*' It was a joke they had between them.

The Magistrate had a full court and the case after hers had a noisy following. He was keen to be done for the day. Her case was over in fifteen minutes.

After the police presented their charges, he looked at the Bail Report.

'Miss Sinclair, I see that you have put yourself forward for weekly urinalysis since the day of the offence and that you have not tested positive in that time. That, and your guilty plea, has convinced me that you are finally growing up and that maybe, with the help of the positive influences you now have in your life,' here he looked over at Patrick who the court supplied lawyer had pointed out, 'you have every chance of, once and for all, removing yourself from this system. You will pay a fine of five thousand dollars, which you may work off through Community Service. You will be placed on a further six-month Good Behaviour Bond which will run concurrent with that which you are already on.'

As she walked out of the courthouse with Patrick, Fiona knew that her real life, the life she was meant to live, was about to begin.

CHAPTER 16

Venice 1737

Paolina's days passed quickly, organising and attending Anna's many rehearsals and performances. Her fear of receiving a formal request from Ruffo for a private meeting with Anna began to subside until she began to wonder if it had been whim, a passing fancy. She started to question too her violent refusal of him. Was it an illogical overreaction, fuelled by her own memories with no basis in the present? *Perhaps Maria was right,* she told herself. *I need to let it go.*

At times she relaxed enough to imagine the glory that was coming Anna's way and wondered, if Ruffo asked again, would she continue to risk Anna's success just to settle an old score? Now that she had stood her ground with him perhaps she could agree to a private meeting for the sake of Anna's career.

But still there remained a niggling premonition, a menacing anticipation. The Marchese of Ferrara had not responded to their letter and Antonio was still owed several instalments from the Ferraro entrepreneurs. Their bank balance was lower than it had ever been. Despite trying to believe otherwise Paolina couldn't help but speculate that Ruffo was behind their increasingly desperate situation.

Until recently, and against her business instincts, she'd allowed herself to be convinced by Antonio that no news was good news, for it meant that all was going to plan. But Antonio did not know of her refusal of Ruffo.

The matter would soon, however, be taken out of her hands.

Maria was visiting to help Paolina with preserving the cherries they'd harvested in the Bishop's garden. They sang and laughed at family jokes while they waited excitedly for Antonio's return from a meeting with the Holy Nuncio, the Pope's representative in Venice.

'Perhaps he is being commissioned to compose another Oratorio for the Holy Father,' Paolina speculated.

'How wonderful that would be for you all,' Maria said. 'I remember the Bishop talking about the last time Antonio went to Rome for just that purpose. It had done Antonio's career a power of good. It was that which catapulted his name across the Holy Roman Empire. Everyone wants what the Pope wants.'

But when the downstairs door slammed, Paolina's stomach lurched. The expression on his face told her that this was not good news.

Maria made a quiet exit, whispering a promise to contact Paolina the following day. 'It is probably some petty church politics, cousin. The Bishop is often summonsed by the Nuncio, to account for one thing or another.'

But Paolina sensed with every bone in her body that his fury was to do with Ruffo. Wiping her hands, she hurried to the music room where she found Antonio writing frantically.

Without explanation, he thrust the letter at her. Her hands shook as she read his scribbling; his anger jumped from the page. She thought she'd prepared for this day. She thought she would be able to calmly tell Antonio about her refusal of Ruffo and why she had done so. She'd even, of late, planned how she would get Antonio to apologise to him on her behalf and perhaps offer him a private recital. 'As long as you and I can be there also, Antonio, I now see no harm,' she'd planned to say.

She did not need to know of what Antonio had been accused. It was all in his response and it was much worse than anything she had expected. Antonio had been publicly degraded, and Anna's reputation was now in ruins.

Ruffo had struck his malicious revenge.

Antonio grabbed the letter back and folded it, ready to be sealed. Her thoughts rushed.

'Please do not send it like that, Antonio. You must let me rewrite it, or perhaps engage a notary to advise you. You are angry and hurt and these words will only inflame the situation. Your response must be crafted most carefully, with dignity and guile.'

'Dignity and guile be damned,' Antonio swore. 'Ruffo's accusations are slanderous. I can no longer go on with this charade, Paolina. He treats me as if I am some minor cleric, beholden to him for my reputation. Damn them all to Hell.'

'You must wait,' she pleaded. Gather support from those whose good opinion of you will counter this accusation. The Bishop, the Doge. Perhaps even the Pope?'

'I have no need of anyone's good opinion or their approval. I am Antonio Lucio Vivaldi. Let my music speak for itself. Besides, it is not on my own behalf I write, but yours and Anna's.'

Paolina recalled the day, months ago, at the market and the rage she felt at the idle gossip about Antonio and Anna. Why had she been so foolish to think it would simply go away? She knew now that Ruffo's dismissal of her and Maria that day had been anything but benign. Was his ego so fragile that a mere refusal would drive him to destroy the lives of three people? Did he send his spies into the streets of Venice to gather scandal, simply to rebuke her for her slight?

As she tried to make sense of the enormity of his response a new and clearer thought dawned upon her.

He remembers what he did. He remembers me and Maria and all the others and he aims to silence me once and for all. With this thought came the fearsome memory of his hand over her mouth as he entered her fourteen-year-old body, smothering the scream that would never be heard.

She ran from the room and vomited until the bile ran dry.

***

The letter went just as Antonio had written it.

Excellency,

After so many manoeuvres and a great many toils the opera is now ruined. His reverence, the Apostolic Nuncio, had me summoned today and commanded me in the name of His Eminence Cardinal Ruffo not to come to Ferrara to mount opera, because I am a cleric who does not say Mass, and because I am friends with the singer Giro. Your Excellency can imagine my state of mind at such a blow. What troubles me most is the stain His Eminence Cardinal Ruffo has attached to these poor women, the likes of which has yet to be seen.

Over the past fourteen years we have appeared together in many European cities and their modesty was everywhere admired, and the same can be said of Ferrara. They make devotions every week to which sworn and authenticated records attest.

For three years I was in the service of the extraordinarily devout prince of Damstatdt in Mantua, together with the above ladies, who were always honoured by His August Majesty with the greatest kindness, and I never said Mass. My travels were always very expensive because I always took along four or five persons to assist me.

I accomplish all the good I can at my writing desk at home, I therefore have the honour of corresponding with nine high princes and my letters travel all over Europe. I have therefore written Signor Mazzucchi that I cannot come to Ferrara if he does not allow me to stay in his house . . . and the above ladies are very helpful to me because they know my ailment well.

These truths are known throughout most of Europe; I therefore appeal to your Excellency's goodness to kindly inform His Eminence Cardinal Ruffo, because this business means <u>my utter ruin.</u>

I reiterate Your Excellency that the opera cannot be performed in Ferrara without me. You can see the many reasons. Should it not be performed I will either have to take it to another city, which is now too late to find, or pay off all my contracts. If his Eminence cannot be persuaded to change his mind I beg Your Excellency at least to persuade His Eminence, the Papal legate, to postpone the opera to release me from the contracts.

I am also sending Your Excellency the letters of His Eminence Cardinal Albani, which I should submit myself. I have been teaching at le Pietá for thirty years without any scandal. I never stayed at the Giro house. Let wicked tongues say what they wish. Your Excellency must know I have a house in Venice for which I pay two hundred ducats and the Giros live in a house of their own very far from mine. I will stop here for I am going to humiliate myself.

I therefore commend myself to Your Excellency's most gracious protection and humbly remain,
Antonio Vivaldi
Venice, 16 November 1737.

CHAPTER 17

Venice and Scotland 1741

It was at a salon concert at *Palazzo Pisani-Moretta* that Robert heard of Vivaldi's move to Vienna. He was at the home of a recent acquaintance, Chiara, the daughter of a wealthy merchant. They were celebrating the most recent *Tiepolo* her father had commissioned.

'The board members and the new music maestro of *le Pietá* were here yesterday to see it finished. Did you know Father Vivaldi commissioned Tiepolo to paint one just like it for the new church? It was just before he left so suddenly for Vienna. They say Tiepolo will paint the great composer himself into it, as an angel overlooking the proceedings. It will be *le Pietá's* acknowledgement of all he did for them.'

Paulo had introduced him to Chiara. Robert knew, it was to divert his feeling for him.

'You know Roberto, the time must come when you move from me. You are still so young and soon I will be an old man and I am, when all is said and done, a commoner. You are nobility Roberto. Perhaps you should think about taking a wife, someone of your own class. It is not uncommon for men like us to have a wife, children even. It will make life easier for you.'

Robert knew he was right, and he was fond of Chiara in the same way he had once been fond of Elspeth. But it was only Paulo who excited him. Yet Paulo had of late been less available. They rarely spent days together anymore and often slept apart. Robert had been jealous of one or two of the young men Paulo had been escorting around Venice, although Paulo had insisted that it was work only.

'I have to earn my living Roberto. You cannot keep me on your meagre allowance. And by the end of the day I am tired. I am an old man you know' he teased.

Robert knew that he was right. His own eyes had been wandering too and there had been more than one young man who had caught his attention. But he could not act. It had been so easy with Paulo, but to make advances to another man seemed preposterous, even here in liberal Venice. So to cover the hurt of Paulo's withdrawal he immersed himself in his flute lessons and his new passion, the history of music. He secured access to Venice's extensive archives which went back to the Eleventh Century. He read about all the music that had been written there and the lives of the composers. He also made a small income by tutoring but was still reliant on his allowance from his father.

He was overjoyed, therefore, on returning from visiting Chiara, to see two letters, one from his father, the other from his cousin, Donald. He opened that one first, for it was Donald he missed the most here in Venice. He had joined the Black Watch and his letters were usually entertaining, full of stories of carefree days spent in the highlands and the camaraderie of his fellow men in arms. But Robert's joyful anticipation soon turned to concern.

I know not where to turn dear cousin. I have been tricked into thinking I would be helping the highlanders, to act as a go between, so that they could learn to understand the King's rule of laws. But increasingly I am asked to detain and even punish good, God-fearing men and women, who do nothing more than voice an opinion that is not in accordance with that of the King. Like all my fellow Black Watch I was chosen and valued for my knowledge of the highlander's ways. But now we are ordered to stamp out even the smallest signs of dissent. We are spies in our own land, Robert. Even Lovat, our leader is disgruntled. Some say he may desert to the Jacobites.

As you know, dear Robert, I care little for the Jacobites cause. Their pompous leaders, the Stuarts, claim Scotland as their own yet they have long since left our shores and know nothing of the highlands and islands. But I must confess I also have no love for our Hanoverian King George either, and even less for his blood thirsty son, Cumberland.

I did not think it would come to this, dear cousin. How was I so naive? What choice do I have now, Robert? To abscond will be treason and I would surely be court martialled, maybe even shot. My mother and father too will be besieged. I am at my wits end to know what to do.

You are wise to stay away, dear cousin. Our country is riddled with discontent and dangerous contradictions.

I hope that, when we meet again one day, we will do so in peaceful times.
Your loving cousin,
Donald Dunbar.

Still reeling from his cousin's distress, Robert opened the letter from his father, certain it would contain details of a transfer of the funds that would allow him to stay in Venice for another year. But his alarm about Donald soon paled against what he read.

Robert,

You must leave Venice at once and come home.

There is great unrest here. Your wayward cousin Donald has absconded from his Regiment. There is a warrant for his arrest. If found he will be tried and shot.

It is thought that he has followed Lovat, who has turned against the King and sides now with the Rebels who intend to bring back the papist Stuart, the pretender. I have publically denounced his actions. I will not have the name of Kerr linked to him.

On your mother's petitioning, and against my better judgement, I am providing a safe haven for his parents, your aunt and uncle, at Newbattle.

*They arrived by cover of night, and have taken up residence in the east
wing. The whole affair weighs heavily upon us all and has taken a toll on
your mother. She takes her meals in her chambers but eats little. She speaks
rarely but when she does it is of times past, of before the Union, as if she has
lost all notion of her privilege and position here, as Lady Kerr of Newbattle.*

*Abroad, the young pretender, Charles Stuart, has come out of hiding in
Rome and we are told he has won the support of France. The traitor, Murray,
is mobilising the Jacobites and has been to France to meet Charles Stuart.*

*Cumberland, of course continues to act for his father but has taken all
able bodied men in the south to join him in his fight against Spain. So it is
down to the few left to hold the North.*

*I say again Robert, you must leave Venice at once and come home. You
will join William in the Dragoons.*

Your Father,
Marquis of Lothian.

Robert left Venice the following morning. He left Paulo to pack up
his belongings and send them on. The Concerto manuscript, once his
prized possession, lay in a corner. He cared not whether it was sent or not.

***

The old sycamore tree greeted Robert as his coach crossed the bridge. It
had stood in the grounds of Newbattle Abbey for nearly three hundred
years. Now its bare branches stretched against the frosty sky like outstretched fingers, knotted and worn by honest toil. The river, still high
after heavy winter falls, raced under the bridge, eager to be somewhere
else. The home field was a white and green carpet of early snowdrops.

From this distance the Abbey, too, looked unaltered, but Robert had
a sense, as his carriage passed the stately gates, that change awaited him.
He passed the family graveyard and a shiver ran through him, wondering
who next would be buried there. He looked up to the window where his

mother would be watching for him and waved. *She will know my thoughts about having to return. But where will her sympathies lie*, he wondered.

The Marquis, his father, waited for him alone at the bottom of the steps. Even from a distance, Robert sensed the changes in him. He wore an official uniform as befit the occasion, but it fell awkwardly across his narrowed shoulders. He leant against the granite pillar as if seeking its support. Robert climbed from the coach, giving the coachman a shilling. He reached for his meagre luggage but a servant, his head bowed, took it from him. Robert sighed, remembering the old order.

Approaching his father, he smelled the stale whiskey; the smell that comes from days of drinking. They embraced like strangers. He felt bones where once there had been muscle. He noticed the tremor in his father's hand.

'So, you have come at last,' the Marquis said. Trying, Robert thought, to muster a growl, but instead it came as a broken rasp. Still, Robert heard the old criticism. He was tempted to quote the Kerr family motto, *Sero sed serio:* Late but in Earnest, but refrained. This was not the time for cleverness.

'At your command, Father, I have come at once. I have travelled for many weeks and thought of nothing but Donald's plight and Mother's welfare.'

'Donald's plight is no longer our concern,' his father snapped. 'His reckless actions have brought disgrace upon our family. Your aunt and uncle now hide like frightened mice. Your mother has eaten little for weeks and her mind, once as clear and sharp as anyone I knew, now wanders. She rambles on about times past, as if she can no longer bear the present. Our friends and neighbours watch us, like buzzards, to see if we too, the Kerrs of Newbattle, will join Murray and Lovat against our one true King.'

Robert felt his father's pain. He knew the Kerrs once had a reputation for swapping allegiances in the past. He knew too that their neighbours had long memories. Despite his abhorrence of these age-old rivalries,

Robert understood how centuries of family history weighed upon his father, like a suit of armour, as restrictive as it was protective. He placed a hand upon his father's shoulder and realised that their roles were now reversed. He was the strong one, the son who would be expected to support a frail, failing father. He'd never thought to see this day and, despite his past anger at his father, it was an unwelcome change. One for which he had not prepared.

'You must not concern yourself, Father. The Kerrs have no real enemies amongst the King's supporters. Surely the Jacobites are few and disorganised. The Stuarts hide away in Europe. They surely can do no real harm.'

As he spoke, William joined them. With no more than a nod of welcome to Robert, William took their father's arm. The Marquis abandoned any pretence of strength and accepted his eldest son's support as William guided him to a nearby bench.

'Much has changed in your absence brother,' William said to Robert, 'and you are wrong to underestimate the Jacobites. We are recently informed that a new association has been formed in Edinburgh in anticipation of the French joining Spain against us. The rumour is that Murray has gone to France to rally support for a rebellion. We will need every man to take up arms.'

William had never spoken to Robert with such earnest commitment before. Even though he had an abhorrence for any talk of fighting, he felt warmed by William's unexpected respect. For years he had yearned for acceptance and it seemed he had now won it. But at what cost? He wondered.

William continued. 'With the Black Watch scattered due to Lovat's betrayal, the highlands are unattended. If they get support from France, the rebels will surely rise up again. It is rumoured the young pretender, Charles, will soon be on our shores, claiming not just Scotland as his rightful Kingdom, but the whole of Britain.'

William's sincerity convinced Robert of the seriousness of the situation. Yet still, in his heart, he resisted. Surely there is another way? He thought. Why is it that men with all their access to education and wisdom are unwilling to consider options other than war?

Turning to his father he began. 'But surely Father you,' he stopped, seeing the weariness in his father's eyes. He turned instead to William. 'Surely we can persuade Cumberland that his strategy will prove tragic for everyone. It will lead to the bloodshed of hundreds, nay, thousands, of our countrymen, both those for and against the King. Is there no other way?'

William looked at him now, as if seeing for the first time, that his brother had truly changed. 'Indeed Robert, your argument has been put to his Majesty already, by the Lord President of Scotland, but he was ignored.'

Robert's thoughts turned again to Donald. 'So, it would seem that our cousin's decision to leave the Watch may well have been made for good reason.'

Before William could answer, their father pulled himself to his feet and stepped forward, his voice hoarse with age and fatigue. 'How dare you! Donald's absconding to Lovat is nothing short of treason. His name will not be mentioned in this house. Do you hear? He is dead to us! It is up to you and William to show that the Kerrs remain faithful to King George. I will have none of this talk of negotiation in my house. It is time to fight! Tomorrow, Robert, you will be sworn into the Dragoons.'

William threw Robert a look, warning him to keep his silence. He led their father into the house. Robert stood for a time before he followed them. He heard the library door close behind them. He was excluded and alone once again. He looked around the empty hall remembering the banquet held in his honour in these very rooms, prior to his departure. Donald, his parents and many of their neighbours had attended. The tapestries had been cleaned and rehung for the occasion. The Botticelli and Van Dyke especially placed and lit. Pheasants were slaughtered and the best wine brought from the cellar. A local fiddle troupe had been employed and the carpet rolled away to allow for dancing. No expense had been spared; it was, after all, an opportunity for the Kerrs to show off their finery.

Robert had drunk too much and danced with many of the local girls; quadrilles and minuets and, of course, Strip the Willow. The hall had filled with laughter as the entire company formed lines and wove in and out, under and over.

It had been well after midnight when the neighbours summoned their coaches, clattering over the bridge. His parents and William had retired too, leaving Robert and Donald alone, contemplating the changes that were upon them.

Robert reminded Donald of their childhood oath. 'Always remember cousin, we are blood brothers until death comes a knockin'.' They'd embraced and laughed, both mourning the life they were leaving behind.

Now, just four years later, the empty hall echoed Robert's sadness, as if it too had lost its importance. He felt its chill. The fireplace lay empty and, for reasons unknown to Robert, the tapestries and many of the paintings had been removed. Only the painting of the Kerr's sacking of Red Castle, centuries before, remained. The sacking, his mother had once told him, resulted in their servants' ancestors coming south to Newbattle. Elspeth, too, had recounted the story of her grandparent's journey south after their highland home at Red Castle had been burnt to the ground by Robert's forbears. Of their marriage beneath the sycamore tree, once they had settled, and of her grandfather's death in the snow. Robert remembered too his mother's story of how Elspeth's grandfather's ghost returns upon the winter solstice.

Elspeth had taught him the plaintive songs of the highlands, sung in the Gaelic of her past and he'd in turn let her play his flute.

Shuddering, he remembered the dancing eyes of Anna Giro and how she'd reminded him of Elspeth. How she had transformed from a child into the Queen Griselda and how the music of the great Vivaldi had transformed him, Robert, from a boy to a man.

Venice now seemed like a fading dream. The music, the salon parties, the carefree indulgences with Paulo, all felt far away. But which Robert did he want to be?

A great tiredness overtook him. He made his way to his room where Elspeth greeted him.

'Welcome home, sir,' she said quietly as she curtsied. 'I am very sorry about your cousin's disappearance, sir. I am glad that you made it home before our departure.'

Despite his despair, Robert startled at the sadness in her voice. 'But where are you going, Elspeth? This is your home.'

'Lord Kerr ordered all servants to cease talking in the Gaelic tongue or be expelled. I did not know he meant while I was singing also. He heard me while I was doing the laundry and ordered that myself and Calum be gone by Christmas.'

'That is outrageous, Elspeth,' he said. 'I shall demand that he retract the banishment.'

Elspeth lay her hand on his arm. 'It is done, Robbie,' she said reverting to her childhood name for him. 'As much as Newbattle has been my home, my heart has always been in the highlands, the land of my forbears. It is a sad time for sure. Family allegiances are being tested on both sides.'

As Robert slumped on his bed, Calum came into the room delivering wood for the fire. He had grown stocky and wore a beard and Robert realised it was Calum who had carried his luggage earlier. He felt ashamed that he had not recognised him, his childhood friend. A yearning for the camaraderie he'd once had with this brother and sister came over him.

'Is there anything else, Sir?' Calum asked.

'Yes,' he said turning to include Elspeth. 'I would have us sit together one last time and listen to your story, Elspeth, of how your ancestors came to Newbattle after the sacking of Red Castle.'

Calum began to protest but Elspeth smiled. 'Come brother, what have we to lose?'

The three settled by the fire just as they had done as children and Elspeth sat for a while, as if savouring the moment before starting the story, a story Robert knew was as precious to her as any heirloom. She slipped into a northern brogue, a lilt that swept away the decades, transporting the three friends back into the highlands of long ago.

It was early in the spring of 1649 when Malcolm and Annie left their highland home forever. They rose before dawn and set out with two of Lord Kerr's - your grandfather, Robbie - men as their guards. They had between them two ageing ponies to carry their meagre belongings. On the first day the four travelled in single file, each lost in their own thoughts, following shepherd's tracks south to the eastern banks of Loch Ness. When finally they set camp, Malcolm built a large fire and, taking his treasured snare and traps, went in search of food, returning before dark with two buck rabbits. The soldiers, craftsmen before poverty had driven them to take up arms, watched on with admiration from a distance as Malcolm skun and gutted his catch, saving the offal in a hessian bag ready for another night's feed.

Annie made short work of cooking the rabbits. Putting them into a battered pot, the only one she had managed to grab from the ransacked kitchen. She covered them with sweet water from the river. Adding a handful of wild garlic, marjoram and juniper she'd collected along the way, she placed the pot on the slow burning fire until the meat was falling off the bones in a creamy sauce.

The soldiers had been instructed to keep close enough to the unruly highlanders to prevent escape, but not to converse with them, for they had magical powers that could lure a man into false security. They were preparing their provisions of potato and turnip, but it was the aroma from Annie's pot that filled the air and set their stomachs grumbling.

When Malcolm beckoned to them they ambled to where their charges sat by the fire, offering up their own humble fare, for it was not the custom, even in the south, to arrive at another man's hearth empty handed. Malcolm thanked them and asked them to sit. Annie added the vegetables to her pot.

They said little to each other while they ate. When the plates had been licked clean Malcolm stoked the fire and took up his battered tin whistle. Annie sat at his side and sang, just as if they were around their own hearth. Her voice carried into the night and across the valley, lamenting some long-ago loss. She sang in the Gaelic, but it mattered not to the soldiers. They heard her sorrow.

Here Elspeth broke into song. Her soft sweet voice stirred in Robert the full weight of his sorrow.

Bidh mi tuille tùrsach deurach
Mar eala bhàn 's i an dèidh a reubadh
Guileag bàis aic' air lochan feurachd/
Is càch gu lèir an dèidh a trèigeadh

I am all too sad and tearful
Like a white swan that has been torn
Sounding her death-call on a small grassy loch
Having been forsaken by all.

When the fire died to coals, they fell asleep wrapped in deer skins, as equals. Three men and a woman with a journey to share ,all dreaming of loves lost and lives lamented.

Elspeth looked up from the fire, holding Robert's gaze. She may have been his junior by two years but sitting here, with the glow from the coals throwing ghostly shadows across the room, she seemed ten years older and centuries wiser. 'Aye,' she said, 'Annie sang in the Gaelic that night, mourning the loss of her home and family, facing her fate with courage as she travelled towards the unknown.' Robert nodded. They both knew what she left unsaid.

'Go on, Elspeth,' he said quietly, 'tell us about the Black Dwarf.'

They continued together, following the shepherd's tracks that criss-cross the highlands. Passing under the majestic Ben Nevis and through Glen Coe where the ghosts of the massacred still cry in the mists. On and on they went, ne'er seeing another soul until they arrived at the River Tay where they were joined by an old shepherd with his bedraggled flock and loyal collie.

That night, camped near the roaring Falls of Dochart, the old shepherd told stories of the Black Dwarf, a creature that roams half way between Heaven and Earth, the self-proclaimed protector of small creatures. His body, barely four feet high, is covered entirely with long red hair and he's as strong as a wolf. The shepherd told of hunters lured by the Black Dwarf to the underworld where they met a gruesome death. His chilling tales, though fantastical, enticed the travellers to pull a little closer to each other and stoke the fire against the darkness.

That night the traveller's dreams were disturbed by unearthly screams. They woke to find themselves surrounded by a heavy mist, muffling all sound, as if they too had been taken to another world. They quickly gathered their belongings, keen to be on their way along the loch, leaving the shepherd fattening his flock on the succulent grass by the falls. But his story stayed with them, like a prophecy of things to come.

It was well into the day before the sun nudged away the clouds, dispersing the mist, releasing them from the spell. As they turned south, the sun lit the top of Ben Lawer, still wearing winter's ivory coat. A vast herd of red deer grazed on the lower slopes. The buck stood above them on a craggy outcrop, his antlers held proud against the sky. Annie made the sign of the cross, praying that the Black Dwarf leave them to their travels in safety.

As they left the highlands the days became longer and warmer. Their journey changed from one of departure to one of arrival; from sadness to anticipation, and Malcolm and Annie spoke of things to come.

Theirs was a simple faith, uncluttered by the push and pull of history, of Protestant against Catholic, of Covenanter against loyalists, of Crown against Parliament. They spoke only of parents and children, of family past and family future. It was Good Friday when, weary and hungry, they finally reached Newbattle Abbey, their new home.

Elspeth paused but Robert needed more. He needed her story to go on forever.

'Keep going, Elspeth. What did they do when they finally arrived?' Elspeth smiled and took a sip of water before continuing.

Annie and Malcolm had always known Lord Kerr, their new employer, had money enough to have servants and soldiers acting for him, but their first sight of the Abbey left them without words. It rose out of the surrounds like an ancient fort, threatening yet comforting. They drew together, clasping hands; foreigners and outcasts with nowhere to go but forward. As they walked up the path, they stopped under the great sycamore looking up into its welcoming branches. There they stood, considering their fate.

Annie could hardly bear to look at the Abbey, its grandeur overwhelmed her so she gazed instead at the neglected back garden, littered with blue bells and snow drops amongst the rampant blackberry vines. Taking Malcolm's arm, she straightened her bedraggled clothes as best she could, raised her head and, with a reassuring smile to her husband to be, they went forward, together.

Calum smiled at Elspeth. 'You tell the story as if you were actually there sister.' Turning to Robert, he took up the story. 'They posted their banns the following Sunday and were married within the month, a week after Annie's sixteenth birthday. Such brave souls for ones so young. And now, Robbie,' he said rising and shaking Robert's hand as an equal, 'it is our turn to be brave.'

Calum left Elspeth to help Robert unpack. As she did Robert looked around. Everything was where it should be but, somehow, everything had changed, as if an artist had taken his brush and washed over the scene with dull grey; as if the orchestra omitted the melody leaving only a melancholic base rhythm. The dark hues of the tapestries hanging on the walls appalled him, so different were they from those of the gold and red he'd grown accustomed to in Italy.

A foreboding settled over him, heavier than his grief, pulling him as if blindfolded, into a strange place, a place of unwelcome stories. A place where everything he loved and valued, lay maimed and broken. He shivered.

'Where would you like me to put this?' Elspeth asked. The manuscript so dearly bought, lay in her hands.

'Ah, so Paulo did pack it,' he whispered. Part of him wanted to take it from her and throw it from the window, so incongruous did it seem now. But he could not. Taking his flute, he played the familiar second movement. Its sadness penetrated the dark and brought with it the simple courage to confront what was ahead of him. If Annie and Malcolm, and now Elspeth and Calum, could face such uncertain futures, surely he too could find a path of his own, protected as he was by wealth and history.

Elspeth's eyes were filled with tears. 'You play so beautifully, Robbie.'

'It is not me but the man who wrote this that deserves your praise, Elspeth. I met him. He was a man of great compassion. Come,' he said passing her his flute as he had done many times as a child. 'Try to play it,' he said. 'You used to repeat the tunes I played when we were young. Do you remember?'

Elspeth tried to play it by ear as she had always done but stumbled a little and stopped.

Robert tore the last page from the manuscript. It ripped oddly, leaving a ragged triangular corner attached. He took pen and ink and transcribed the first sequence of the tune in its most basic form. Its simple notes tripping up and down the stave.

'Here,' he said, 'see how they go up and down just as the sound does. The blacked-in notes are short, the open ones longer.'

Elspeth played again, this time with more confidence and for longer. When she smiled and her eyes lit up, Robert thought of Anna. He pushed the memory away.

Venice was gone from his life. He turned over the torn off paper and wrote:

To Elspeth. May she live a long and happy life, full of music and magic.

Composed by Antonio Vivaldi and transcribed by your friend always, Robbie Kerr.

Then he took the flute from Elspeth and wrapped it in the scrap of paper. 'You must take it with you.'

'I will keep this with me forever,' she said.

***

Their departure was not as planned. Elspeth was with Robert and his mother when William came to arrest her. He pushed past Robert and grabbed Elspeth by the arm. Robert saw the glee in his eyes and the fear in hers. William's blood rose and he thrust his brother aside so he was standing in-between Robert and his childhood friend.

'What are you doing?' Robert demanded.

'She was caught passing on a note written in the forbidden tongue of the highlands. Father and I were informed and we found her there with your sister and her husband reading the note,' he said turning to their mother. 'It was from their traitor son, Donald. Your little friend and her brother are spies for the Jacobites, Robert. They must be held to account. Father has ordered they be taken to Edinburgh prison and charged with treason.'

Robert turned to Elspeth in dismay. 'It was just a letter for your aunt, sir,' she said. 'From Donald Dunbar of Mochrum, your cousin.'

The mention of Donald enflamed his temper, but soon a quiet calm overtook him. 'Come. We will go to Father and sort this matter out,' Robert said, gently leading Elspeth from the room.

His father and aunt and uncle were gathered in the entrance hall. Calum had been brought in from his work in the garden. The siblings were flung together, quivering like frightened lambs.

Robert asked to see the letter. Together he and his mother read it. She had the Gaelic and had taught some to her youngest son. Neither had dared use it at Newbattle for many a year.

Robert waved the letter at his father. 'You must release them at once. This was a mission of compassion, Father. Not a note between Jacobites, plotting rebellion. A letter of reassurance, from a loving son to his mother.'

Robert's mother too pleaded her servant's case. She knew however that to back down was not an option her husband would entertain.

'Bring forward their departure if you must but I beg of you husband, in the name of goodness and mercy, release them from this charge that will surely lead to their deaths. Banish them today and they will no longer be able to carry messages of any sort from the north.'

Elspeth and Calum left that very day. Each carried a small bag on their shoulder. The only possessions from a life of servitude. Robert was the only Kerr to see them off. He wondered if Elspeth had taken the flute but guessed she would not have. She was a sensible girl and would instead have made room for more important necessities.

As they reached the sycamore tree, Elspeth turned and waved. Robert prayed that she be safe. He thanked God too that his father had never learned Gaelic for if he had it would surely have been the gallows for the two highlanders. He burnt the letter as soon as they'd been pardoned of treason. If his father had thought to get another Gaelic reader to intervene, Robert and his mother too, would have been convicted. As he watched the siblings cross the river, he tried to imagine the hardships they would face as they made their way back to their clan land. But he could not.

Who of us is truly free, he thought turning back to face the Abbey? Its shelter was a comfort, its history a weight, its call to duty could not to be denied.

CHAPTER 18

Australia 2010

The autumn sun fell across Fiona's bed. A multi-coloured crochet rug lay across her feet and the rose-pink quilt smelled of lavender. She could see the kitchen table with its linen tablecloth and on it, a small bunch of white daisies lifted their faces in welcome. This is what home feels like, she thought with a smile, as she pulled on an old dressing gown Teresa had lent her.

Patrick hadn't said anything but she knew his mum was due home soon and she still hadn't found anywhere else to live. She hated the thought of going to a hostel, but without a rental history, she'd had no luck finding anything. Besides, there was nothing within her budget in the inner suburbs and she wanted to stay close to Teresa and Patrick. Employment, too, seemed out of her reach, although she'd scored a few hours a week waiting tables at the Black Bull.

She flicked on the clock-radio. She'd taken to listening to ABC FM Classic in the mornings. A Bach violin concerto was playing. Its optimism was contagious. I'll find something, she thought.

When it finished she played her *Cappercailie* CD. She loved the way the lead singer sang the old Gaelic songs and how even the band's own tunes had a traditional feel. When it got to the *Four Stone Walls* track she wondered if it had anything to do with Culloden. She'd been reading how after the battle there, people had been forced out of their homes and forbidden to speak Gaelic. She remembered how her grandmother always got teary when she spoke of Culloden, as if it had been recent, not three hundred years ago. The song's words rang in her ears.

If it kills I will surround myself with four stone walls,
A little pride upon the shelf and four stone walls around me.

'I don't think I'll ever have my own four stone walls,' Fiona said to Patrick, one night as they listened to it together after a few beers.

'What about "a little pride upon the shelf"?' He asked. Fiona laughed. 'Yes I have a little of that now. But I want to have my own place to call home. I've never had that.'

Patrick nodded. 'I do get that. I was lucky that I couldn't get my hands on my superannuation while I was drinking and partying. When Mum offered to buy this house with me, I jumped at the chance. She said it was a good investment to see me settled. It's in both our names and we share the mortgage.'

Fiona wondered what it felt like to have family to back you up. For the first time in a long time she felt that old anger at Vonnie. 'You've left me high and dry you bitch,' she muttered as she pulled her backpack out of the wardrobe. It was empty except for the two black garbage bags Teresa had used to clear out her room at Wesley. It seemed a lifetime ago. She looked around at her meagre belongings. Not much, she thought, but more than I've had for years.

Patrick knocked on her door. She picked up some dirty socks and threw them in the wash basket and pulled the quilt up over the unmade bed. Even as a child she'd hated having people in her room, yet with Patrick, it didn't bother her. They'd ended up in bed together one night after a session at the Bull, but they'd both agreed that it had been a mistake.

'Patrick, I think I need a friend more than a boyfriend.'

'Yeah, I know what you mean. It felt a bit like cuddling my cousin or something.'

Putting the backpack on the floor, he sat on the bed beside her. 'Fiona, I've been thinking. If you want, when Mum gets home, I could clear out my study and you could stay there. I hardly use it since I've got my laptop.'

Fiona's heart leapt. Kindness still took her by surprise. 'Are you sure? I wouldn't cramp your style?'

'Style? I'll let you know when I get some "style" for you to cramp. No seriously, I think it would work fine.'

'If you think so, then I would love to stay, but only 'till I can get somewhere of my own. Getting rental is hard, especially with no history. I'd pay rent at the going rate for a room and I can keep on cooking for you and your Mum.'

'That's a deal then. Just one rule.'

'Yeah, what would that be?'

'If you get some "style" yourself and you're going to bring a man home, or for that matter, a woman, I have to meet them first. Give them the big cousin tick of approval.'

She laughed, picking up the backpack and threw it at him. The garbage bags fell out and, with them, two letters. She picked them up. They were dated two months earlier. A vague memory of Teresa saying something about letters the day she'd left Wesley came back to her.

One was from Centrelink regarding her dole, the other was hand written and had a UK stamp on it. It was addressed to the last Trust house Vonnie had lived in. Someone, probably the tenancy officer from the Trust, had re-addressed it care of the prison. Then it had done the rounds in Corrections ending up at Wesley House.

She recognised the address on the back as that of Vonnie's brother, Andy. Her hands shook as she opened it.

The Bairn
13 Dairy Road
Clanachan
Oban

Dear Fi,

I am sorry it has taken me so long to reply. I'm not one for letter writing and you said that you had no fixed address when you wrote. I hope this finds you. I used the last address I had for your mum.

I was so sorry to hear about her death. She was a good sister to me when I was young. We weren't so close once we grew up, but I think you already know that. Mum, your Gran, told me that Vonnie never really recovered from your dad dying. The drink is such a hard thing to give up for some. Even still, your letter about her death came as a shock. I didn't ever think that I would never see her again.

You said in your letter that you were doing fine and I hope that's still the case.

Your Gran's will has finally been settled. It got caught up in a lot of legal red tape. I am the executor with your Aunt Jeanie. Mum didn't have much money, as you know, but there is a bit to come your way. You know your Gran loved you and your mum dearly.

We're all fine here. My two boys, your cousins, have both taken up with local lasses and are working at the fish farm. Your Aunt Jeanie and I don't go far- just to Oban for our supplies and to Glasgow when we have to. We go to the Willow tearooms there and pretend that we're posh for a day.

Fiona laughed imagining her six-foot uncle in a genteel tea room.

If you write me your current address, I'll post you a cheque for what is coming your way. It's only £1,300 I'm afraid. Not sure what that is in your money but as we say here "don't give up your day job." The lass at the bank is Joe's girlfriend and she said she'd do the transfer for me.

We all miss you and remember some good times together with you and your mum. If you are ever coming this way be sure to come to see us. We live a quiet life but you would be most welcome to stay as long as you like.
Love always
Your Uncle Andy
PS. Jeanie says I'm to tell you there's a box of old stuff from your Gran, too. It's in the cupboard under the stair if you ever get here.

She passed the letter to Patrick, her faced lined with tears. As Patrick read it, he put his arm around her. 'At last,' he said. 'A lucky break. You deserve it, you know.'

'It's weird. I'd almost forgotten about Uncle Andy and Aunt Jeanie. When Gran died, I felt as if all my connections with Scotland had disappeared.'

She reread the letter. 'I remember Andy carrying me up to the shops on his shoulders. He'd sing all the way. His boys were just babies then. When Mum started drinking and rowing with Gran, they all kept their distance. They didn't even come to see us off when we left. But then again, maybe Mum didn't invite them.'

'They seem pretty keen to keep in touch now. Hey orphan, you've got a family.'

The day Patrick's mum, Maureen, came home they had an afternoon tea with vegemite sandwiches, Anzac biscuits and lamingtons waiting for her.

'We thought you might have missed this fine Aussie fare,' Patrick joked.

'Ireland's not the other side of the world you know,' said Maureen. 'Oh well I guess it is, but you know what I mean. It's so easy to get there nowadays. Just twenty-four hours and you're there.'

That night Fiona thought about what she'd said. *All these years I've been building it up as if it is a lost planet but really, if a sixty-year-old can do it, surely, I can one day.*

Fiona wrote straight back to Andy. It took her a long time to decide what to say. In the end she kept to the bare minimum. The cheque arrived a few weeks after the court case.

'$2,300. It's enough to get me to Scotland,' she said in answer to Patrick's question, 'but I'd have no money to come back to.'

'Maybe you won't want to come back,' he said.

Fiona shrugged. 'Maybe. I don't know why, but it feels like running away. I want to have something solid behind me. I feel like I've been running all my life.'

Patrick helped her set up a video link phone call at Christmas time with her lost family from Scotland. Her nerves at seeing them, and even more significantly, them seeing her, were almost enough to override the huge curiosity she felt about them.

Uncle Andy looked a lot thinner than she'd remembered. It made him look like her mum. She'd never noticed that, when she was little. He still had a full head of snowy white hair though.

Jean looked exactly as she remembered her. The biggest shock was to see her cousins as men. One of their girlfriends was there too. She was very pregnant. Aunty Jean hadn't mentioned that. Family secrets? Fiona wondered, although nobody seemed to be hiding it. She reminded herself that it was 2010 there, too. Time hadn't stood still and the strict family that Vonnie had always ridiculed had moved with the times.

Their accents carried her back to her childhood. They exchanged awkward small talk about time differences and the weather contrasts before Jean blurted out, 'Oh, Fi, you look so much like your dad.'

Fiona saw Andy throw her a look. 'I hope that's OK to say?' Jean said. 'We were awful fond of Gregor. He had a lot to put up with.' This time Andy took over.

'What Jean is trying to say is that we really miss your dad. His death shook us all up. Your mum and you included.'

'I don't remember much about him, really,' Fiona said, 'and I don't even have a photo anymore. Mum tore most of them up and the one I had was thrown away when I was...'

She still hadn't told them about prison. Luckily, Aunt Jean always filled any gap in conversation.

'His mum came to Gran's funeral.'

Fiona stiffened. 'Really? Vonnie had always said she hated us and didn't want anything to do with us.'

'Aye, that was probably true for a good while lass,' Andy said. 'But when her husband, your grandfather, died, Mum saw it in the paper and sent her a card. They kept in touch after that. I think your Gran tried to tell your mum.'

'She never wanted to talk about Dad, let alone his family,' Fiona said, her voice breaking a little. Some subjects still managed to floor her. Patrick, who'd stayed close by came and sat alongside her. He took her hand and she gave him a squeeze of gratitude. This was harder than she'd expected.

'Have you got her address? My other grandmother?' Fiona asked. 'Do you think she would want to hear from me?'

'She would I'm sure,' Jean said. 'She's a bit of a toff and thought your ma was below your dad, right enough. But you're her granddaughter after all. And you're different from your mum.'

Not as different as you think, Fiona thought. She spoke to each of her cousins. They asked about the beaches they'd seen on TV and if she'd been on the Great Ocean Road. She didn't want to tell them she'd hardly ever left Adelaide, so she bluffed her way through the conversation.

When it seemed everybody had run out of things to say, Jean came back into vision.

'Now, I told you there's a box waiting for you here, didn't I? Just some old recorder and photos and I think some music or something. Your Gran insisted it all be given to you personally. Not posted over.

Probably her way of making sure you come here. So, when are you coming do you think?'

'Well I've applied to go to University. I'll have to see if I get in or not.'

'That's the girl. Your Gran would have liked to hear that. You always were a clever lass. Yes, get qualifications first and then you can do what you like, where you like.'

'Not like us she means,' her eldest cousin chipped in from behind, ruffling his mother's hair. 'We're still here, getting under her feet.'

'Eating me out of house and home more like,' Jean laughed.

They all said their goodbyes and promised to talk again soon.

'Bloody hell,' she said turning to Patrick as the screen shut down. 'I can't believe my mum would do that to me. Another grandmother and she didn't think I should know?'

Patrick passed her a beer. 'Families, heh? You just don't know what they will do next. Will you contact her?'

Fiona shrugged. It was all getting too much.

'Well it's up to you now, Fiona. Scotland. Uni. Family. All yours to make decisions about.'

The letter from the university came a week after the Skype conversation. 'I've gotten in. I've gotten into do a BA,' she said jumping around the kitchen grabbing Patrick as she did.

'Of course you did. Never doubted it. What subjects will you do? Can you choose?'

They read through the university website together. There were even a couple of Music History subjects that looked interesting.

'What about Scotland?' Teresa asked when they next met for coffee. 'Family is pretty important.'

Fiona nodded. 'I know, but I would feel like I was running away again. No, I've decided. I'll get a degree and then head off. And I've also decided to find myself a one-bedroom unit near the uni. I can use some of Gran's money to set myself up and save the rest for when I want to go.'

'Patrick will be disappointed,' Teresa said, fishing for the low down on their relationship, or so Fiona thought.

'Well his stomach will, although his mum will start doing the cooking again once I go. Anyway, we'll see each other often enough at the Bull. He can invite me for dinner as often as he wants. I'll be skint as always.'

She saw Teresa's questioning look and laughed. 'Patrick and I are just friends, Teresa. Besides, I'm not looking for more complications in my life.'

As she waved goodbye, she remembered her pathetic crush on Paul and thanked God that she hadn't acted on it.

***

The unit was tiny but big enough for her. She set up one corner with her music stand and hung the photo of Vonnie and Gran that she'd managed to keep next to one of her dad that her other grandmother had sent.

She picked up the photo of Gregor and made a decision. The phone rang three times before a woman's voice answered. Her accent was very different to the Oban family, more formal.

Fiona said hello. It took her grandmother some time to work out who she was talking to, and Fiona could tell she was nervous.

'Why are you ringing, child?' The woman asked.

'I'm ringing because you're my grandmother,' Fiona said. 'I thought you might like to hear from your granddaughter.'

'Yes, of course dear,' her grandmother said. 'Are you still in Australia? It's such a long way away. What is it you do there?'

Fiona filled her in on her studies and living on her own. She'd seemed impressed about her going to uni, although she didn't really ask much about it. Fiona turned the conversation back to what she really wanted to know.

'Was my dad a drinker, like my mother?'

'No. No. Gregor was hard working and sober and I miss him every day of my life, Fiona. It's not natural burying your son. If it hadn't been for your mother...'

She stopped short of finishing the sentence, but Fiona's anger flared and she wasn't going to let her off the hook. 'If they hadn't got pregnant with me, he might have not been on the rigs at the time of the explosion. Is that what you mean?'

She could hear sobs at the other end of the phone but Fiona's anger kept her from saying anything to console her grandmother.

'I'm sorry, Fiona, I can't do this,' her grandmother said. 'I've spent many years despising your mother and trying to forget I had a grand-daughter I would never see. Now I know Vonnie's gone too, well I don't know what to think anymore. One thing I do know, is that Gregor loved you more than anything in the world.'

Now it was Fiona's turn to go quiet and she reminded herself that it was an old lady she was talking to. 'Perhaps we should meet sometime. I hope to be back in Scotland one day.'

She put down the phone. Another stone dislodged, if not turned. She locked the door of her unit and put on her Capercaille CD and sang *Four Stone Walls* at the top of her voice.

CHAPTER 19

Vienna 1741

The handful of mourners including six choir boys dispersed quickly from St Stevens after the graveside service. The local priest had advised Paolina to dispense with the music, but she'd refused despite the extra cost. She'd chosen the second movement of the flute concerto to be played as they carried his coffin to the rear graveyard, remembering how deeply it had moved him, those two short years ago. A cloud crossed over the weak Viennese sun as they lowered him into the earth, as if brushing aside an insignificant life. Ashes to ashes, dust to dust.

Paolina and Anna were the last to leave. Around them the graves of Vienna's poor were soberly marked or not marked at all. The pauper's graveyard was all they could afford. Antonio had visited there himself during his last days, insisting that they spend no more than their means allowed.

'Worry not Paolina. It is my music that will live on. I have no need of a grand headstone in this uncaring foreign city.' His last desperate attempts to be received by Duke Ulrich had indeed been met with uncaring silence. When finally the disease - the malady he'd battled since that storm-wracked night of his birth some sixty-three years before

- overtook him, he breathed his last rasping breath with his beloved Giro sisters at his side.

Back at their rooms, Paolina clamped down the lid of her travel box. Their landlady, the saddler's wife, Fraulein Wahler, had arranged the transport for Antonio's few belongings to be sent back to his family in Venice. It was only Anna who had accumulated more than could fit in a single container.

'The Mingotti brothers will send someone to collect my things once we arrive at Piacenza,' she instructed Fraulein Wahler. She had joined their troupe with Antonio's blessing.

'You must follow your heart, Anna. Your voice is well suited to their repertoire. There is nothing for us here in Vienna.' While travelling with them, she met her fiancé, Count Landi.

As they waited for the coach that would carry Anna back to her new life, Paolina realised that for the first time in her life she was to be alone. She could not prevent the ripple of excitement that, for just one moment, interrupted her sadness.

'You must come soon and live with me, Paolina,' Anna insisted. 'The Count has bought a sweet apartment for me and, once he is free to marry, we will move into his villa. How tedious these rules about periods for grieving are. His wife, God bless her soul, has been gone for a year already now. Still, his family insist he not marry yet. I am sure if I were well-born there would be no such problems.'

'If you were well born you would not have to lower your standards to sing with such a common ensemble,' Paolina remonstrated. Their arguments about Anna's decision to abandon the sophistication of opera to perform with a troupe of barely known musicians had coloured their relationship since coming to Vienna.

Anna took her hand. 'Let us not part like this, sister. You have done everything you could for me and I will always appreciate it. It is not your fault that we fell on hard times. Had the Ferrara opera gone ahead, who knows where we would have ended up. But it was not to be.'

Paolina had never told Anna of the vitriolic accusation made about her and Antonio, although Paolina suspected Anna had heard rumours enough. In spite of it all, Anna had gone to Ferrara that following season. The mediocre reviews she'd received bothered her much less than they had Paolina.

'They are buffoons. A few overrated merchants amongst a hundred peasants. Even their Cardinal is a provincial clown.'

'Ruffo,' Paolina gasped. 'Did you meet him?'

'Oh yes. He insisted on having a private recital, but I invited two of the chorus to come with me to keep me from being bored. He could hardly stop shaking when he took my hand,' she laughed. 'He muttered the whole time, something about Mantua and the Giro girls.' She mimicked his antics, making even the horrified Paolina smile. 'I could not make out what he was saying, so I laughed and told him he was too old for sad memories. He looked surprised as if he did not know he was old. That made me laugh even more.'

The relief that swept over Paolina was quickly replaced by an intense guilt. Had her reaction to Ruffo, the reaction that had undoubtedly set in motion the censuring of Antonio, really been so futile?

She had no one with whom she could talk about it. Antonio was dead, Anna leaving, and Maria too far away. She knew she should have told Antonio of her encounter with Ruffo at the Bishop's villa, but the timing never seemed right. Once, lying in their damp bed at the back of the Wahler's simple apartment, she told him that she felt responsible for the hard times they found themselves facing. But before she could explain he dismissed her thwarted confession.

'There were many in Venice who wanted to sideline me, Paolina. No, it was time for me to leave, of that I am sure. Perhaps, if the Emperor had lived, I would have continued to enjoy his patronage and the fame I once had. But it was not to be. And his son had no interest in my music. Besides, I am tired Paolina.'

And so, the story was never told. 'Secrets,' Paolina muttered to herself as she took one last look around the room that had been her residence but never her home. 'Am I to always be the holder of secrets?'

She thought too of their last visitor in Venice. The only person, it seemed, who still valued Antonio as much as she did. Lord Kerr had come to pay his respects and to thank Antonio for the many hours of pleasure he'd had listening to his music during his time in Venice. He was leaving the following day, to face up to a life he neither wanted nor felt equipped for. She'd felt sorry for him. He seemed so lost and angry.

'My father has summoned me home. He is preparing to make war on our fellow countrymen,' he said with a shrug that belied the grief in his voice.

When he left, Antonio played the second movement of the flute concerto again, as he had when they had first met. Paolina watched as he played and saw then the truth she had been trying to hide from. Their move to Vienna would not be a start, but a finish. Not a tempestuous finale but a slowing, quiet finish, a *ritardando*.

Financed by the sale of all of the works Antonio had ever composed for *le Pietà*, they had slipped out of Venice, as quietly as a gondola on a foggy night.

A knock at the door signalled Anna's coach's arrival. 'I will come to Piacenza once you are settled, Anna,' Paolina said, hugging her sister goodbye. 'But first I want to return for a time to Mantua, the home of our birth and where our parents are buried.'

She was using the excuse of a nostalgic visit to Mantua but her reasons for going there were now much more significant. Maria had, that very day, sent news of Ruffo's death. There was to be a grand funeral and Paolina would attend. Would she pray for God's forgiveness for a flawed man? Or would she demand from the Almighty that he be condemned to eternal damnation.

She had not yet decided.

CHAPTER 20

Culloden, Scotland 1746

A bitter wind blew across from the east. They'd camped just outside of the village known as Nairn from where the Jacobites had fled just days before. Robert dusted off his coat and checked his musket once more. He wondered if red had been chosen for the uniform to cover the blood that would soon be spilled. He tried to summon up the thrill of battle, the exhilaration of a near-certain victory. But all emotion had left him. He was dead inside; as dead as this barren, desolate moor. Trancelike, Robert felt he was watching himself from above, powerless to resist the pull of fate. Like a deer cornered, he would face his foe with resignation and dignity.

All those around him were calm and orderly. They'd celebrated Cumberland's birthday, his twenty-fifth, with brandy and extra rations. How odd, Robert thought, to be honouring a birth as they prepared for death; that of their enemy and, maybe, their own. He suspected his company felt the same for there had been none of the usual coarse hilarity that accompanied a celebration. All had gone to bed early. Robert wondered what they thought of as they fell asleep, possibly for the last time.

He'd lain awake watching the moon be slowly engulfed in a dense fog, imagining sounds of the enemy approaching. When he slept, he dreamed of hunting. But not of large, wild beasts run viciously aground by triumphant men; of rabbits, small and comical, scurrying cleverly from children. He was with his cousin Donald in his dream. They laughed together as the rabbits escaped them, balls of fur disappearing down hidden burrows. But when Robert turned to his cousin, Donald too had disappeared, leaving Robert alone and frightened.

The dream's gloom lingered heavily upon him when he responded to the five o'clock call to arms. He rose and marched through the clearing fog towards his destiny on Drumossie moor.

As word came through that the rebels were ill prepared, scattered and hungry, a heightened optimism, not felt since their crushing defeat at Prestopans, rippled through the troops. Robert tried again to summon an eagerness for battle. He sought to feel again the rage, hot and flaring, he felt seeing Elspeth's face as she was hauled into the great room to be charged with treason. Yet still he remained numb. He tried to rekindle the quiet smouldering rage he'd felt at having to abandon his dreams of art and music. A rage that had given way to the undeniable call to duty. Duty to his father and the Kerr name.

But he felt nothing. No rage, no duty, not even remorse. He was as if dead.

They formed three lines across the moor, their red coats like a solid brick wall, a wall of power and privilege. Robert stood at the ready with the rest of Barrel's men at the far western end. An eerie silence fell over the moor until the unnerving rallying sound of the bagpipes rent the silence and the rebels advanced, their curious array of tartan skirts and farm apparel anything but uniform.

The Red Coats held fire until the rebels were but thirty yards away. At Cumberland's command, they fired their first deadly volley. Clansmen fell, like scythed grass, their bodies lying at odd angles on the ground as if playing some childish game. Slowly the blood began to seep through their garb. No child's game, this.

Taking up their bayonets, Barrel's men moved forward as one, towards a small mound. The rebels - what remained of them- surged forward and were upon them, broadswords raised. They took the higher ground and all but one of Barrel's men retreated to regain advantage.

Only Robert, Lord Robert Kerr, remained on that grassy knoll. Some said he smiled as two rebels surged forward, swords heavy in their hands. One wore the bold red and green of the Dunbar tartan, the other the MacBean plaid. Robert rallied at the last, as if awakening from a dream. He thrust his pike at one of the rebels but then abruptly drew back, incredulous.

The man that stood before him was the one man in the world he could not kill. Donald Dunbar of Mochrum.

Witnesses said the two men stood transfixed; both immobilized, both defenceless against their shared history. With a deathly cry, the other rebel, MacBean, swung his broadsword and split Lord Robert Kerr's skull in two.

CHAPTER 21

Australia 2011

Getting back into study was harder than Fiona had expected. At twenty-four she felt like the elder citizen in most of her lectures. What she found most difficult at first was keeping her concentration on one thing. There was so much she wanted to read. Unlike many of her peers, she loved the tutorial sessions and attended them all in person, if she could. Online was just not the same.

One of her elective subjects was in Eighteenth and Nineteenth Century English Literature. She'd always enjoyed reading, but the language in the likes of the Waverly novels was a challenge. She persisted because she loved the way they drew her back in time. She'd chosen the Walter Scott novel because it was Scottish. It was also about the Jacobites and she remembered her grandmother talking about them. She recalled a reference to it when she'd been reading about the mystery Concerto but couldn't quite remember what it had said so she re-read that article, too.

She had read it several times when she'd first begun her quest to solve the mystery of the tune. But back then she'd focussed mostly on Vivaldi. Reading it again now, another aspect caught her interest.

Lord Robert Kerr... was killed as a young man fighting for the British Government against the Jacobites at the Battle of Culloden (1746). His bloody demise was widely noted but unfortunately little else is known about him. (Woolley p6).

Somehow she'd rather hoped he'd been fighting with the rebels because that might give her a lead to how her Gran new the tune. But as an aristocrat and a Red Coat the likelihood of him being the link was remote.

She did an internet search on Culloden. The pictures of the battle field brought back the memories of when she went there with her grandmother. She'd only been about eight but she remembered because her Gran had gone quiet and gripped her hand till it hurt.

'I can feel the ghosts, Fi,' she'd said. 'Our people fought here for the Jacobites. What a waste. So many were killed. They didn't have a hope against the Red Coats.'

Fiona seemed to remember she'd said something that day about her flute too, but she couldn't remember what. Why would she have been talking about a flute on a battlefield? Fiona wondered as she fell asleep that night.

She dreamt of being on a battlefield with Vonnie and her Gran. They were looking around at all the dead bodies, mostly wearing tartan, some with red coats. Vonnie wanted to sing a song but Gran told her to be respectful and played her flute. Fiona woke to the sound of her tune in her ears. Was she really *dreaming* her tune now? As she dressed there was a knock on her door.

'Morning love,' Maureen said. 'I didn't wake you did I? I was just nearby and thought I'd come and visit you in your wee room.'

Fiona ushered her in, moving some books from her only chair while she put the kettle on. Maureen pulled a packet of biscuits from her bag and took one out after offering them to Fiona.

'Patrick said it was small. He wasn't lying was he? Are you sure you're comfortable here, pet?'

'I'm fine, Maureen. It is tiny but there's not much housework and I can walk to uni.'

Maureen picked up one of the books on the table. It was about Culloden; one she hadn't got to yet. 'Now what's a nice young woman like you doing reading about Culloden? Is there not enough tragedy in today's world without reading about the past atrocities?'

'Do you know about Culloden?' Fiona asked.

'Oh yes. My mother was Scottish. A Macleod. She met my da when he went to work in the mines near Glasgow. He took her back to Ireland after I was born. Ma would talk about the Jacobites as if they were her best friends.'

'Have you been there then, to Culloden?'

'No, no. It's not for me to visit the place of the dead. I only go into cemeteries when I have to. What's your interest in Culloden?'

Fiona told her about the mystery tune and its association with the famous battle.

'Is Culloden near to where your Gran lived? Perhaps that's the connection.'

Fiona shook her head. 'No, but I went there with her once and I remember she said something about a flute, her flute I think. I seem to remember she said that one of her great-great grandfathers was killed there. I think she said that his wife had once worked for one of the Red Coats, but that seems unlikely, don't you think? I'm pretty vague about it all.'

'I guess people take work where they can,' said Maureen. 'There were even plenty of Scots who fought for the King. The Jacobites were mostly from the highlands and islands, as far as I know. But some families had brothers and cousins fighting against each other.'

'I'm trying to find out more about it and if it has anything to do with me knowing the music. I remember hearing something about a massacre even after the battle.'

'So, you've not heard of the Butcher then?' Maureen asked, motioning for Fiona to take a seat on her own bed. Fiona smiled to herself. Maureen had a way of commanding the room, even in someone else's house.

'I think his name was Cumberland,' she went on taking another biscuit. 'It was him who led the Red Coats. But he wasn't satisfied with winning the battle at Culloden. He ordered that any highlander who had supported the so-called rebels be slain. He even had the young pipers who piped them into battle killed.'

'Some say it was the beginning of what became the Clearances, the worst cases of genocide that has ever taken place on British soil. Anybody who was remotely connected to the Jacobites were either killed or driven from their land. The old clan system was destroyed. The wearing of the tartan and speaking Gaelic was forbidden.'

'But both my grandparents spoke Gaelic, so it must have survived.'

'Somehow it has and there's been a resurgence of attempts to keep it going. Kids are learning it in schools now in some areas.' Maureen continued to flick through the book.

'Look up the name Kerr,' Fiona said. 'That was the name of the person who bought the Concerto from Vivaldi. The Wooley chap wrote that he had been killed there.'

Maureen pushed her glasses higher on her nose. 'There is one here. Listen to this.'

When the rebels made some little impression on Barrels regiment it proved fatal to Lord Kerr, who, observing his men's giving back, remained a few yards forward, alone. He had struck his pike into the body of a highland officer but before he could disengage himself was surrounded and cut in pieces. Excerpts of Report from Culloden, The Scots Magazine April 1746 p189- 193.

Maureen sat back in her chair. 'Men! Always so ready to destroy. If they knew how hard it was to bring life into the world, they may not be so keen to obliterate it.'

Fiona took the book from her and read it for herself. A sadness crept over her. 'I know it sounds weird but I've come to quite like this Lord while I've been reading about him. This is such a sad ending and it just seems so opposite to how I want to think about him. On one hand, he obviously loved music and, on the other, he went into battle to kill his fellow countrymen.'

'Perhaps we should cut him some slack.' Maureen said foisting another biscuit onto Fiona. 'To be fair, he probably didn't have much choice and he did get himself killed. Unusual I think for a Lord to be in the frontline like that. They usually hid in the backlines. Much like the wealthy do now. It's still the sons of the poor that join up. Patrick was thinking of joining up you know. But they threw him in jail instead.'

Fiona looked up to find Maureen watching her. Patrick had said he hadn't told his mum anything about her, but she wondered if Maureen was fishing.

'I've been inside too,' Fiona confessed. 'Patrick helped me out by letting me stay in your flat. I'll always be grateful to you both.'

Maureen pushed the biscuits aside and sat tall in her chair. She was nodding as if Fiona had passed some test. 'So are you finished with all that then? I don't want Patrick getting back into old ways.' Fiona felt the atmosphere change as Maureen continued to watch her closely.

Ah, so that's why she's here, Fiona thought. A random visit to see what she would find. She's not as gullible as she makes out.

Fiona thought for a while before answering. In the past she would have been offended by the visit and the intrusive questions. She would have retorted that it was none of Maureen's business. Now her interest felt, if not supportive, at least genuine.

'I've done it before,' she began. 'I stayed clean for twelve months when I was with my boyfriend. It's still early days for me, Maureen, but I've never had so much to lose as I have now, thanks to Patrick and Teresa and you. I can't say I don't think about using sometimes, but mostly I'm loving being clean and having a life.'

Maureen nodded. 'Well, you can add me as someone who is on your side too, Fiona. But if I see you dragging my boy back into using you won't know what hit you. Now,' she said, slapping her legs as if starting a new conversation, 'let's have another cup of tea and give me another look in that book. I want to see what it says about the MacLeods.'

CHAPTER 22

Australia 2015

Fiona first met Ben during her third year of uni at one of her courses. He seemed too good to be true. Too good for her, at least. He wasn't what she would call handsome, in fact some would say geekish, but his soft voice had a calming effect on her. She'd guessed at his Indian background, although his accent was pure Aussie.

'Both my parents were born in Mumbai,' he explained on their first date. 'They came here when I was six. They're living in the Middle East now, working on an engineering project for an NGO together.'

Ben was studying archaeology and they'd worked on a paper together about the dating of musical manuscripts. He'd come to the Bull with her once or twice, although he confessed to preferring synthesized gamers music. He'd been keener than her to get serious and for twelve months she'd tried to ignore his attention, not quite believing that someone so normal could be interested in her.

'He'll run a mile when he finds out about prison,' she said to Patrick.

'What's the worst that can happen, Fi? He's a really nice bloke and he clearly adores the ground you walk on. If he does a runner when you tell him, or it doesn't work for other reasons, so be it. It'll hurt for a while, but you won't die from a broken relationship.'

After six months of dating they finally slept together and they'd hardly been apart since. He hinted a couple of times about moving in together but she avoided the subject by making jokes about it. They were celebrating her invitation into the Masters course, his PhD and appointment to a tutoring position when he asked her again. This time he would not be put off and it was starting to make complete sense. As it was they were both paying rent and only using one place at a time. Besides, she no longer felt the anguish of losing her independence. Ben was not the sort to take over.

Before she let herself say yes she told him about prison. She'd come close to telling him a few times but had lost courage. It all seemed like someone else. Fiona knew she couldn't make this next commitment without coming clean.

He'd been shocked about her being in prison, but he'd been more nervous about her drug use. 'I've never really met anyone who has used illegal drugs. Well just dope I suppose. As a Sikh I shouldn't even drink,' he said, raising his glass of wine and smiling.

'It's been almost five years now since I last used anything. I can honestly say I am just not interested anymore and being in jail seems more like a bad nightmare. She said. 'Do you still want me to move in?'

'I only know you as who you are now, and I trust you to stay that person,' he said.

Ben and Teresa helped her pack and move her belongings. Teresa turned on the radio which was set, as it often was, to the classical music station. They told Ben as they worked about the day they'd heard the Vivaldi tune.

'While you're in Scotland you could probably see the manuscript that guy found, if you have the right introductions.' Ben suggested. 'Now that I have doctor in front of my name, I might be able to help arrange it, if you need? I've heard the archive rooms in Britain are a bit precious.'

When she closed the door to her tiny flat for the last time, she sang the *Capercaillie* tune as a goodbye. 'Thanks for being my four stone walls and giving me a little pride upon the shelf,' she whispered. As she drove to Ben's house in her tiny car packed full of her things, she hummed the Vivaldi tune and let the sorrow of the past years flow from her.

***

The luxury of eight weeks with no study to do stretched out before Fiona. She was working one night a week at the Bull and doing some childcare for Teresa and Paul's twins. She planned to give up the pub job and get a position supporting international students to settle into Adelaide, but until uni started again in January, the days were deliciously empty.

It gave her time to think about all that had happened and what she really wanted to do next. Her Masters was the obvious answer but something niggled at her that it was not the right move. Not yet anyway. So, when Teresa showed her the advertisement on her phone for a six-month tutor position at an Adult Education College in Scotland, it had all seemed so right.

'It was in my emails this morning,' Teresa explained. 'I get a lot of stuff through because of my teaching websites. It's the "must have a commitment to students from diverse life experiences" that made me think of you, so I looked at where it was and nearly fell over.'

Fiona scrolled down. 'Newbattle Abbey! But that's where the Concerto manuscript was found.' She read further:

Newbattle Abbey College was founded in 1937 when the 11th Marquis of Lothian gifted his 16th Century home and estate to the Scottish nation. We offer adults the opportunity to experience a high-quality transformative learning experience within an historic heritage site. http://www.newbattle-abbeycollege.ac.uk/

The candidate must be eligible to enrol in a Masters program for study in the area of Music History or Musicology.

'And look,' Teresa said taking the phone back and scrolling down. 'One of the subjects they offer is Eighteenth Century Influences on

Scottish Music. That's right up your alley, isn't it? Your friend Vivaldi was 1700's. Looks like he'll be popping up in your life again. You might even start channelling him again,' she teased.

Fiona spoke to Ben about it that night. 'I won't apply if you don't want me to. I've just moved in.'

'Are you crazy! Of course you're going. You've always said you should go back to Scotland.'

'But what about us?' Fiona was surprised at how the thought of a future without Ben seemed impossible.

'If we can't be separate for a few months, we haven't got much. Six months will fly past. I'm going to be flat out with the tutoring job and I can come over in the mid-year break.'

'I'll think about it,' she said, going over in her head all the reasons she could think of to say no. She still hadn't applied when, a couple of days later, she got a phone call that would help make her decision.

It was Aunt Jean, telling her that Andy was ill and if she wanted to see him, perhaps she should come soon. 'He's bearing up pretty well so far, but you never know what's around the corner.'

'I think I'm more afraid of facing up to my family than taking the job.' Fiona admitted to Ben one night. 'What do I tell them about my jail time?'

'Tell them as much or as little as you want, Fiona. You'll know the right thing once you meet them again.'

As she finalised her travel arrangements she began thinking about the mystery of the Vivaldi tune. She'd hardly done anything about it since she'd started studying. She'd taken a couple of subjects in first year that focussed on baroque music including Scottish baroque, but nothing had emerged that explained how she knew the concerto tune. She'd searched out Lord Robert Kerr's name once and found he'd been a member of the Edinburgh music society, but there was still nothing that explained how her grandmother knew the tune. She'd asked her

Uncle Andy about it once during one of their phone calls, but he didn't seem to understand what she was on about.

Vivaldi himself, on the other hand, had become a big part of her research. She'd done a major essay on him and had been curiously saddened when she learned that he'd died *impoverished, anonymous and unnoticed*. Her essay focussed on his, and indeed Venice's, commitment to the *le Pietà* girls. She'd been tempted to compare in her essay how contemporary Australia treated its unwanted children but had been advised by her lecturer against it.

'It's a bit too political for a Music History subject,' he said.

For your middleclass sensibility, Fiona had thought. But she'd taken his advice and received a high distinction. She often listened to the flute concerto; it was part of her study playlist and when the second movement came on she would stop what she was doing and give herself over to its magic. As her studies became more demanding and life more fulfilled, the aching need she'd once had, to solve the concerto's mystery, faded.

Now, with the prospect of working at Newbattle Abbey, her curiosity fired up again. The thought of being at the college where the manuscript had last been located was almost too strange to be real. Mystery tunes weren't something easily explained.

***

Teresa dropped Fiona at the airport. Climbing out of the car she handed her the flute. 'I'm going to be on a good wage and living rent free on campus, so I will be able to buy my own soon. Perhaps you can give it to another "disadvantaged crim".'

They'd often joked about Teresa's slip up, all those years ago. They hugged so tightly that Fiona could hardly breathe. Teresa muttered something about hating goodbyes and climbed back into the car, tooting wildly as she pulled away.

Ben found her in the check-in queue. Her hands were sweating and heart racing. She checked her bag three times for her passport while shuffling to the head of the line. Ben put her case on the scales and calmly held her hand as she answered all the usual questions and went towards security. She went straight through. Ben was pulled aside for explosives testing.

'How can you be so calm?' She asked. He laughed. 'It's par for the coarse for us darkies. Anyway, I've done this dozens of times, Fiona. It's your first international flight for what?

'Twelve years.'

'No wonder you're nervous.' She thanked the universe once more for his easy-going nature and clung on tight when they hugged farewell.

'See you in twenty-six weeks,' he said. Just like him to calculate in weeks not months to make it sound better, she thought as she waved goodbye. She disappeared through the International gateway.

Her nerves settled a little as she watched other passengers arrive. Some, like Ben were treating it like a bus ride, others seemed agitated and excited like her. With thirty minutes still to go before boarding she pulled out an article she'd selected to read on the flight, but her mind would not settle. When the call finally came to board, she took a last look at the Adelaide hills and began the next stage of her new life.

They'd been flying for about an hour before Fiona remembered the article. It was one of the readings for the course she would be tutoring. It was about Vivaldi and quoted an Eighteenth-Century commentator:

There is no doubt... that Vivaldi's opportunities in Venice were drying up. He is an old man with a mania for composing. I have heard him boast of composing a concerto in all its parts more quickly than a copyist could write them down. To my great astonishment, I have found that he is not as well regarded as he deserves in these parts, where everything has to be fashionable, where his works have been heard for too long, and where last year's music no longer brings in revenue.

The reason why Vivaldi, now aged 62, ventured on a final journey in 1740 remains mysterious....

We first get wind of his imminent departure (from Venice) in a resolution debated by the Pietà's governors on 29 April 1740.

"It has been brought to our attention that our orchestra needs concertos for organ and other instruments to maintain its present reputation. Having heard also that Reverend Vivaldi is about to leave this capital city and has a certain quantity of concertos ready for sale, we shall be obliged to buy them..."

Death overtook the composer a month later. When he breathed his last, on Thursday 27 July 1741, he was living in the house of the widow of a saddler named Wahler, hence its description in the necrology as 'saddler's house'.

Vivaldi....an excellent performer on the violin and a much admired composer of concertos, once earned over 50,000 ducats... but through excessive prodigality died a pauper in Vienna.

p 68- 70, The Dent Master Musicians, Vivaldi, by Michael Talbot,

Fiona frowned. Vivaldi dying in such impoverished circumstances and sinking into anonymity might explain why the manuscript lost importance with Robert Kerr and his family, but it brought her no closer to solving her mystery.

CHAPTER 23

Argyll, Scotland 2015

'Cabin crew prepare for landing.'

Fiona thought she'd never heard sweeter words. Everyone had warned her that long haul flights were horrible, but she wasn't prepared for how dreadful she would feel. She'd followed Ben's advice and tried to keep to Australian time for the first half, then UK time for the second, but she still felt as if she'd been dragged through a bush backwards. Her eyes were red, her skin dehydrated despite a gallon of moisturiser and her hair looked like that of an eighty-year-old. She was glad she'd booked into the Glasgow hotel for the first night. The idea of getting on a train to Oban now was unthinkable.

The shuttle bus dropped her quite near the hotel. She booked in and had a long shower.

'Stay awake as long as you can so you go to bed at night time,' Ben had said. She donned some clean clothes and walked out into a Glasgow drizzle. She remembered some of the names: Argyle Street, Sauchiehall Street, Queens Street station. The orangey-red brick buildings, which a brochure she'd picked up at the hotel told her were a mixture of Georgian and Victorian, gave off a warm glow in the late afternoon sun. All around her the course but comical Glasgow accent felt familiar and comfortable. She made her way to George Square and sat until late afternoon, watching the workers, shoppers and tourists go about their days. She pondered over the difference between Adelaide's statue of a matronly stern Queen Victoria and the one in front of her, a young woman astride a horse leading the charge. How easy it is for art to make what it wants of reality, she thought.

An intense sense of release began to spread through her as she realised the joy of being anonymous in the middle of a big city on the other side of the world. Her paranoia of being known in Adelaide had gradually faded over the years but it wasn't until this moment, sitting in this strange yet familiar city, that she realised how much fear she had carried with her through the years. Fear of other ex-prisoners trying to drag her back to old ways, fear of seeing old school mates who would question what had happened to her since leaving school, but most of all fear of meeting up with the women from Wesley House and being accused of killing Harvey Brown.

She knew at a rational level that administering a drug to stop a consenting adult who was about to rape her was justified self defence, but the guilt and the fear of being found out had never left her. She'd come close to telling Ben but decided that it was a story he didn't need to know. Now, with the relief she felt sitting amongst the pigeons of Glasgow, she realised she had been carrying these fears with her all this time.

The bell from a nearby clocktower told her it was five o'clock and the overwhelming need to put her head on a pillow led her back to the hotel. She slept for twelve hours.

The train trip between Glasgow and Oban was vaguely familiar. She seemed to remember cold draughty carriages full of men who'd drunk too much. These carriages were new and full of well-heeled tourists. She found a window seat and took out a book. But once the train was out of the built-up city she had no time for reading as the wonders of Scotland opened up around her. How had she not remembered the vastness of the mountains and the blue, bejewelled lakes? When had the memory of the distant snow-capped peaks disappeared? Was it just that these things weren't important to a child or was it that she had become too troubled to notice? A familiar ache for that child filled her. Why had she let her go? How had she let the joy she had once felt be smothered by abuse and neglect? Why had she chosen the oblivion of drugs to the ecstasy of nature?

Across from her sat a young girl arguing with her mother to be allowed to look at her device. Her petulant innocence reminded Fiona that she too had been innocent; powerless against the forces that were to come. She made eye contact with the fraught mother and smiled. *Don't be angry,* she thought. *Don't let her go.*

She followed the trip on her phone map, the names of places and landmarks embedded somewhere deep in her memory, seemed to welcome her home. Loch Lomond, Ben Lui, Crianlarich, Tyndrum, Loch Awe. They swirled in her mind like hands reaching out to her, drawing her into their history. A memory emerged, of a conversation she'd had on this very trip with her grandmother.

'You've got the *sight* Fiona. There's some that have it and most that don't. It comes to me too. Look after it lass. It will help you when you need it.'

Fiona wondered what she'd meant, although she remembered too that she often known and felt things that she couldn't explain. But it had all disappeared when they left Scotland and she hadn't thought of it since.

She must have dozed off because soon they were pulling into Oban. She'd wanted to be fully ready for this meeting. Calm and aloof. Assured and self-contained. Her anxiety, which had all but disappeared from her life, began to stir and dark thoughts crowded in. What would they think of her, this family that she both wanted and dreaded? She looked at herself in her phone and fluffed some life into her hair. Putting on some lipstick she tried to convince herself it should help to turn her into the woman she was meant to be; a confident graduate, taking up employment as a tutor. The red just seemed to accentuate the doubt in her eyes. She wasn't ready to be that person yet.

The platform had almost cleared when Jean bustled towards her, sweeping Fiona's fear of awkward silences aside.

'So sorry, hen. I wanted to be here when the train pulled in, but Andy insisted on staying up to greet you. I wanted to tidy a few things away and he does get in the way trying to help. He's had a good day but he's very tired. He'll probably just say hello and then be off.'

She grabbed hold of Fiona's largest case and was half way back to the car before she stopped long enough for Fiona to utter a word.

'I really appreciate you putting me up,' she managed to get in. 'I'll only stay until-'

Jean turned to her as if in shock. 'You're family, Fiona. Andy would be most put out of you're thinking of staying anywhere else.'

Fiona smiled and shook her head. 'I didn't want to assume. Especially with Uncle Andy being sick.'

'You'll be just the tonic he needs to keep him going a while longer, hen. Look at you,' she said slamming the boot down and taking her niece by the shoulders. 'The image of your father.'

Andy was standing at the door as the car pulled up to the house. It was a grey stone semi-detached double story house topped with a small window under a slated roof.

'You'll be in the wee attic room,' Jean said pointing to the window. 'Andy has moved into the spare room, so he doesn't disturb me. So he says, but I'm afraid I'm a light sleeper and I hear every groan. Still, it's probably for the best.' Fiona heard the sadness in her voice and wondered what it felt like to be sleeping alone after so many years.

'The attic room will be fine.'

'We've just had it repainted and it's got a lovely view.'

By the time she got out of the car Andy stood propped against the front doorframe. She'd thought so often about this moment but nothing in her experience prepared her for the rush of love she felt as she gazed into his azure blue eyes. He'd always looked like Gran, but now it was as if she was again with her. They hugged for so long that Jean had to bustle them aside.

'Look at you two blubbering liked old fools' she said, a smile as wide as her face. 'Does my heart good, so it does. Look you've got me greetin' now!'

Andy had prepared a small supper of tea and shortbread. Jean did most of the talking, Fiona answered her questions as best she could from within her sea of emotions. Andy hardly said a word, simply gazing at Fiona and nodding as if answering some inner questions.

When Jean began bustling away the supper things Fiona suddenly realised how tired she was. She said goodnight and made her way up to her room. Despite her tiredness she didn't want to sleep. The joy of being with family was almost too much for her. Looking in the multiple mirrors of the old dressing table she began to wonder who she really was. After Jean had come up to say a final goodnight, she'd discovered Gran's old wooden flute in the battered suitcase left for her. A scrap of paper with her tune on it should have seemed surreal, but perhaps because her jet lag was distorting her sense of what was normal it had seemed just one more miracle for the day.

Fiona finally went to sleep dreaming of flutes and suitcases and of standing at the beginning of a long winding road unable to move, until she realised she could fly.

***

Jean was clearing the table by the time Fiona made it downstairs the following day. Another twelve-hour sleep, and she seemed to have avoided the worst of any jet lag.

'Help yourself to cereal and toast, lass. I have to go out for a while. Can you mind your uncle for me? He insisted on getting out of bed and is waiting for you in the downstairs bedroom.'

Fiona made them both a cup of tea. Andy was sleeping in his recliner chair when she found him. The chair's floral design gave her the impression it had been bought for a woman, her Gran perhaps. When he was awake he looked so much like her, but here his head dropped to one side and his mouth slightly open, she saw not her Gran but her mum in her last weeks. On the table next to him was spread a large sheet of paper. She tapped him gently on the shoulder and he opened his eyes.

'Ah lass it's so good to see you,' he said trying to stand. Fiona sat on the bed next to him and with a look of relief he sank back down.

'I'm so sorry you're unwell Uncle Andy. Is there anything I can do?'

'You've done what I needed you to do already. You're here.'

They spoke for a while about Vonnie and Gran. Fiona had thought of a hundred questions to ask: about her mum growing up, about her and Gran fighting, and why he thought Vonnie took to the drink. But now it all seemed too hard. He was so frail. So they talked instead about his boys and Gran's last years. Soon, however, he seemed impatient with the small talk and motioned to the table beside him.

'Take a look at this, lass. It's a family tree I'm working on. I started with all the names that Mum had talked to me about and went from there. Jean says I'm a wee bit obsessed. Look here's you and there's your mum and your gran.' He pointed out their names and she saw his too, alongside Jean and their boys.

'There's a space here for the new wee one when he or she arrives. Will you put that in? I want you to keep it going Fiona, the family tree record. My boys aren't interested. They're more the outdoors type. Mum always said you were the one with the brains. I started it before she went, and she said I should pass this on to you.'

Fiona looked at all the names stretching back to the first person, a female born 17th April 1746. 'Margaret Elspeth MacBean.'

'You've really been able to trace back that far?' She gasped.

'Aye, you'd be surprised at what you can find on the Scotland People site.'

She looked at all the names of her mum's cousins and recalled only a few. She traced them back to that top name again. 'Margaret Elspeth,' she whispered. It was some minutes before the date struck her.

'1746. Wasn't that the date of the Culloden battle, April 1746?'

Andy pulled the chart towards him for a better look. 'You might be right, lass. I'm not much of a one for history like that, not like your Gran. No, family history is one thing, battles and Kings, now that's something else.'

He sank back again and laughed. 'Fancy you knowing about Culloden, coming all the way from Australia. I don't think my boys even know about it.'

'Well I have done a history major at uni and I went there once with Gran.'

'Aye. Mum was often on about it. She used to say we had people killed at Culloden, but I never paid much attention. Look here,' he said rummaging around in a folder of printed documents. 'Does that say Inverness? I didn't put any places on the chart, they take up too much room, but I seem to remember that Margaret Elspeth MacBean being born in Inverness.'

Fiona took the page from him and went to the window for better light. It was a copy from a hand-written parish record. The writing was very untidy and loopy and some of the entries were badly smudged. The title at the top of the page was clear enough: Registry of Baptisms, Inverness, 1746. Andy had put a mark half way down the page against an entry that had escaped any smudging. The left-hand column said MacBean. The next column took some deciphering, but it she worked out that it said: "Margaret Elspeth, born 17th April. Father Gillies, 36, and mother Elspeth Margaret Fraser, 34."

'Uncle Andy, Inverness is near Culloden, isn't it?' She asked.

'Aye it is,' he said closing his eyes as he let out a sigh.

Fiona checked the document again. There could be no mistake. Margaret Elspeth MacBean was born right there, where history was being made.'

'Why is the mother's name down as Fraser?' she said more to herself than Andy.

'It's the Scottish way,' he replied, eyes still closed. 'Women are named in the records with their maiden name.' Fiona knew she should leave him to sleep but her curiosity won over.

'Did you try to find out more about her parents, Gillies and Elspeth?'

'Aye I did but I had no luck. Perhaps you will do better, Vonnie.'

Fiona startled at being called her mother's name and was about to correct him when she realised he had drifted off. She gave him a kiss on his cheek and was about to leave when he stirred. He sat forward, wincing with pain and grabbed her hand tightly. 'Did you get the old suitcase? Mum said I must give it to you in person. She was very insistent.'

Fiona nodded. 'Yes. Jean gave it to me. Uncle Andy, I found some music in it with Gran's flute. It has some sort of inscription on the back. It's too faded to make sense of. Do you know anything about it?'

Letting go of her hand he relaxed again as if he'd accomplished some important task. 'Only that Mum insisted you get it. She said she had told you about it when you were wee. About a great-great something grandmother and a mansion of some sort, near Edinburgh.'

'It's only I played the tune written on the pieces of paper last night. It's the same one that…' How could she explain the mystery to him when it made no sense to her? 'I think it is a tune Gran used to play. I wonder why she wanted me to have it?'

'She said she'd had the *sight* about it being important that you solve the mystery. Those were her exact words. What mystery, she never said but I knew better than to question the wisdom of the *sight*.'

Fiona recalled again her grandmother talking about having the *sight*. She was about to ask Andy more when he began coughing uncontrollably. The wracking sound frightened her as she watched him gasping for air.

She helped him into his bed and gave him some water. The coughing stopped. She phoned Jean to check what she should do about the coughing. 'I'll come home now. Sit with him will you Fiona, till I get there.'

'Jean's on her way,' she reassured Andy. 'Can I get you anything else?'

'Play it for me Mum,' he muttered. 'The tune you played last night.' Being mistaken for her Gran wrenched at Fiona's heart. She didn't want to leave Andy but she knew that playing for him was the right thing to do. He was breathing normally when she got back from her room with the flute but his face had turned a horrible waxy colour. A colour that Fiona remembered only too well. She played until she heard Jean arriving home. Leaving them together she heard their intimate whispers of love. Andy slipped into unconsciousness later that day.

Fiona played the flute at his funeral. It was one of the hardest things she'd done but she could have sworn that Gran sat by her side throughout.

***

Fiona took the long way around to Newbattle. Catching the bus to Inverness, she stayed overnight there so she could visit the Culloden museum and battle ground.

As she walked onto the desolate moor, she remembered her Gran's reaction all those years ago and wondered if she was having the *sight* that day. Perhaps not because, now as an adult, she too felt the spiritual impact of the place where so many people lost their lives. She thought of Elspeth Margaret MacBean making her way into the world at the very same time as so many were falling.

A map she'd picked up at the Visitor's Centre showed where each side had lined up. She made her way to where the King's army had formed and located the marker for Barrels dragoons. While all the history she'd read left little room for sympathy for the Red Coats, she strangely felt as much an allegiance with Lord Robert Kerr as she did to the Jacobites. She recalled the gruesome details of how he'd met his death and wondered again how the man who had once owned her tune came to such a wasteful end?

She took her flute out of her backpack. She'd convinced herself that she wanted to bring it for security reasons and that was partly true, although her accommodation seemed very safe. But she'd had a strong urge to have it with her as she'd gotten ready for the day.

As she began playing the second movement of Vivaldi's *Il Gran Mogul* Concerto the rest of the world dropped away and she saw in front of her the image of a young woman, a maid servant and a forlorn but well-dressed gentleman. They hovered before her, smiling and nodding.

As the last note faded so did the images and her grandmother's words came back to her, 'It'll help you when you need it.'

Fiona looked around. A small crowd had gathered to listen. Some had coins in their hands looking for a busker's box. Fiona searched their faces. None of them looked anything like the images she'd seen. She knew she should feel frightened, but she didn't. Embarrassed at drawing attention to herself, she shoved the flute back into her bag. Making her way back to the Visitor's Centre she wandered around the exhibits and began to watch a video of a reenactment of the battle that changed Scotland's history. It took her into the fray. The sound of cannon and gunshot firing and of men screaming as they were slaughtered was more than she could bear.

She went outside just as a bus load of school children spilled out into the car park. Their gleeful laughter, excited no doubt to be free of the classroom for the day, brought her back from the horrors she had been imagining. She'd planned to go to Cawdor Castle but decided she'd had enough gore and supernatural for one day. Stories of Lady Macbeth seeing the illusion of a dagger and of witches making prophetic claims was more than she could manage. She yearned for some concrete reality, so went instead to Inverness Library in the hope of finding more about Elspeth Margaret's parents, Gillies MacBean and Elspeth Fraser.

The library sat behind the bus station. Its rather dirty façade of columns and steps gave it a look of neglect. Fiona was glad however that it's absence in the tourist guides meant that it was quiet and being used by what she guessed were all local people. Armed with a folder containing some of Andy's certificates and charts, and a photocopy of the inscription scrap of paper accompanying the flute, Fiona approached a rather bored looking librarian.

The woman's face lit up when Fiona explained what she was looking for. She ushered her to the family history section and helped her log into a genealogy website. It was a different one than Andy had talked about, so she was hopeful of finding out more.

'What years are you looking for?' the librarian asked.

'The last date I have is a birth in April 1746. I'm hoping to find more about the mother.'

'Oh! That was at the time of Culloden,' the librarian said. 'You're lucky to have found that. Lots of records were either not kept or destroyed. Was the mother from these parts?'

'I don't know. I think she may have been in service near Edinburgh at one stage.'

'Well perhaps you should check in that county then, although often people in service didn't make it into the archives.'

She showed Fiona how to look at the Lothian area information and was about to leave when she noticed the photocopy of the inscription on the manuscript. 'That's very old writing.' Although keen to begin her research, Fiona appreciated the woman's help so she gave her a short version of what she had been told about Elspeth.

She had a closer look at the photocopy. 'Well that could be Elspeth,' she said pointing to the "El... and did you say it was a Vivaldi tune. Does that "....di" there fit with that?

Fiona almost grabbed the photocopy from her. How could she have been so blind.

'I think you're right. I can't believe I didn't see that!'

The woman nodded. 'Glad to help, hen. You know if you can't find anything in the official records you might get them from the estate she was in service at. It would be rare for a servant to be named, but you never know.'

Fiona sighed. It was such a long shot because she didn't know anything about Elspeth other than she'd given birth to Margaret Elspeth.

A group of young women came in with their babies and toddlers. Most of the women were younger than Fiona and the children between two and five. A pang of sorrow gripped her as it often did when she saw little children. She'd never felt guilt or remorse about the termination, but she wondered what being a mother would feel like.

The librarian's voice broke through her thoughts. 'I'd better go and see to these. It's the Gaelic for babies reading session. Good luck with your search,' and without taking a breath she broke into Gaelic as she shuffled the mums to a room in the corner. Fiona remembered the woman who'd sung in Gaelic that first night at the Black Bull and a fresh wave of loneliness swept over her, until she remembered too how frightened and anxious she'd been and realised, not for the first time, how different she'd become. Resolving to phone Ben the next day she spent the rest of the afternoon trying to find out more about Elspeth.

'How did you go?' The librarian asked as she made for the door at closing time.

'I found a marriage record but there was nothing on there about where they'd been born.'

'Welcome to family history research,' the woman smiled. 'It's one step forward two backwards most of the time.'

***

The Edinburgh bus was already at the station when Fiona arrived. A small queue had formed waiting to board. Most people had only small overnight bags, so she felt a little embarrassed at her two cases. I'm moving for six months, she felt like she needed to explain. But she heard Ben saying to her. 'Actually, nobody really notices you, Fiona. You've turned into the invisible person you always wanted to be.' He'd said that to her once when she'd been too scared to go to a music festival. She knew that for most people it would be an insult, but Ben knew just the right thing to say. She boarded the bus feeling confident and brave again. Ben is so good for me, she thought as she settled in to scenery watch for the next four hours.

As they drove through the back streets of Edinburgh she craned to see the castle but only got a glimpse before the bus turned into the coach terminal. Her plan had been to get on a local bus to Newbattle but the sight of a string of taxis was too inviting and soon she was back in the countryside again. She'd arranged to be met at Dalkeith, the nearest town, so she took the taxi there. Although she was a little earlier than expected a woman of about Teresa's age was already waiting. She approached her as she unloaded her cases and paid the taxi driver.

'Fiona Sinclair?' The woman asked.

'Yes, that's me. You must be Shona.'

'Smart move getting a taxi when you have all this luggage. The driver would have been pleased with the fare too, they usually only get to drive from the station into the old city. It drives them crazy with all the one ways and tiny back streets.'

Fiona noticed her accent, so different from her aunt and uncles. It sounded slightly familiar.

'Aberdeen,' Shona answered when she asked.

'I grew up there. Well, between there and Oban. Till I went to Australia.'

They had the usual, 'where in Australia? Is that near Melbourne? I have a cousin there,' conversation as they settled into Shona's small car.

'So you've never been to Newbattle before? You're in for a treat then. You were lucky to get a live-in room for the semester. They're usually kept for students only. The rest of the teachers live off-site and, to be honest, we prefer that. Teaching the students is one thing, living with them quite another.'

Fiona could have told her a lot of stories about a life of sharing accommodation with people far worse than students.

'The management agreed to me living in because I'm from overseas. I guess. I'll be tutoring the Music History subject and I've enrolled in a couple of subjects myself.'

'Yes, I know. Never heard of that before, but good on you. You're in my Celtic studies subject. But you've already got your degree, right?'

'Yes. A BA with a history major. I thought while I'm here I might as well get to know something about the local history.'

'Well it'll be good to have you, although it will be strange to be teaching one of my colleagues. I'll have to be on my best behaviour,' Shona said. Fiona could hear the slight aggravation in her voice.

'I'm not a teacher, just a tutor,' Fiona reminded her. 'I'm sure I'll learn heaps from you, including how to keep a group of adult students on track.'

Shona nodded. Fiona knew she'd said the right thing and had maybe won an ally.

As they turned off the main road and through the grand gates of Newbattle, Fiona let out an audible gasp. She'd googled the site many times, but it had not prepared her for actually seeing her home for the next six months. The gates themselves were massive pillars and a long drive led up to the Abbey. Although it was massive and could have been imposing, it had a welcoming feel to it. The main building was symmetrical like most manor houses, but it had a wing on one side only. It was adorned with an elegant turret. On the other side a low wall with an assortment of square, rectangle and arched windows. A barn-like building stood off to the side and behind the main building Fiona could see a four-story tenement type residence. Its grand but irregular presentation had a warm and welcoming feel. The words *irregular pearl* came to Fiona and she remembered how important it had been to her all those years ago to realise she was not wrong or bad, just irregular.

'I told you, you were in for a treat,' Shona said, no doubt noticing the now gleeful look on Fiona's face. She went on to chatter about what were the original buildings and which were the new additions, but Fiona could barely follow her commentary.

They turned left past the barn and pulled up in front of the four-story building.

'This is where you and the students are housed,' Shona said. 'I guess as staff you get the pick of the rooms. I suggest the top floor if you don't mind the stairs. If there's going to be a quiet space, it'll be there, and the views are rather grand.'

'Yes. I'd already decided on that when Neil, the principal, asked,' Fiona said.

As Shona helped her with her luggage, she could see the back of the Abbey and a formal Italian style garden. It seemed more imposing from this view. She saw the two statue-like sundials she'd read about. One of them, old Lord Kerr and his wife had given to each other as wedding presents. Being here felt a little like walking into a movie set.

'Just leave these here for now,' Shona suggested stacking her cases inside a small closet. 'They'll be safe enough. We can walk back to the front entrance. Neil said to bring you to his office.'

They talked a little about the students who were enrolled for the semester and went past the top end of a grave yard.

'All Kerrs,' Shona said. Fiona wondered if Robert Kerr had been buried there or if they buried soldiers where they fell.

Entering via massive doors they made their way through a small reception area which opened into a larger area. Before her an intricately carved divided stair case opened out its arms. Fiona imagined Robert Kerr standing at the top playing his flute to welcome friends. The flooring, a patchwork of browns, reds and orange created a sense of warmth and endurance.

A man appeared at the top of the stairs and came to meet them. Fiona had to fight hard to dispel the notion that it was Robert come to greet her.

'Welcome Fiona, I'm Neil.' Fiona shook his hand and reminded herself that she was here as an employee, not a tourist.

'I've asked for coffee and cakes to be brought to the great hall,' Neil went on. 'I like to meet my new staff here just as the old Kerrs would have welcomed their guests.'

Fiona was grappling for words when Shona gave her apologies and squeezed her hand as she said goodbye.

'Don't worry, we all felt pretty overawed when we started,' she whispered.

The walls of the dining hall were covered with carved wooden panels, portrait paintings and tapestries. Three rectangular paintings, more colourful than the rest, caught Fiona's eye.

'Italian,' said Neil. 'Brought back from Venice by one of the Kerrs I believe.'

Fiona had to force herself to stop looking at them and concentrate on what Neil was saying.

'...And coming all the way from Australia. But we knew you were the best person for the job. Your high distinction grades along with your obvious passion for music and history is exactly what we want. Of course, the fact that you too returned to education after a break means you will have sympathy with the challenges our students face. Some have even had, shall we say, less than salubrious pasts. But none of that matters here.'

'I do know what it's like starting again,' Fiona responded. Perhaps one day she would tell him more about herself and her own *less than salubrious* past. She'd been surprised they hadn't asked for a full police check, just for crimes against children.

'And I did some tutoring of first years in my final year. I particularly liked working with the mature age students.'

'Well welcome,' Neil said raising his cup of coffee as a cheer. 'And please make use of all the resources available to both staff and students.' He waved his hand as he said this, and Fiona gazed again around the room as Neil reached for a folder full of forms she needed to fill out. The sight of the books, obviously bound long ago, lining one of the walls reminded her of the suggestion of the Inverness librarian.

'Are there any old records belonging to the Abbey stored here?'

'Not many. They're mostly in the National Archives in Edinburgh. They acquired all that was here in 1937 when the Kerrs bequeathed it to the government. They stipulated it be used for adult education.'

'How would I go about seeing them, do you think?'

Neil gave her a strange look before nodding as if he understood. 'Of course. You're an historian. I can arrange for you to get a reader's card. You'll just need some ID and a local address.'

They spent the next hours signing paperwork and discussing the students enrolled in her topic.

'They're a mixed bunch. Mostly people who left school early for various reasons. Financial mostly, but we've got some young mums, and men who were persuaded to take up a trade but who always wanted to study. We've even got an ex-prisoner. I'm not breaching confidentiality. He's quite open about it.'

Fiona could feel Neil watching her closely and for a second she began to panic that he knew her past, but soon realised he was waiting for a negative reaction. Something about his open attitude made her want to be honest.

'I've been in trouble with the law myself at one stage.'

'Well, you'll fit right in,' said Neil. 'You provided me with some really good referees who all checked out. You're an example of how people can change, I guess. The Kerr's motto is *Ser Sed Serio*. It means "late but in earnest" and pretty much describes the students here.' He packed up the folder and walked Fiona to the door. 'I'm sure you can find your own way back.'

Fiona had three days to settle in before the students arrived. Her room was simple but comfortable. Good to his word, Neil helped her with the necessary paperwork to access documents in the archives. The building was off Princes Street in Edinburgh. Fiona had phoned ahead and ordered an estate log book to be made available to her. It was dated 1737 to 1746 and was the last of its kind in the Kerr's collection. She wondered if it was a coincidence that they were no longer kept after Culloden.

It had been laid out on a cushion to protect the spine and she was given gloves to handle it. Her nervousness was matched only by her anticipation. She knew it was a very long shot that she would find any clues to her mystery. But if her Elspeth had any connection to Lord Robert Kerr this would surely be the place she would find it.

Each section was marked by the year of its completion. The records were written in old style hand writing and were hard to decipher. Most of the entries were of farm activities. Some were about the garden and many about the hunting and fishing stocks.

She examined each page for names but found no clues to her mystery.

Turning to the 1741 page she noticed a change in the entry hand writing. It was a list of names against which was given an age and occupation. A type of census of the estate, she assumed. Heading the list were Lord Mark Kerr and Lady Margaret Kerr. Third on the list she found him, Robert. The man the musicologist had reckoned as being the most likely to have bought the manuscript.

She ran her finger further down the list of names, all servants, lady's maids, herdsmen and gardeners. About to abandon her search when she let out a squeal.

There she was, Elspeth Margaret Fraser, 29, lady's maid. Fiona's heart raced. Was this possibly the same Elspeth Margaret Fraser? Her academic mind was telling her that this was neither conclusive nor corroborated evidence. But the name and the age were right.

She continued to look at the list but nothing else seemed relevant. She was about to finish for the day when she saw an entry in yet another hand.

I, Lord Robert Kerr, this day banish Elspeth Fraser and her brother Calum Fraser from Newbattle Abbey and from the county. They must leave forthwith. Miss Fraser has been found guilty of passing on information from the enemy. When interrogated Miss Fraser stated that she was guilty of passing on information but has pleaded for clemency for it was an act of compassion she said, not an act of treason. When questioned, she told the inquiry that she had merely passed on a letter to Lord and Lady Dunbar of Mochrum, guests of Newbattle and family to Lady Kerr. The letter, she said, was that their son Donald Dunbar was alive and well and had joined forces with Lord Lovat to support the Jacobite cause.

I support her plea for clemency. She is to be pardoned from the crime of treason, which would attract a punishment of death by hanging, and instead be banished from this estate. Her brother, Calum, too is banished.

Fiona read the entry three times. Her heart pounded and tears streamed down her cheeks. Her many time great grandmother charged with treason! And then saved from certain death by the very man who had bought the Concerto from Vivaldi.

There was just one more thing she needed to do.

She searched the catalogue and found the reference to the *Il Gran Mogol* manuscript. When it finally arrived, she gazed at each page, caressing them, absorbing their history. She barely managed to contain the tears at touching a document that both Vivaldi and Lord Robert Kerr had once owned. Turning to the very last page she saw, as she knew she would, the torn corner. A triangular tear. Taking the scrap from her bag, she fitted it into place. As the two came together Gran came to her side for the last time and played her tune.

Epilogue

Elspeth woke late from a troubled sleep that April morning. The child inside her had stirred most of the night, its tiny limbs pushing and kicking, as if trying to find a way out. A blood-red dawn slashed the sky before it finally quietened, releasing Elspeth to finally snatch an hour of sleep.

Waking, she reached for the warmth of Gillies' body before she remembered yesterday's terrible truth. She hurried to the window. The snowdrop covered field was empty of men, although a score of daffodils defying nature's odds, displayed their yellow bonnets.

She'd married Gillies MacBean soon after her return to the Highlands. He'd found her at the side of a *burn* washing her hair and singing a sad refrain. Bewildered with hunger and grief, all she could manage to tell him was of her brother's body lying two days walk from there.

'He would not eat so that I could,' she told Gillies. 'When he fell the rocks smashed his bones. I was with him when the last of his breath left him.'

As the days passed and she began to recover her strength, warmed and fed in Mrs MacBean's cottage, she told how they'd been turned away from the grand home where her family had worked for generations.

'We walked for days, catching a ride when we could. But we lost our way and hadn't seen man nor beast for days. When the weather set in our food began to come to an end.'

Gillies nodded. They'd had an unusual start to autumn with storms coming from both the north and the west. He'd taken Elspeth to his mother's and, with a group of clansmen, set out to retrieve Calum's body. When the clan chief realised who she was he'd showered her with praise for the part she had played in the Jacobite cause.

'The information you passed on helped bring about the victory at Prestopans. They'd fed and clothed her and settled her eventually with a cousin.

''Tis not right for an unwed woman to be under the same roof as you,' Gillies's mother had insisted. But Gillies, recently widowed, was smitten from the first. Their wedding celebrated not only their love but the hope of another child to keep the clan blood going. Elspeth welcomed him to her, knowing she was back where she belonged.

But belonging is soon destroyed when great men decide on war.

Gillies's nephew, a boy hardly big enough to mount the horse that carried him, had come the day before, begging food and dry clothes for the bedraggled troops.

'They are already gathered in place at Inverness, Gillies, awaiting the Red Coats advance,' he said. 'The Prince says we will have the element of surprise if we advance by night, and Lovat's man Donald Dunbar of Mochrum, says we need every man. You're to come with me Gillies MacBean and you too will be part of a glorious history.'

But Elspeth had pleaded with Gillies. 'Our child will be born soon. Let the young ones go. I need you here.'

In the end duty to clan and the lure of fame and glory was too great for Gillies. 'Charlie Stuart is sure we can beat them once and for all, Elspeth,' he implored. 'Those Red Coats canna' keep us highlanders doon. We won Prestonpans and took Edinburgh, did we not?'

And now her bed lay empty.

Pulling on her dress and boots, she searched again from the window for any sign that more news had come. She hoped to see the men returning, the Saltire flying. But the field between her cattleman's cottage and the big house was empty. The quietness shouted of loss. She remembered the morning's red sky and wondered if it had been a forewarning. The image of Calum's broken body came to her and without warning she saw in her mind's eye the battlefield strewn with men, cut down, slaughtered. She stroked her stomach as if trying to keep her black thoughts from the child. She knew she should go straight away to the laird's house where the women and children of the clan would be assembled. But she was in no hurry to hear the bloody news.

'You must come first now,' she whispered, pushing her welling grief away. The women who'd attended her during the morning sickness had said that a child could be stricken by a mother's thoughts long before it saw the world for itself. She took up her flute that lay always by her bed and unwound the scrap of paper, the only sheet music she possessed. She played the sad refrain just as Robbie Kerr had taught her all those years ago. She wept for what was to come. But the haunting tune would not let her give up and she rejoiced for the life she was about to create.

By the time she arrived at the big house the women were gathered around the same wee boy who had days before been full of hope. Their faces told the tale.

'I scarpered as soon as the Union flag had been raised. They are dead, almost to a man,' the boy wept. 'Slaughtered! And it did not stop. Even when we lowered the Saltire they drove forward.'

'And the Prince?' One of the women asked.

'Turned back and fled, like a coward.'

Elspeth sat beside him and took his hands. 'Where are they, those who were saved from death?' She asked.

'Rounded up, to be tried for treason, they said. Your Gillies and Donald of Mochrum led our charge against Barrels Regiment. They escaped the first volley and charged forward. On seeing us in such numbers and with such fury on our faces, the cowardly Red Coats retreated a little. All but one. He stood alone. I saw Mochrum reach him first and the Red Coat raised his pike, as if to charge. Then, Elspeth, it was as if time slowed. They stood staring at each other as if a strange force came over them.'

The boy frowned with the memory. 'Then Donald of Mochrum did the strangest thing. He lowered his sword and hung his head. I thought him slain!'

Elspeth nodded for the boy to proceed. 'And Gillies. What did my Gillies do?'

The boy shook himself and looked into Elspeth's face. The room went quiet. 'It was then your Gillies stepped forward. He raised his broadsword and slew the King's man. Lord Robert Kerr, they said it was. Split his skull Gillies did, from crown to collarbone. Before,' he stopped.

Elspeth held tight her swollen belly. 'Go on, son.'

'Before your Gillies too was overrun.'

The child within her startled as if aware of the bloody history being made around her and Elspeth felt the warm wetness on her thighs announcing the start of a new life.

Author's Note

Vivaldi's Lost Concerto is a work of fiction inspired by true events. Some of the characters and stories are based on real people whose lives have been recorded in the annals of history. But history has his own bias and gaps, so I have interwoven with the known facts; the creations of my imagination, the playthings of fiction.

For those who want to learn more about the real lives of the people I have plucked from history, and explore more about where and how they lived, I have created a short bibliography of the works that have informed my research. And because this novel would never have emerged without the music, I have listed some of the pieces of wonderful baroque and traditional Scottish music that inspired and guided me into the worlds I came to occupy whilst writing.

Bibliography

Ackroyd, P. 2010, *Venice: Pure City,* Chatto & Windus Vintage, London

Ellero, G. and Urlando C., (editiors) *The Pieta in Venice,* 2011, Instituto Provincial, Venice

Goy, R., Venice. *The City and its Architecture,* 1997, Phaidon Press Ltd., London

Heller, K..,1997, *Antonio Vivaldi. The Red Priest of Venice*, Amadeus Press, Portland, Oregon

Sardelli, F-M. ,*Vivaldi's Music for Flute and Recorder* 2007, Alderhot, England

Talbot, M. 1993, *Vivaldi,* J.M. Dent, London

Wooley, A. *An Unknown Concerto by Vivaldi in Scotland,* 2010 Unpublished

Wright, T. Esq., *The History of Scotland, from Earliest Times to the Present Time,* (undated) John Tallis and Co., London and New York

Discography

Capella Istropolitana, *Vivaldi, Famous Concerti* , 1990, Naxos

Capercaille, *Secret People,* 1993, BMG (UK) Records Ltd.

Emma Kirkby, The Brandenburg Consort, Roy Goodman, *Vivalidi Opera Aria and Sinfonias,* 1994, Hypernion Records

Europa Galante, *Il Diario Chiara Music from La Pieta in Venice,* in the 18th Century, 2013, Glossa

Catheine-Anne McPhee, Mairi Mor, 1994

Vivaldi World Premier, *Il Gran Mogul*, Katy Bircher, Le Serenissima

Acknowledgements

Of the many people who have supported me in the process of my writing I will name here just a few.

My beta readers Sonya, Lynnie (also proofreader extraordinaire), Marilyn and Rose who helped shape messy drafts into a final coherent whole.

My writers groups: Marion Writers, who waded through the very first drafts eliminated the many "that's" and "had's", and the Novelist Circle, whose ongoing feedback on my next piece of work has also flowed back into this first novel.

And finally, my family and friends who have bravely asked 'How is the novel going?' and done a marvellous job of feigning continuing interest over the last six years.

www.ingramcontent.com/pod-product-compliance
Lightning Source LLC
Chambersburg PA
CBHW021421110726
47901CB00008B/2251